She held her breath.

"The email was simple," he said. "It said Protect Isabel."

Her heart stuttered and her breath blew out in a whoosh. "It said what?"

"Protect Isabel. Two words. And we were unable to find the source. Not even Felicity was able to find the source, and Felicity is the atom bomb of IT. Someone seriously does not want to be found. But that someone also wants me to protect you. To keep you from harm."

Isabel watched his eyes and saw the truth of what he was saying. "I don't understand. I can't understand. There's no one left in the world who cares what happens to me."

Joe's face turned even grimmer as he took her chin and turned her head to fully face him. "That's not true, Isabel. Not anymore. I care what happens to you."

And he kissed her.

Also available from Lisa Marie Rice and Carina Press

Midnight Vengeance
Midnight Promises
Midnight Fire

MIDNIGHT SECRETS

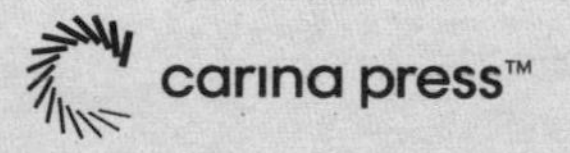

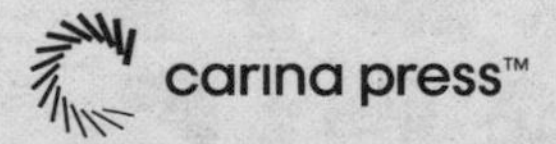

ISBN-13: 978-0-373-00323-5

Midnight Secrets

This edition published by arrangement with Harlequin Books S.A.

www.CarinaPress.com

Printed in U.S.A.

To my husband and son, the loves of my life.

Acknowledgments

Many thanks to Christine Witthohn and Angela James.

MIDNIGHT SECRETS

ONE

Portland, Oregon

THERE SHE GOES, Joe Harris thought. Isabel Lawton. The most beautiful woman in the world, and his next-door neighbor.

And she cooked for him.

Isabel Lawton, gorgeous mystery. One huge question mark. And a wounded woman.

Something bad had happened to her, something she never talked about. Of course, she didn't talk about much of anything personal, but she particularly didn't talk about whatever had happened to her.

Joe kept tabs on her. Because she was a wreck—weak and vulnerable. And because…well, because.

Joe's house was surrounded by vidcams. As a former SEAL, he believed there could never be such a thing as too much security. And he lived by the specops maxim: one is none, two is one.

So he had 360-degree coverage that he could access at any time and was always on view on a monitor in the kitchen. He was sipping a cup of coffee leaning against the sink when he saw movement on the monitor.

Isabel. Dressed for a cold-weather walk. Carrying something almost too heavy for her. He had to clench his jaw and mentally nail his shoes to the linoleum floor to keep from opening his door and taking that heavy thing she was carrying from her.

She wouldn't want that. And he didn't want her to know he was keeping an eye on her.

So he watched as she slowly made her way up his walkway onto the porch and bent slowly and painfully to place something in front of his door, then slowly and painfully went down the steps and down his gravel path to the sidewalk.

When she was gone, Joe opened his door and saw a huge pot. It smelled like it had just been dropped from heaven. He picked it up and carried it into his bare-bones kitchen. It was still hot, she'd just cooked it.

He lifted the top and drew in a deep breath. Beef stew. Sort of. Not like the beef stew in a can that tasted like dog food mixed with dog shit that his dad had opened when he remembered to feed his young son. Which wasn't often. Joe had learned early the fine art of can opening. No, this was perfect beef stew with some kind of special spices that nearly brought him to his knees.

She'd also cooked for an army, so his buddies would get to share, as usual. Maybe he'd call an extra poker night. After eating this, they'd let him win by default. Except maybe for his buddy Metal, nicest guy on earth except when playing poker, when a hidden mean streak always flared up.

Joe always won at poker, always. Drove Metal wild.

He wished he could share it with *her*, but Joe knew by experience that Isabel wouldn't eat it with him. She was friendly but reserved. Not cold, but gun-shy. It wasn't because of anything he'd done, that was for sure.

Joe was big and rough but he took care to control his

voice and his movements around her. On his very best behavior. Any other time, he'd have made a play for Isabel, right from the first moment. Any red-blooded male would have, and his blood was redder than most. But he hadn't. Not because he didn't want to, but because he hadn't had any moves in him when they'd first met. He'd been lucky to be alive and upright.

An IED on the last day of his last mission, a month from separation of service, had reduced him to rubble.

Taliban karma.

Two months in a coma, four operations and four months of unrelenting hell delivered daily by his best friend and sadist Metal, who oversaw his physical rehab. And now, here he was, almost as good as new.

Now. *Now* he could go after the most beautiful woman he'd ever seen, a woman who intrigued him like no other. But the fact was, she was still in bad shape.

Isabel wasn't as good as new. She was still as shaken and unsteady as the day she'd moved in next door to him three months ago.

She was looking particularly shaky as she made her slow way along the sidewalk. She'd turned left at the gate. Outside the gate there was left and there was right. Left was to a small park about five blocks down, right led eventually to the Green, a big meadow about a mile away where people played Frisbee and flirted in the summer and jocks ran in the winter, with a shopping mall on the other side. When Isabel was feeling better, she went right. If she went left it meant she didn't trust herself to stay out for long.

It wasn't his business, really, but the thought of her falling down on her walk was like acid on Joe's brain. So after texting his buds Jacko and Metal—Neighbor lady brought food come for poker if you get back early, otherwise our regularly scheduled transfer of money to me tomorrow—he went looking for his ancient black watch cap and black running gear and suited up.

Once outside, he couldn't run, he'd pass her in a minute and he wanted to stay behind her. So though he felt like a jerk, instead, when he was worried about her, he walked fast then stopped to do stretches. Luckily there wasn't anyone around to look at him, because they'd think he was insane to stretch longer than he walked. He looked like a fool.

Which was cool, because that's how he felt. Awkward and clumsy. Joe was usually pretty smooth with the ladies. He'd never had a big problem attracting them and he'd never wanted one he couldn't have. It had all worked out really well until Isabel.

She tied him up in knots.

A month ago, Isabel had come home limping and he'd rushed out the door. It wasn't a sprain, thank God, but she'd banged her knee badly. He'd patched her up the best he could and had Metal come over to be sure. Metal had been their team medic and what he didn't know about injuries wasn't worth knowing.

No one else had come to her, for her.

Isabel seemed to be alone in the world, which baffled him. She was so beautiful his jaw had dropped the first time he saw her, talking to the moving guys. Good thing she wasn't looking his way otherwise he'd have scared her off. He couldn't take his eyes off her.

She'd been sick, that was easy to see. She'd clearly lost a lot of weight recently. Joe knew all about that. He'd dropped from his fighting weight of 210 to 150 by the time he was released from the hospital. When he'd walked with two crutches outside the rehab unit's doors, the skin seemed to drop off him. If they'd put him in old smelly clothes with a hat and a guitar on a sidewalk people would have been lining up to drop coins in the hat out of sheer mercy.

He'd worked hard and was back to 180, and it was all muscle. He'd get all the way back to 210, most of it thanks to Isabel's cooking.

That first day had started it. The moving guys had been total shitheads. They clearly'd had another delivery before the day's end and had simply dumped her stuff as fast as they could and left. Some things they'd even left on her front lawn.

He'd never forget that sight of her, lost and lonely in the middle of boxes and a few pieces of good furniture shoved up against the wall. He'd knocked on her open front door and she'd turned to look at him and *pow!* He was lost.

"Hey," he'd said gently, "I'm your next-door neighbor. Joe Harris. Need a hand?"

Bones, his orthopedic surgeon, had given him strict instructions to use the cane until the end of the month. Bones had also said that with anyone else, he'd order the use of two crutches for the next two months. But Bones knew Joe was a former SEAL and he knew it was pointless trying to stop Joe from pushing forward with his rehab.

However, Bones had been really strict on using at least the cane for the next four weeks and had given Joe a long, boring lecture on load-bearing coefficients and fusion time and yada yada. It had all made sense at the time and Joe had been following doctor's orders like a good little patient.

But seeing that beautiful woman trying to tug a couch toward the wall…well, he couldn't do it. Just couldn't sit by and watch. He tossed the cane and spent the afternoon helping her unpack. His bones had ached that night, but what the hell. Though he was just back on his feet, he was still stronger than she was. So he'd carried in boxes from the lawn, set up some furniture, unpacked her books and when he saw that she couldn't take it anymore, he'd gone back to his place and stared at the wall for an hour, seeing that face.

The next morning he found freshly baked cinnamon buns and a pan of banana bread outside his front door.

That first week became a pattern. He helped her set up her stuff and he'd find amazing things to eat outside his door.

She didn't talk much and he didn't press her. Something crappy had happened to her—he recognized the thousand-yard stare of someone who'd seen bad shit. The bad shit had gone down fairly recently, too. Once, the sleeve of her sweater rode up and he saw a big scar where something had sliced her. He knew scars. That couldn't have been more than six months old.

Also—it looked a lot like a knife scar and he'd stopped what he was doing as a fit of rage overtook him.

Someone had knifed her?

Some fuckhead had taken a knife and *sliced* her? He knew knives, was good with knives. Knew what knives could do to the human body. In many ways, a knife could be more devastating than a bullet.

Isabel had caught his look, quietly pulled her sweater down over her forearm and turned away. It couldn't have been more plain if she had shouted the words. *I don't want to talk about it.*

She was clearly traumatized. She couldn't talk about it? Fine. He knew all he really needed to know anyway. Amazingly beautiful, really sad, incredible cook.

Messed with his head and his gonads.

The rest would come later, whenever she felt like talking.

And if someone had done this to her and he found out who that fuckhead was? The fucker was a dead man walking.

So Joe had resigned himself to waiting it out until she felt comfortable enough with him to talk about it.

God knew he had time on his hands. He wasn't going anywhere. The doctors wouldn't let him go to work for another month, though he was itching to.

His rehab was hard but he was on the mend and it was a steadily upward trajectory. Metal wouldn't let it be anything else. Sometimes Jacko showed up, too, at the gym, to spot him. Metal knew everything there was to know about physiology and Jacko was a world-class gym rat so between the two of them he was putting himself back together again in record time.

He had friends, he had the full support of his company, ASI.

Who did she have?

Nobody. Except him.

She wasn't looking well at all today. The ground had frozen overnight and there were unexpected pockets of ice.

Joe had good balance but Isabel didn't.

Isabel might need him.

Joe headed out.

"I THINK IT might be time to pass on to phase two," the voice on the phone said.

"All right," Hector Blake answered and there was a faint click and then silence.

The voice, as always, had been put through an anonymizer and was a metallic tenor. It could be anyone—man, woman or child—there was no way to tell. The software program was created to disguise any identifying characteristics. Though Blake would bet good money it was a man.

Blake could bet good money because the voice at the other end of the line had made him several billion dollars overnight, and so he could be an alien from Aldeberan for all Blake cared.

Still, he had a mental image of the man, sitting at a desk somewhere.

The office would be ordered and plush, full of comforts. There was something prissy about the voice. The anonymizer changed the timbre and tone of the voice but couldn't change the syntax, the small pauses, the vocabulary.

So, Blake had built up this image of an elegantly dressed, fussy man sitting in an elegant office, dispensing orders like God. Just about as powerful as God, actually, because the man was planning on bringing down the most powerful country on earth in several stages.

Phase one had been a resounding success. So he supposed it didn't really matter who the voice belonged to.

He remembered clearly the day the voice had called. First of all, he'd called on Blake's personal cell, which was interesting in and of itself. Very few people had his personal number and Blake took care to keep that number low. He had a very busy, highly successful law practice. His office had ten lines and he had two—one for internal calls and one for outside calls. His staff answered his phone at home and very few were forwarded on to him. He had two cells for business and one for personal calls, which he rarely used. The person who'd called that day had called him on his personal cell.

It had been clear immediately that the voice was altered. Right away, Blake had been both intrigued and irritated. He was a busy man and silly games bored him.

Until the caller told him what the call was about and Blake sat up straight, electrified.

This was—this was illegal and treasonous and immoral.

And yet highly profitable. Almost unimaginably so.

When Blake had asked who was talking, the voice answered, "Call me M."

Blake had hummed the Bond tune but nobody laughed on the other end.

Blake would never have believed that someone would approach him with a plan this terrifying, this audacious. But M had, and over the course of an hour's conversation a day for several weeks, his reaction shifted from never to maybe to yes.

And then they'd started talking details.

It had come at a moment in Blake's life in which he was becoming a shade depressed and a little bored. He'd been born for great things and, yes, he'd accomplished his fair share. He'd turned his family's small estate into a big one. He'd founded a successful law firm specializing in international law and he'd published so many articles in the field he was considered an expert. He'd advised the State Department and the European Union and the United Nations on aspects of treaties.

He'd been an ambassador for two years. To Andorra, it was true, but it was enough to be called ambassador for the rest of his days.

He'd run twice for the senate and won both times, but his time there had been boring and the experience soon grew stale.

However, in spite of all his success, marriage one had broken down—so many years ago he could hardly remember her face—as had marriages two and three. He had no children except an out-of-wedlock girl in Southeast Asia he occasionally sent money to.

None of his ex-wives spoke to him, though they cashed his checks readily enough.

Blake had made his mark, but it wasn't enough.

What M proposed was enough. God, yes. More than enough. It would put Blake right up there in the history books with Alexander, with Charlemagne, with Napoleon. One of the most powerful men ever to have lived.

Viceroy of the Americas.

Every time he said that title to himself, he smiled secretly. It was becoming so real to him, his own manifest destiny, that current reality was starting to fade. And yet—it was *reality* that somehow seemed a veiled scrim, almost invisible.

He found himself caught up in plans for the After, completely taken up by what the world would be after the plan came to fruition, completely forgetting that the plan hadn't been implemented in full yet.

It had begun, though.

He was wealthy beyond belief and soon he would be powerful beyond belief.

Viceroy of the Americas.

The Washington Massacre had been phase one and that had been a resounding success.

One extra special fillip to the Massacre was that it had taken out the Delvauxes, the whole brood. Simply swatted them away, like you would with pernicious flies.

Officious pricks, every single one of them.

The Blakes and Delvauxes had been friends for three generations.

Everyone thought Blake and Alex Delvaux were friends when the truth was Blake despised Alex, always had. Hated all the Delvauxes, actually, with their shock of blondish hair, athleticism and charisma. Kennedys for the twenty-first century. Seemingly destined for greatness when there had been no greatness there, just mediocrity and good cheekbones.

It had been his distinct pleasure to arrange for the Massacre to be at a campaign party announcing Alex's candidacy for the presidential nomination.

Wiped almost all of them out.

All in all, over fifty Delvauxes killed. Every single one, actually, except for one.

Blake frowned.

Why Isabel Delvaux had been spared was beyond him. The utter vagaries of chance. She was a pretty thing, some kind of food maven, completely inconsequential. Her survival was a quirk of fate. She wasn't political in any way, as many of the Delvauxes had been. Had gone on record as being against her father's campaign, but for personal reasons not political reasons. Most of the Delvauxes were highly political and very vocal. Had any of the political Delvauxes survived the blast, Blake would have had them put down by his team because none of them would stand still for phase two.

Blake let Isabel be. She wasn't going to make waves. She was a shadow of her former self and had changed her name and crossed the country to live a recluse's life in Portland, Oregon.

It was a very good thing that it looked like Isabel could barely stand on her feet, because she'd seen things she shouldn't have. For one electric moment that night, in the midst of the Massacre, their eyes had met and Blake saw that she'd realized something. Then the building had blown. He thought she'd died together with the rest and had been astonished three days later to discover she was in a coma at George Washington University Hospital.

He'd been very tempted to send a kill team to her. There was so much chaos everywhere that it would have been easy to slip into her hospital room and inject an air bubble in the IV line.

In the end, he'd decided to wait it out and he'd been right

But he kept an eye on her, checking in at intervals. She remembered literally nothing from the night of the Massacre.

If her memory ever came back, Blake would have her put down. He had a man in Portland keeping an eye on her.

No, Isabel was no threat.

So, now they were passing on to phase two.

He got up, poured himself a thirty-two-year-old single malt and sat down again, admiring the view outside his windows.

Viceroy of the Americas. He smiled and took another sip of his 1983 Macallan.

TWO

Portland

IT WAS FREEZING cold and windy, but Isabel Delvaux, now Isabel Lawton, went out anyway. Her daily torture session—a one-hour walk. It had to be done. If she didn't grit her teeth and force herself to go out, she'd never leave the house.

Staying in her house forever. It scared her that the thought didn't scare her.

The wind was as raw as she felt. She had three layers under her down coat but the wind made her shiver anyway. Probably because of the exhaustion. It had been another horrible, sleepless night. Just like the night before and the night before that and like tomorrow night would be. She hadn't had one decent night's sleep since the Massacre.

The night she lost her whole family, the night she lost everything.

Don't think about it. Her daily—hourly—mantra.

Don't think about Mom or Dad. Or Teddy or Rob. Or—God!—Jack. There hadn't been anything found of Jack to bury.

Don't think about her aunts and uncles and cousins—all gone. Her tribe—gone.

In a moment she could remember only in her nightmares, her life had been swept away and what was left was the husk—a shell of a woman who couldn't eat, couldn't sleep, could barely walk.

She made it past the gate and after a moment's hesitation turned left. It was a shorter walk to the park, there was no way she'd make it to the Green. Already her body was screaming for her to turn around and go back home. Close her front door behind her, curl up on the couch and stare at the wall until the light faded.

No. Keep on walking.

There was a stone wall fronting her house and she put out a hand to steady herself. It was in pristine shape, thanks to her incredibly helpful next-door neighbor, Joe Harris.

She'd left her largest pot filled with boeuf bourguignon on Joe's doorstep. She could barely choke down yogurt herself but having Joe to cook for made cooking fun again. Running through her endless list of recipes for something Joe might enjoy was the one bright spot in her day, though she probably didn't need to stretch and be creative—he seemed to like more or less everything she cooked for him.

Joe was always so incredibly grateful, as if she'd gone out, sheared wool off sheep, carded it, spun it and knitted him things. Or butchered the cows and harvested the wheat. As if she'd done this amazingly complex and elaborate thing just for him. It was only cooking and it kept her sane. Well, sort of sane. Sane had gone out the window on the night of the Massacre.

It barely compensated Joe for what he did for her. Everything in her house was in perfect condition. Joe would scour the place for things to fix or improve. She didn't trust herself to drive but last month Joe had started driving and he drove her everywhere she wanted.

He'd been as messed up as she was when she'd moved here three months ago. But Joe had moved on. He'd used a cane that first day and he later told her he'd been on crutches the week before. The cane disappeared a few days after she arrived and every day after that he celebrated some milestone in putting himself back together again.

He was still thin but he was all muscle.

Yeah.

A wave of heat shot through her. Just thinking about him made her weak at the knees and her knees were already weak.

When doing repairs, Joe wore an ancient tee that was soft and thin from so many washings that every single muscle was visible through the thin cotton. When she'd first set eyes on him, thirty pounds ago, he'd been all muscle and sinew. Now he was even more muscle and sinew. Even when thin, his shoulders had still been the broadest she'd ever seen. Though, of course, in her previous life, muscles weren't important in her crowd. She'd known more men with money than men with muscles.

Muscles were better. Who knew?

She often caught herself staring at him as he stretched or reached for something, trying to keep her jaw from dropping. He was just…magnificent.

Watching Joe move became her new favorite thing at a moment when all her favorite things had been taken from her.

He was pure sex, whether standing still or moving.

Such a waste to have a guy like that for a next-door neighbor. Enticing, but out of reach.

Because the fact was that sex had fled from her world. There were the occasional nonmenopausal hot flashes when Joe was doing something manly around the house but they were rare. Mostly, she felt numb. And cold. Dizzy spells would come and go, leaving her shaken and sweating.

She had continuous flashbacks of when she'd woken up in the hospital, completely alone because her entire family had been wiped out. The nurse who had told her that had burst into tears. That horrible moment was never covered by the gauze of memory. No. Horribly, her flashbacks carried the emotional weight of living through the horror, again and again.

Isabel carefully masked what she felt about Joe because, well, what would a man as vital as Joe want with a shell of a woman like her? He'd put himself together in three months and she was exactly as he'd found her that first day—dazed, halting, wounded.

She wasn't getting better. She was getting worse.

These were thoughts she had a billion times a day. Buzzing round and round and round in her head like angry bees. It took an almost physical effort to wrench those thoughts in another direction. Joe was off-limits because she had no business yearning after him, not in the state she was in. That day—the day she found out she lost her family, the day she lost her life… She backed away from those thoughts as fast as she could. *Don't think about that.*

So many things she couldn't think about. Things she chased from her head the instant they appeared.

No past, no future. What was left was the here and

now. *Pay attention to the here and the now,* she told herself constantly, *because it's all you have.* The here and now, though, was vicious. She suffered from crippling bouts of dizziness that attacked her without warning. In the supermarket, shopping, in bookstores, in the bank, even at home. She'd suddenly feel the world swirl around her, no shape or meaning to anything. The ground would feel shaky under her feet. The only thing to do was freeze. She'd done that in the bank and in the supermarket and it had taken everything she had not to faint.

She'd stood in the middle of the bank's lobby and in the frozen produce aisle, unable to move, feeling nauseous and dizzy, and wishing with all her heart she could just press a button and be home, in her bed, with the covers pulled up over her while she waited for her wildly pumping heart to slow down.

It had felt like a heart attack and she'd gone to the emergency room twice. It wasn't a heart attack. It was her craziness, it was her broken heart. No hospital in the world could fix that.

Fix it. How? Nothing short of the miraculous restoration of her family to life could work. She was in a deep hole and it kept getting deeper, blacker. The second time she went to the hospital in an ambulance, she found herself hoping she was about to die. Just put an end to it.

That really scared her. As much as the outside world did.

The outside world terrified her, because she could never be sure she wouldn't simply pass out.

Think of something else.

Okay. What?

It always came back to him, her neighbor, Joe. That

made her dizzy, too, only in a good way. No matter that she couldn't even think about sex, about relationships, no matter that she was alone in the world in a way that nobody could understand. She couldn't be with anyone. She was too crazy. But…though she knew thinking about him was perfectly useless, her thoughts always circled back to him.

He always moved with grace and economy, even when he'd been barely upright. He watched her carefully with those keen brown eyes of his, the color of a hawk's eyes, that seemed to see everything so clearly. He seemed to take his cues from her. When she was really down, which was most of the time, they barely spoke. He came in, fixed something for her or carried something for her or set up something for her and then left.

On the days that were just awful and not horrible and she had the energy to talk, they'd carry on a conversation. Nothing personal, oh, no. The weather, maybe, though Portland weather wasn't very interesting. Mostly wet. It was either getting ready to rain, raining, or rain was coming. They discussed the hell out of the weather.

Then, her cooking, which he seemed to find miraculous, which was a laugh. He was a former SEAL. Those guys could send a slingshot around the moon, they could kill with a pinkie, they trained hard to be the best soldiers on earth. All she could do was cook, but he seemed to find that ability fascinating. Since he was helping her so much, she offered to teach him how to cook and he eagerly accepted her offer. It turned out, though, that he was severely cooking-challenged. Everything came out burned and oversalted and disgusting.

But that was okay. She liked cooking for him. It gave her something to do. And since he seemed to have some kind of rota system of buddies stopping by, she cooked for them too.

She had the world's best TV and sound system, carefully put together by Joe. She could probably receive TV signals from outer space. There wasn't one creaky door or drawer in the house. He took her bathroom's leaky faucet as a personal challenge and not a drop had fallen since.

Wow. She stopped and blinked. She was almost at the park and she'd had very few bad thoughts along the way. Thinking of Joe had carried her from her house to the park, though the thoughts were useless. If she wasn't such a head case, she'd have been thinking of her future, of what to do with her life instead of mooning over her gorgeous, built neighbor who had better things to think about than her.

Okay, Isabel, now focus, she told herself sternly.

Describe your surroundings. Be in the moment. That's what a psychotherapist told her when she consulted her. She couldn't sleep and wanted something that wasn't pills. Pills were awful. They didn't work but they did render her a numb walking automaton during the day. Anything was better than taking sleeping aids, even insomnia.

Focus on your surroundings. Her surroundings. Well, mostly single family homes. It was a residential neighborhood, which was what she liked about it. The small park, whimsically called Strawberry Fields, was coming up. It was a pretty park even with bare trees and gray evergreen bushes. You could see the flower beds that would blossom in spring. It would be glorious in summer.

Would she still be here in summer? Yes. Probably. Because...where else would she go? Back East was full of memories, no way. There was always California, much nicer climate. But Portland suited her. Everyone was friendly without being obnoxious. Lots of concerts. It was so green. Very little crime.

Joe Harris.

She sighed. Joe Harris was so something she should not be thinking about. Focus on something else. Focus on...that cute little pup trying desperately to dig in the flowerless flower beds. He was making it his life's mission. His mistress was pulling so hard on the leash he rose on his two hind legs, the two front legs scrabbling in the air.

Isabel laughed. She nearly looked around to see who'd done that, it felt so weird. *She'd* done it. The laugh had come from her. You'd have to be dead not to laugh at the pup, tongue lolling out its smiling mouth, scampering to leave its mark on the park.

Its mistress—a young girl with golden hair tucked up in a Peruvian Chullo hat—was bending over, finger raised, doing her best to teach her pup etiquette. The pup barked and licked her finger. There was very little etiquette-learning going on.

Isabel laughed again. The pup rolled its eyes toward her and barked. Their eyes met and the pup barked again, grinning and slobbering, straining now in her direction.

Was that dog *flirting* with her?

Isabel was not far from the small enclosed doggy section of the park, a square filled with sand where dogs could play and do their business. Owners took them off the leash to enter the small enclosure. The girl walked the puppy over to the doggy section. At the entrance, she bent to unsnap the leash.

Instead of heading into the doggy park, the pup took off like a rocket, making a beeline for Isabel, fur rippling with speed.

The girl straightened, gasped, called out to her dog. “Freddy! Freddy! Come back here right now! Bad dog! Bad dog!”

Freddy paid his mistress no attention at all, leaving the ground several yards from Isabel, leaping straight at her.

Isabel froze. The pup was heavy. It was going to be a big dog. It was big now. Hurtling straight at her, it was going to knock her to the ground and she didn’t have the reflexes to get out of its way.

The dog barked, hit her in the chest, trying to lick her face. Isabel slipped on an icy patch, stumbled back and…

Didn’t fall.

Something big and strong caught her, kept her upright.

She looked up, startled.

Joe.

Freddy was barking and writhing at her feet. He barked enthusiastically, put his paws up and wriggled, trying frantically to lick her.

“Down, Freddy,” Joe said sternly. “Sit.”

Freddy sat, butt wriggling on the ground.

Joe had barely raised his voice.

The girl came running up, face scrunched in apology. She held her hand out to Isabel. "Oh, gosh, I am *so* sorry! Are you okay?"

Was she? Isabel patted herself down. She'd expected to hit the ground hard, but hadn't. It had happened in a flash. The dog jumping on her, guaranteed to bowl her over and then whoosh, like magic—Joe was suddenly there.

"Yeah," she said cautiously. "I'm, um, fine."

She looked up, way up, at Joe's grim face. Sober, harsh features, standing there like a rock, big hand holding her arm.

"Thanks," she said and he nodded.

Her voice seemed to unlock something in the puppy. It scrambled up, tail wagging furiously, body language clear. It wanted to jump on her again.

"Down," Joe said firmly again and Freddy plopped back down.

The young girl looked at Joe wide-eyed. "How'd you *do* that? Freddy doesn't obey me at all. How'd you get him to sit?"

Isabel took pity on her. Being female, the girl was probably blaming herself for a ton of dog-training inadequacies.

"Joe here is a former navy SEAL," she explained kindly and the girl's face smoothed out. Clearly she wasn't inadequate. No one could expect her to show a SEAL's ability to command.

"Oh." She looked up at Joe. "That true?"

He nodded seriously. Isabel looked carefully and saw that Joe was biting his lips not to smile.

"You're not—you don't..." The girl took a deep breath and blurted it out. "You're not a dog trainer, are you? Because man, I would pay anything to get Freddy to obey me like that."

"Sorry," Joe said in his basso profundo voice and the girl slumped. "Not in that line of work."

The girl sighed and bent down to clip the leash to Freddy's collar. Freddy shook, hindquarters up, front paws extended. His hindquarters braced. The girl pulled at the leash but it was a big puppy and she had no hope of stopping another jump at Isabel.

And then Joe worked his magic, this time with one sharp movement of his big hand. Freddy subsided.

Isabel exchanged glances with the girl.

Yep. You had to be a SEAL to be able to do that.

With a smile, the girl walked off, an obedient Freddy trotting alongside her.

Isabel looked up at Joe. "Thanks," she said again and he shrugged.

FUCK, THAT WAS CLOSE.

Joe had excellent balance, always had. Even after being injured, he'd never fallen, not once. He also had superb spatial awareness. When that rambunctious pup made a leap for Isabel, Joe had been able to see the consequences exactly as if it was a game of chess. Isabel was standing next to a steel post holding the wooden slats of the enclosure. She was in the exact right spot to ensure that she'd bash the back of her head against the steel post, drop and smash her head against the concrete piling. Maybe bounce off the wood, too, and get sharp splinters while she was at it.

He'd seen it, as inevitable as geometry. Which was why he broke land speed records getting to her and breaking her fall.

Joe knew how to make his face a mask. Nobody saw what he didn't want them to see and he knew he wasn't betraying the absolute panic he'd felt at the thought of Isabel cracking her head open. He'd watched one helmetless marine die when he fell and cracked his head on a rock.

Isabel, dead. Fuck. Not going to happen, not while he was around.

She was pale but she sketched a smile. "That puppy needs some manners."

"She'd better hurry up and teach him some because Freddy's going to grow up to be a big dog," Joe said sternly.

He had no patience for those who acquired animals they couldn't handle. That woman could have cost Isabel a bad concussion, or worse.

"So," he said, holding her elbow. He'd rather put his arm around her waist, but one way or another, he was going to be touching her. Isabel looked pale and shocky. She was *not* going to fall. "Since I'm here, do you want to walk around the park or are you ready to go back?"

"Back," Isabel said immediately. She peered up at him, frowning. "How did you happen to be here at exactly the right time? Are you Superman or The Flash?"

"I didn't go for my run and I wanted some exercise. I like this park and I just happened to see you and see that dog come running at you," Joe lied cheerfully.

Because the truth would have sounded too creepy. *You looked unsteady on your feet so I followed you, and made sure you couldn't see me.*

"Well, you showed up just in time, like a superhero." She smiled at him. Her smiles were rare and they lit up her face. Joe should have felt bad about lying to her, but he didn't. She wouldn't have been smiling at him if he'd told her the truth.

"Ma'am?" He stuck out his elbow at an exaggerated angle and she put her arm through his. "May ah have the honah of accompanyin' you home?" He laid on a thick ole-timey Southern accent. Rhett Butler offering Scarlett his arm.

"Why, sir." She batted her eyelashes extravagantly. "It would be mah pleasure."

He was playacting but…whoa. It wasn't hard to imagine her in some big ball gown, curtsying. She had such an old-fashioned beauty to her, made up of fine features, huge eyes with eyelashes that were like fans and perfect ivory skin. Those eyelashes of hers were so long they could create a breeze when she fluttered them.

She frowned, the playacting completely dropped. "Joe?"

Whoa. He'd been standing there staring at her like a total moron. The playacting had allowed him to study her face. He rarely looked at her for long because he didn't want to come across as creepy, because really? He knew he could stare at her for hours and wouldn't that scare her away.

"Raht here, ma'am." He nodded and tipped an imaginary top hat. "Okay, let's go."

They walked back slowly, because Isabel wasn't a fast walker and because he wanted to stretch out their time together. And it was no hardship walking slowly. Not with Isabel by his side.

She was watching the ground. Yeah, he recognized that. He'd spent two months walking carefully, watching every step. But he knew exactly why he had to watch his feet for months after being able to finally get out of bed.

He'd been blown up. He'd died and come back. He'd been really messed up there.

Why was she watching the ground so assiduously? Why was her balance so off? Why did she have to walk so slowly?

What the hell happened to you?

The words were there, on the tip of his tongue. She'd been wounded, hurt in some way. That was clear. But how? He'd caught that one glimpse of a scar on her forearm and that was it. It was a nasty one but not life threatening. She always wore long-sleeved sweats in the house and outdoors she was dressed for cold weather so basically he had her face and hands to judge by and they were…perfect.

Maybe her bad wounds were covered up. He'd have to see her naked to know.

And bam, just like that, the image of a naked Isabel rose up before him and his dick stirred in his pants. His very first hard-on since almost dying.

Oh…shit. His dick had been dead meat between his legs since the IED. Nothing had stirred it to life. When he'd discreetly asked Metal, he'd gotten a hard stare. *Dude, you nearly died. As a matter of fact you did die and they shocked you back to life. That's major trauma and you're lucky to be alive, you ungrateful fuck,* Metal had said. And then Joe got a long lecture about how penile erection was one of the last functions to return and that he was an ungrateful shithead who by the merest chance wasn't bones in the ground and…

Metal started getting heated up and Joe had held his hands up and never asked again. And truth was, there was no time for women in his life after the IED, there was just long, painful rehab.

And then Isabel showed up and she fascinated him and intrigued him and he was vastly attracted but his dick basically stayed down. There was the added factor that she was clearly a traumatized woman and he wasn't going to come on to a woman who looked so vulnerable.

So it was like this balance they'd achieved. She didn't flirt and he didn't push because neither of them was in a position to do something about it.

Except now…

Shit. It was just his luck that his dick surged to life at the wrongest possible moment. Before being blown up and dying, Joe would have said that an active dick was never a bad thing, but right now it was.

True, his parka reached midthigh and he had on heavy cold-weather camo pants from his navy days, but still. He had to work not to walk funny.

He couldn't even think of something else, something to make it go down, not with Isabel *right there*, holding his arm. That was boner material, just her touching his arm through about a billion layers of clothing.

Christ, a dead man would get a boner with her around. The fact was that he hadn't died that day. He'd lived and now his entire body was on the same page.

The top of her head reached his shoulder and, looking down, he saw absurdly long lashes, high cheekbones and an impossibly lush mouth. She was wearing a knit cap rimmed with pale mink fur, shiny mink-colored locks escaping from it.

Silvery gray eyes moved to look up at him and he shifted his gaze just in time. He didn't want her to catch him staring at her.

"Are you having a poker night tonight?" she asked with a slight smile.

"Not tonight." Shit. "Do we make too much noise? Sorry."

She shook her head. "Oh no! Not at all. I don't hear much, just the occasional shout or groan. I imagine they correspond to a win or a loss. Do you do much losing?"

"Nah." He'd always earned extra money with poker. He could beat the pants off Satan himself. "But I'm sorry if we bother you."

"It's actually kind of…nice hearing you guys." She bit her lips as if she'd already said too much. Her voice sounded wistful.

Was she lonely? Wow, that was a thought. And yet—she had to be. To Joe's knowledge, he was the only person she saw. It seemed so outrageous to him that a woman as beautiful and as nice as Isabel could be lonely, but there it was.

Joe was really lucky. His company, Alpha Security International, was like a big, extended family. He'd been blown up at the end of his deployment in the military and ASI had carried him on its payroll since then, even when he'd been in a coma and had begun the series of operations that put him back together. ASI was mainly made up of his BUD/S buds who had shown their support in every way.

He had his teammates and soon would join them full-time in the job. They were like a family, tight and strong. Anything he needed, he got. And as soon as he was fully functioning, he'd be there for them, too—no question. He knew he was soaking up help, but that was the way families worked, wasn't it? When you reached out for a helping hand, it was there.

His family hadn't been like that, his old man would have been more liable to knock Joe down than extend a helping hand but Joe was no dummy. He'd seen how good families worked and it was like a little miracle.

Where was her family? Who cared for her? Why was she so isolated?

He burned with questions he wanted to ask her. *Who are you? What happened to you? Where are your people?*

"You can come over anytime you want," he blurted. "Poker game or not. You play?"

She smiled and shook her head. "I'd lose every cent I had if I played poker. I don't have much of a poker face and I can't keep the cards straight in my head. Clearly, you can."

Oh, yeah. After a day or two, he'd be kicked out of any casino in the country for card counting.

"You can sit beside me and be my good luck charm," he said and she closed up. Bam. Just like that. Face as blank as that of a doll.

"I don't bring anyone good luck," she said softly.

Well, fuck. If a beautiful classy woman considered herself a jinx, what could he say?

They were back home. He walked her up to her front door. He opened his mouth to say something, anything—*do you want to come over for the lunch you cooked for me? Do you want to go for a drive? Do you want to go to bed with me?*—but before he could put his foot in it, she smiled at him, thanked him again and disappeared into her house.

Joe was left staring at the wooden door that was exactly like his until he snapped out of it and entered his own house. He had some paperwork to get through—he had to read through a contract ASI had signed with a local bank and which would be his first job for them at the first of the month—and he had some laundry to do.

What he did was head for the shower. He needed a long, cold one after his walk with the most beautiful woman in the world, Isabel Lawton.

But first, he had to check his email. There might be another contract for him to look at.

He shucked off his parka and sweater and boots and socks, standing barefoot in front of the keyboard.

There was an email from Jacko—We're on for tomorrow! Metal's bringing beer.

So—poker night tomorrow was confirmed.

And another email from an address he didn't recognize. In the subject line: READ ME. It smelled of spam but if it had passed his spam filter, it was worth a look.

He clicked it open and felt his face tighten as he stared at the message.

PROTECT ISABEL

Do you want to come over and watch while we play poker?

Oh, God *yes.* Isabel had had to bite her lips to keep from saying that. She'd lied a little. The guys *did* make a lot of noise but she just lapped it up. Sometimes she sat in a chair close to the living room window that faced his house and listened to the rumble of deep male voices, closing her eyes and imagining she was home again, with Jack teasing their father, the twins, Teddy and Rob, chiming in.

Joe and his friends swore like the sailors they were. She heard more four-letter words in one evening than she normally did in a year. They were profane and funny and something else. There was affection there as they called each other names. It was absolutely unmistakable. Affection and fraternity. The kind of affection and fraternity that had existed among the Delvauxes.

The men were all close friends, a tight and unbreakable union, like her family had been.

And just like that, it took her. The room swirled and her head went light and her knees wobbled. She sat down heavily, still in her coat and boots, and bent her head low between her knees. In the very beginning, when thoughts of her family made her dizzy, she'd have to head as fast as she could to the bathroom, where she'd vomit the contents of her stomach together with her misery into the toilet bowl.

Maybe it was a mark of progress that she no longer vomited, but just felt dizzy. She sat, head bowed low, trying to ease out her breathing until the room stopped spinning. No tears, though. At times she thought she'd cried out all the tears her body could possibly hold. It had been months since she'd cried. Not because she didn't want to but because tears wouldn't come. The tears had dried up inside her, just like all the other emotions. Now she felt as dry and shriveled as a husk of corn. Most days she was surprised the wind didn't just carry her away, she felt so insubstantial.

She wasn't here. She was a ghost. She had already died only her body hadn't noticed yet.

The only thing that told her she wasn't actually dead were those flashes of heat when she was near Joe Harris. He seemed such a nice man, but she didn't dare tell him he reminded her that she wasn't dead.

It sounded so weird, so incredibly neurotic. Yes, she'd lost her family. But he'd been blown up. In battle. Her own physical injuries paled next to his. Her spirit had broken, not her bones. His spirit hadn't broken at all.

Who knew if Joe would or even could understand that? He seemed so…straightforward. So sane. He'd probably had a Putting Joe Harris Back Together Program going the instant he woke up after the explosion. Yeah, that sounded like him. He probably had some kind of timetable for recovery, and was moving ahead with it, step-by-step.

Get wounded, do rehab, get better.

Whereas she was still mired back at step one. Lose family. She'd never really gotten beyond that in any way. Every night when her nightmares woke her up, she felt the pain of their deaths every bit as keenly as when she'd woken up in the hospital and the nurse had given her the news. She relived that, night after night after night, in some hellish endless loop, but was never able to remember anything else in the morning, only grief and horror and terror.

When the dizziness passed, Isabel stood, exhausted. She hung up her coat in the hallway and moved to the kitchen for a glass of water. Her feet were shuffling and she had to remember to pick them up, to walk normally. Every single thing she did had to be done like a child learning it all for the first time.

Except…except walking back home. That had been great. Arm in arm with Joe Harris she'd felt almost normal for the first time since the Massacre. He'd kept pace with her, moving as slowly as she did but making it seem perfectly normal. She had a feeling that if she'd crawled, he'd have crawled right alongside her.

Clearly, he could walk faster than that. Hell, he ran

almost every morning. But coming back from the park, he'd kept step with her without making any kind of big deal about it. And it had felt just great. Arm linked with his, feeling him so big and warm and strong at her side, well…she'd felt strong too. Just a little. It wasn't like the old days when she was fit and happy and energetic. Those days were over, maybe forever. These days she felt a hundred years old.

But she'd definitely felt better with him by her side. She didn't need to watch her feet. He wouldn't let her fall if she tripped. So for the first time in what felt like forever she'd walked with her head upright, seeing the street for the first time. Acutely aware of the big man by her side. Wishing they could walk together forever.

But that was crazy. He was just walking his nutso, next-door neighbor back home because she'd nearly been knocked over by a dog. Couldn't even be trusted to take a short walk to a nearby park.

Oh, God she was so *tired* of this! So tired of being a pale shadow of herself, so tired of not sleeping, so tired of feeling guilty because she hadn't died together with her parents and her brothers and her aunts and uncles and cousins.

Yes, she should have said. *I'd love to come over.* Sit by his side while he played cards, listen to the male banter, laugh at their corny jokes. They'd probably watch their language around her but she didn't care. Teddy had passed through a stage where *fuck* was a noun, a verb, an adjective, an adverb and an exclamation. He'd been so funny.

Isabel sat down and ducked her head back between her legs as the dizziness came back, together with a pounding headache.

She missed her family. So. Fucking. *Much.*

Would the pain ever go away?

Would it have helped if she'd accepted Joe's invitation? Could she shed this dry husk of sadness that enveloped her, just for one evening? Go back to her old self?

No dizziness, no sudden crippling bouts of sadness, just a sense of play among strong, confident men.

She liked guys. Growing up with three brothers had given her a sense of ease around men. In college, it had been a game the girls played—finding new and inventive ways to describe the dumbness of the guys. They were fine for fucking but none of her friends stuck to one guy for long. One of her friends, when asked why she'd dumped the date du jour after only a couple of nights, simply rolled her eyes and said, "The Y chromosome." And everyone laughed and understood.

Not Isabel. Granted, guys could be clueless most of the time but they never took offense and she loved their take on things. Her best friends in college had been two jocks who were smart as whips but who were having big problems passing the obligatory English exams. English profs objected to jocks almost on principle. So she coached them through the exams and they kept her car running and everyone was happy.

Could she have that with Joe and his friends?

Maybe if she reached out. But she hadn't been attracted to her two jock buddies, not at all. Sex hadn't been any part of the equation. She *was* attracted to Joe, so maybe that wasn't a good idea.

Joe was hot. In every sense of the term. She hadn't really understood it completely when her friends said that a guy was hot. Usually it meant he had money, or tons of charm or dressed well. Mostly, though, in her circles, it meant he had money. Money left her cold. The fact that a guy was rich wasn't in any way a factor in attraction as far as she was concerned. She'd moved among the wealthy all her life and if there was one thing she knew, right down to the ground, it was that money did not make a person a better human being.

Joe didn't seem to be rich but he was definitely hot. And by hot she meant he made her hot. Or at least that icy crust around her heart melted a little when she was near him, or thought of him.

But if grieving, semi-crazy Isabel Lawton thought Joe Harris was hot, then lots of other women did, too, guaranteed. And he was a former navy SEAL. Ever since she discovered that, she also discovered that SEALs were considered rock stars. The hottest of the hot. Women lusted after them, they were babe magnets. There were calendars of bare-chested SEALs and they sold like crazy. SEAL seemed to be synonymous with sex.

She hadn't seen women flocking to Joe's door but then he was often gone. Who knows where? And with whom?

And she really had no business thinking these thoughts because she was barely human these days. She wasn't good company for herself, let alone for someone else.

And sex. God. She'd enjoyed sex back in the day, but now? Now she shuddered if someone got too close to her. Claustrophobia clawed at her in an enclosed space with too many people. Her hands and feet turned to ice and her stomach churned and panic rose in her throat. Walking with Joe had been really nice but who knew how she'd react if it ever came to intimacy? She'd freeze, surely. Curl in on herself, incapable of reacting like a woman.

Isabel rested her head against the back of the couch. Sadness and weakness nearly overwhelmed her.

Was this going to be the rest of her life? Missing her family like crazy. Unable to stop grieving them. Nightmares every night. Despair and exhaustion her constant companions during the day.

These thoughts were toxic thoughts, just as surely as if she was taking poison, drop by drop. She couldn't go on this way. She was dishonoring her family, who had loved life and lived it to the fullest. Though the dizziness and the nightmares were beyond her control, her thoughts weren't. She could control her thoughts, or at least try to.

Doing something. That was usually a good antidote. But do what? The house was spotless. Her accounts were in order. She'd neglected her food blog for so long she had no more followers, so that was out.

Food.

Okay.

She'd cook something else for Joe, to thank him for saving her from the big bad slobbering puppy. Baked ziti. A hearty recipe a friend's Sicilian grandmother had taught her. He could freeze the pan and share with his buddies over poker some other time.

The thought energized her enough to propel her from the couch and back into the kitchen. Her hands took over. When she cooked she rarely had to think. Her hands just did the work without much input from her. It was magic.

So she switched on her cook setting and went along for the ride.

There was something so magical about food. Food and sex, the eternal healers. In her heart of hearts, if someone put her feet to the fire to make her tell the truth, she thought food was better than sex. More reliable as a source of pleasure. Good food never let you down like people did.

Before the...before. Before, she'd been making a name for herself as a food blogger because all of it interested her. *Foodways*, her blog was called. Well, it had been called that when it was active. Now it was dormant, dead. She still got puzzled inquiries from fellow food enthusiasts who hadn't put together that Isabel Delvaux of *Foodways* was one of *the* Delvauxes, the political and artsy family. The family that had died in the Washington Massacre.

The contacts were falling off fast and other food bloggers had picked up her readership. *Foodways* was dead. Last week she'd even canceled her personal *Foodways* email address.

But in its heyday *Foodways* had received hundreds of thousands of hits a day. A million and a half readers. A best of collection of her posts had been published and enjoyed a modest success. Before...before. Before, she'd received several offers from publishers about writing a big book about the history of food, about food folklore throughout the world, including recipes. She'd been in negotiations with a major publisher when...

When the bottom dropped out of her world.

Memories usually carried sharp-cutting edges, slicing deep, making her bleed. It was only in the kitchen that she was able to chase memories away.

Right now she resolved to make the best pan of baked ziti in the history of the world for Joe. She'd put it into the biggest pan she had and leave a note on top that he could freeze the pan until the next poker night if he wanted. All he'd have to do was take it out of the freezer and pop it into the oven an hour before his friends were due to arrive.

Not the microwave oven, she'd have to add that to the note. She knew the attraction microwaves held for bachelors.

The real recipe, the true one, for baked ziti took hours. It was something only a grandmother could possibly cook. And, well, Isabel, who had hours to kill. Great aching vast oceans of hours to kill.

So she set to it, making the sauce from scratch, making almost a hundred tiny flavorful meatballs, undercooking the ziti because they'd finish cooking in the sauce in the oven, grating the scamorza cheese. It was a rich dish full of carbs and fats and protein. The kind of dish you'd need if you were walking across Antarctica.

Not the kind of dish she could eat, though she could certainly cook it. That was another thing that had fled from her world that night, together with sleep. An appetite. She'd always loved food and now most food tasted like cardboard, like a simulacrum of food. No matter what the dish, whether she'd prepared it or a master chef had, she couldn't taste anything. Her stomach often clenched shut so tightly her abdominal muscles hurt.

Months ago, she'd have vomited if her plate was too full. Now she'd learned to nibble at the blandest, most tasteless things possible. Dry toast, small bowls of plain rice. Nothing with taste and color.

Right after the Massacre she'd completely lost her desire to cook. Cooking was recently reintroduced in her life, thanks to Joe. He helped her so much with things she couldn't do that she knew she had to do something in return, something she did know how to do.

Crazily, cooking for Joe didn't make her dizzy or nauseous. She could cook the most elaborate dishes and as long as she didn't have to eat a bite of them, she was okay.

Like now, putting together the ziti dish, delicious smells coming from the stove top, and all she felt was pleasure.

She'd often toyed with the idea of actually inviting Joe over for dinner, instead of leaving something on his doorstep like the cooking fairies. He went out of his way for her so much that cooking a meal and serving it was the least she could do.

The thought even gave her a crazy kind of pleasure. She'd started over completely here in Portland, getting her furniture from IKEA and her linens from Bed Bath & Beyond. But she'd shipped over all her culinary equipment and her Limoges dinner service and the Delvaux silver cutlery. She could wow him with an elegant meal as a thank-you.

It was so incredibly tempting. Not spending an evening nursing a cup of lukewarm milk, with the TV on to a show she wasn't watching, simply so she could hear the sound of human voices. So she wouldn't feel at the bottom of a deep well, the only person in the world. Having Joe over would be fun. He was an interesting guy and, well, there was that hotness factor.

But…she wasn't an ordinary woman. She didn't do well in company. The days of bursting into tears with people around her were over but that didn't mean she was back to normal. She could throw up. She could become so dizzy she'd faint. She could lock herself in the bathroom because she couldn't deal with him.

They were all fun possibilities. She didn't trust herself at all. Joe helped her because she was visibly wounded and still relatively weak. He never asked, bless him, and she never said what was wrong. Keep it like that. Let him think she'd been in an accident and was putting herself back together again.

Because the truth was much blacker and bleaker. The truth was that she *had* been in an accident that had torn her family from her but she *wasn't* putting herself back together again. Maybe she'd be like this for the rest of her life, unfit for human company.

Missing her family like crazy, for the rest of her life.

Put like that…put like that maybe all she really was good for was to cook things for someone who'd suffered but who was pulling himself out of it.

She swiped angrily at her eyes as she finished the pan of ziti and started making naan bread.

THREE

"WELL?" JOE ASKED Felicity impatiently, ignoring the nasty look Metal was shooting at him. Everyone always treated Felicity with kid gloves. Apart from the fact that she was Metal's love and Metal would pound anyone who was disrespectful to her, she also earned a hell of a lot of money for the company as their in-house computer guru.

And she beat everyone's ass at video games.

"Sorry, Joe." Felicity Ward, soon to be Felicity O'Brien, pushed herself away from his desk where she'd been using her own computer. Some kind of woo-woo piece of tech that could have been time-traveled from the future, it was so advanced. Felicity had taken one look at his laptop and sniffed in disdain. "Whoever sent you that message is scary good. I can't identify the IP. Believe me when I say that's unusual."

Oh yeah, he believed Felicity. She was a computer genius and ASI had snatched her up, right after she'd unmasked an international conspiracy. An international *nuclear* conspiracy no less. She was smart in everything but she was off the charts smart when it came to IT. If she couldn't track down the sender of the mystery message, no one could.

"Whoever sent it must be as smart as you," he said.

Felicity smiled and waved Metal, who'd risen from his seat, down. It was a pillar in Metal's thought system that Felicity was the smartest person on earth. "Yeah. Hard as it is to believe."

"Scary stuff," Metal rumbled.

"Yes." Joe nodded his head sharply.

It *was* scary stuff. Someone Felicity couldn't ID had sent a message about Isabel. That blew his mind. That someone knew about Isabel and that that someone knew she was connected to him. How could that happen?

"So," Felicity said. "Let's look at the object of the message. Isabel Lawton. Who is completely off the grid."

Joe frowned. "What do you mean?"

Felicity was frowning, too, only at her monitor. "She almost doesn't seem to exist. No Facebook page, no Twitter handle, I can't find any trace of her educational or job background anywhere in the US. I've found plenty of Isabel Lawtons but they're either too old or too young and no one fits what you've told me about her. Which, frankly, isn't much." She sighed and turned a serious face to him. "You'd almost think she is me."

Hmm. Felicity had grown up in the Witness Protection Program. Her father had been a famous Russian nuclear scientist who had defected and Felicity had basically been undercover her entire life. She'd changed names several times during childhood.

"Like…a spook?" Joe asked. "Or a spook's daughter or sister or—" He swallowed. "Someone's wife? Maybe the wife of someone dangerous? And she's run away from him?"

That thought burned in his chest. Isabel married to an abusive husband. It was a thought he didn't want to have but it sort of made sense. Instead of being a woman of mystery maybe she was a woman on the run. Maybe someone was after her, which would explain how she seemed always on edge.

If that was the case, her running days were over. Joe wouldn't let anyone hurt her. No one was going to touch her. Except him.

"Not a nice thought," Metal said.

Metal hated abusers as much as Joe did. They'd both been sick at heart when they'd had to negotiate with a warlord in Helmand for safe passage for a convoy of marines. The warlord, who was in his sixties, had called in his pregnant wife, a girl in her late teens, to serve them. Her shaking hands had spilled some hot tea on Joe and the warlord had punched her in the face.

Joe and Metal had kept their faces bland because the mission was an important one with the lives of a marine battalion at stake, but they didn't forget. It had been Joe's immense pleasure to find the warlord's head in his crosshairs after a double cross had cost the lives of fifteen marines. Pulling that trigger and seeing that fucker's head explode had been one of the great pleasures of Joe's life.

"What do we know about Isabel Lawton, besides the fact that she makes the best boeuf bourguignon I've ever tasted?"

"The best what?" Joe and Metal said in unison.

Felicity rolled her eyes. "The best boeuf bourguignon. Hello? What we had for lunch and which we all agreed was fabulous?"

"Oh." Joe sat back. "The beef stew."

Felicity rolled her eyes again. "Yeah. The beef stew."

"Great stuff," Metal said.

It had been. They'd practically inhaled it. The instant Joe had seen that message he'd invited Metal and Felicity over for a late lunch, making it clear that if Felicity didn't come along, Metal wouldn't get to eat.

It was a threat with bite. By now, getting a chance to eat whatever Isabel cooked was a fought-over privilege. Joe got points for Isabel's cooking.

So they'd eaten and then Joe had shown Felicity the mystery message.

"Was she a chef?" Felicity mused, tapping on her laptop's nearly invisible keyboard. The keys were barely raised and allowed Felicity's hands to float and conjure up miracles with what looked like the merest strokes. "Have any chefs gone missing lately?" She briefly consulted a website then sat back. "No."

For an instant Joe was distracted from the problem of someone stalking Isabel. "There's a website for disappeared chefs?" he asked, astonished.

"No, dummy." Felicity shook her head. "I consulted a list of notable chefs and wrote a little algorithm to check for people who were on last year's list but not on this year's lists. There were ten people missing but they were all men. Three had died and one is doing time."

Joe slid his eyes to Metal. Felicity had done all that in less than a minute. "She's scary."

Metal grinned smugly. "That's my girl."

"Well, someone knows enough about Isabel to know that we see each other on a regular basis and that's scary, too." Joe ground his teeth.

"Does she see other people?" Metal asked.

"No." Joe's voice was abrupt. Issue closed.

Metal recognized that tone but Felicity didn't. "How can you be so sure?"

The good thing about Felicity was her smarts. The bad thing about Felicity was her smarts.

"I just know," Joe said, his tone chilly enough to get a frown from Metal.

Felicity's head cocked as she studied him. She wasn't afraid of him in any way, which was good but damn, Joe wished they were in the military and he could shut her down with a command.

Though it was entirely likely that if Felicity was in the military she'd be a general by now. Head of Cyber Command.

"You keep tabs on her," Felicity said.

Joe sighed. "Yeah." He made an impatient gesture. "It's not like I'm stalking her or anything. She's not in a good way and to tell you the truth, she worries me."

There, that sounded normal and sane. Concern for a neighbor, no more no less.

"Plus, she is a fabulous cook," Felicity said dryly.

"Yeah, there's that too."

"And probably beautiful, judging by the expression on your face."

Busted. Joe sighed. "Yeah. She's a looker."

Metal rested his arm against Felicity's seat back and she leaned into it, the movement so natural because she'd probably done that a thousand times.

Metal was a lucky guy. Felicity was a looker, too. Joe and Metal were old enough not to be attracted by looks alone. As a teenager, Joe'd been turned on by just about any girl who didn't make dogs whine and cringe. The pretty ones had been like catnip. Experience had taught him the hard way that pretty features didn't mean shit. He'd met some vain and vicious pretty women and his radar was fine-tuned for that. Felicity and Isabel didn't ping any of his warning buttons.

Like Isabel, Felicity wasn't vain or neurotic about her

looks. She and Metal were lovers, but they were also a team. A pretty cool one, too.

The same with a lot of guys in ASI. At first, Joe had thought it was something in the water out here in Portland. A lot of the guys were in tight, solid relationships. Maybe because the two owners, John Huntington, aka Midnight, and Douglas Kowalski, known as the Senior, had fantastic marriages. Jacko was also engaged to a looker. They were crazy in love, too.

Weird, so many solid couples in one place.

"Someone knows you're interested," Metal said soberly. "Otherwise that message doesn't make sense. You don't tell someone to look after their neighbor unless you know there's some relationship there."

"And you don't take high-level precautions to hide your identity," Felicity added. She touched her magic computer. "This guy, or this woman, employed a lot of difficult tricks to hide his or her identity. It's not just a question of an anonymizer. The person who sent the message had to take a number of steps to hide their identity, and not easy steps, either. That person had to work, and work hard, to hide from me."

She said it without false modesty. Felicity was the best of the best and she knew it.

"Someone's watching you," Metal said. "No way around it."

"Or watching Isabel." Joe didn't know which thought bothered him more.

"And you're not catching it." Metal shook his head. "I don't buy it. You've got good situational awareness. You haven't noticed anything, anything at all?"

Joe shook his head.

"Security cams," Felicity said suddenly and both men turned to her.

"What?"

But she was too busy communing with her laptop, fingers flying over the keyboard. She sat back and turned the monitor so he and Metal could see. Joe's eyes widened.

She had some kind of map of their street with an overlay of security cameras with their field of vision. His street with projected cones over several houses.

"Okay, these are the security cams on your street, including yours and Isabel's. Someone has probably hacked into some of them."

"Not mine," Joe said heatedly.

"No," Felicity said softly. "I set yours up myself and they are not hackable."

"And I set up Isabel's system using your equipment and software." So nobody had hacked his vidcam system or Isabel's.

"What about the vidcams in the neighborhood," he asked. "Are they hackable?"

Felicity had kept up the computer patter, fingers flying. "Oh, yeah," she said and turned the monitor toward him. He and Metal bent forward.

And shit. Sure enough, there was his front doorstep, front and center of the camera view of his neighbor across the street, Edward Crawford, a retired doctor. Isabel's doorstep was at the edge, barely visible. But when she walked down the small paved path to her gate, she'd be visible.

Felicity scrolled, from vidcam to vidcam, and he got a choppy view of his side of the street down to the park, where security vidcams took over.

"Are these vidcams hackable by someone who's not you?" he asked.

"Oh, yeah," Felicity said. "You'd need a little nimbleness and savvy but they are hackable. You don't have to be me to do it."

Again, she said that without false pride. She knew how good she was.

Joe swallowed. "Have they been hacked?"

Felicity frowned. "Now, that I can't say. Because I'm assuming that whoever is doing this is pretty good. Good enough to cover his traces." She gave a half smile. "Or her traces. I'm assuming it's a guy, though."

"Yeah."

"You still have that same email address? You didn't change it to Joe.Harris123 did you?"

Felicity had a thing with passwords and email addresses. All of her passwords were created using a randomizer—and she remembered them all—and her email address was impossible to guess.

"Yeah." Joe rubbed the back of his neck. "You pounded that home to me. To all of us. So not only is this guy following me and following Isabel, he—"

"Has a stake in this. He cares for some reason," Metal said.

"That's the thing that has me worried." Joe looked at his friend who was looking as grim as he felt. "Someone is watching us who cares. And reaching out and touching me. So, yeah, he's saying I need to protect Isabel but how do I know he's a friend?"

Felicity's pretty face was scrunched up in thought. "I'm not too familiar with tactics, not like you guys are, but didn't he just show his hand? For what purpose, if not to focus you on Isabel?"

"And you're already pretty focused," Metal said, jabbing Joe with an elbow. Metal was a strong guy and his elbow jabs would knock over a lesser man. Joe wasn't going to give him the satisfaction of budging.

"I mean, what does he have to gain?" Felicity persisted. "So I think we're going to have to take this message at face value." She held up a slender hand and started counting the points off her fingers. "One, he's probably not in town. He's at a different location and can't make it in time if she needs immediate help. Two, he's on Isabel's side. I think we need to simply assume that. Otherwise the message makes no sense. Because if he wanted to hurt her, he wouldn't have alerted you to his presence. Three, he's been able to peg Joe as a good guy and as someone who has a stake in Isabel's safety. To reveal himself like that to Joe, he has to have done some digging. Though Joe's military history is probably heavily redacted as to specific missions, the facts are publicly available. He'd know you were a SEAL. And he trusts you. So I guess in a way we're starting to get a picture of him."

"Okay." Everything Felicity was saying made sense. "So now what do I do?"

Felicity cocked her head and smiled.

"Uh-oh," Metal said. "I know that smile."

"We do two things." Her fingers moved on the keyboard. "First, we answer the guy."

"Okay." Joe sighed. "So, what am I going to say?"

"You already said it," Felicity declared, showing him the message she'd sent.

You bet your ass I'm going to protect Isabel.

She stood up. "And now I'm going to go visit our mystery woman."

Joe's eyes widened. "Wait!" he said but it was too late. Felicity moved fast when she wanted to. In a second she'd grabbed the pot the beef stew had come in, and which they'd washed, and was out the door.

Joe and Metal looked at each other when the door closed.

"She doesn't take no for an answer," Joe finally said, glancing at his friend.

"Nope." Metal shook his head. "She doesn't. And she usually does exactly as she pleases. But living with her, I have learned one thing and that's that she's usually right. So I've learned to stop worrying."

And he had her back. That went without saying. Metal was always there for her and always would be.

They sat in the silence of the house and simply waited. As SEALs they'd been taught patience the hard way—through pain. So they were perfectly capable of waiting anything out. Because clearly, Felicity wasn't just dropping off the pot. She was staying at Isabel's, God only knew for how long.

"So," Metal finally said, looking at him keenly. "Isabel."

"Isabel," Joe nodded.

"She's pretty." Metal had seen her when he'd tended her knee.

"Yeah," Joe sighed. "Very."

"Pretty women can be dangerous."

"Can be," Joe agreed. "But she's like Felicity. Nice, not nasty. But she's also...damaged. Something's happened to her, only I don't know what and she isn't talking. It's like there's this huge no-go zone she's created and I don't have the courage to step into it."

Metal gave him a sidelong glance. Joe had courage

in battle. He'd proved that time and again. He'd spilled blood time and time again, once in saving Metal's ass. But it was true. Squeezing info out of Isabel that she didn't want to give—he just couldn't go there.

"What?" He met Metal's eyes. "You're not gonna make a crack?"

"Nope." Metal zipped his lips. "If there's one thing I've learned lately it's the power of women. She doesn't want you to know something, you're not gonna know it until she wants you to."

Joe nodded. Man, yeah.

He'd been present when CIA agents interrogated jihadists and their methods had been brutal, even the psychological ones. Necessary, but nightmare inducing. Joe was down with breaking terrorists. The thought of coercing Isabel in any way, however, made him nauseous. But damn, he wanted to know her deal, find out what happened to her.

Because the truth was, there was that really ugly suspicion rolling around in the back of his brain. He couldn't get it out of his head that she'd been abused. It wasn't something he wanted to think about but it stuck in his head like a nasty burr. That first day—she'd been hollow-eyed and terrified. Joe knew that look. None of his teammates had had it, of course, they bent but were never broken. But Joe'd spent the better part of a decade in war zones and he'd seen shell-shocked civilians. They had that same look.

Actually, it drove him bugfuck crazy, the thought of someone hurting Isabel. He could picture it in his mind and it was almost more than he could bear. Isabel's skin was delicate, incredibly fine. The idea of her covered in bruises made his heart beat faster with rage.

Of course, he couldn't go anywhere with these thoughts. Who would he talk to about it? Metal and Jacko would just look at him funny. And he couldn't ask Isabel because she wasn't talking.

Because if Isabel was on the run from some man, if that cryptic message was from someone who wanted her to be safe, well whoever sent it had sent it to the right guy. Joe had never backed down from a fight and never would. And to protect Isabel? He'd go to the wall.

"What are you thinking?" Metal asked. The guy looked like a WWE wrestling champ, a big slab of meat and Joe had seen people treat him as if he was a few sandwiches shy of a picnic. Nothing could be further from the truth. Metal was sharp—he just had nothing to prove and he liked being underestimated.

So Joe knew better than to lie to Metal. But he could put a little Vaseline on the lens and misdirect.

"Trying to figure out what's wrong with Isabel. What happened to her."

Metal narrowed his eyes. "You figure she's running from some guy who hurt her."

There it was, out in the open. Joe sighed. "Yeah. I think about it all the time. Drives me nuts."

"I hear you," Metal said. "Every time I think about that fuckhead slicing Felicity open, I can't see straight."

Felicity had been coming to visit her friend Lauren and instead she'd been met at the airport by a guy who wanted to kidnap her for what was in her pretty head. Felicity had escaped because she was Felicity, but not before getting a nasty knife wound. Metal said it still gave him nightmares.

"Men who can do that…" Joe trailed off. Men who could do that weren't worthy of being called men.

"Yeah." Metal looked grim. They both got sick at the idea of men abusing women and children.

"So, suppose a guy like that is after Isabel?" It was his worst nightmare. "How would I know about that if she's not talking? This guy could just show up one day…" He shuddered.

"Like the email said—protect Isabel."

Fuck, yeah. Joe opened his mouth to answer when the front door opened and Felicity came in together with a gust of cold air. She was carrying something big wrapped in tinfoil and set it on the kitchen counter.

Felicity started slowly taking off her gloves, picking at each finger, enjoying the attention. One glove, the other…

Joe couldn't stand it. "Well?"

"Well?" she echoed.

"What did you find out? Did you guys talk?"

"Yes, we did. We chatted. And she said absolutely nothing about herself. But she didn't have to. One look at her and I knew. I'm surprised you didn't figure it out yourself."

Joe followed her out of the kitchen. "Figure what out?"

Felicity sat at her computer. Joe could swear that she didn't touch the keyboard but it suddenly lit up. He'd often wondered if she had arranged her software to mess with their heads. When she was gone from her computer it automatically shut down. When she sat down in front of it, it automatically turned on.

"Who she is," Felicity answered. Her fingers flew over the keyboard.

"So." Joe bent as a number of photos appeared on Felicity's monitor. "Who is she?"

She pointed at the screen. There was some kind of political event, someone at a podium, surrounded by other people. Joe peered closer and frowned. The person at the podium was Alex Delvaux. Joe had been in-country and then in rehab so he wasn't too up on politics, but it looked like a rally. He remembered that Alex Delvaux had been contemplating a run for the presidency before being killed, together with his entire family, in the Washington Massacre.

Felicity placed a fingertip over a woman in the background on the podium. The features weren't clear, all the faces were a blur. She was good-looking but all the Delvauxes were good-looking. Had been good-looking. Now they were all dead.

"So what is it?" he asked, impatiently. He wanted to know what she'd found out about Isabel.

"Here she is. Your next-door neighbor." Felicity tapped once on the face. "Isabel Delvaux."

Washington, DC

PHASE TWO WAS tall and distinguished-looking, with a shock of iron gray hair and craggy features. Phase two was also dumb as a rock, which Blake was counting on.

"Hector!" John London stood up with a fake smile showing fake teeth, manicured hand outstretched. Nice dry handshake. "Sit down, sit down! Can I offer you something? Cup of coffee? They have a nice Colombian roast, hill country beans. Or maybe a cup of tea? Loose leaf Darjeeling, none of this tea bag shit."

"Tea would be fine," Blake murmured, knowing better than to ask for a drink, which he would have preferred. London was an aggressive teetotaler, having been a drunk half his life. He was a dry drunk, incredibly vain and a massive hypocrite.

Blake had hated him for thirty years.

"Wife and kids?" Blake asked, sitting across from London in an old cracked chesterfield. The Voyagers Club, founded in 1895, was proud that it hadn't updated the decor in over two hundred years. There were no more explorers in the upper reaches of America's elite, but the old tradition of what happened in the Voyagers Club staying in the Voyagers Club still reigned. As old-fashioned as it was, some pretty high-tech people went over it weekly, checking for spyware. It was as safe a place to talk serious business as existed in Washington.

Elites need safe spaces and this was one. A lot of secret business had been done here and it had never escaped these walls.

"Wife and kids are fine," London said easily. They all hated his guts, as Blake knew. London had two kids. One was a high-functioning cocaine addict who worked on Wall Street and the other was on her fourth husband. London's wife was a dedicated fashionista who disliked her husband but who wanted ferociously to be First Lady.

Well, Blake was here for that very reason. A reason that had vast geopolitical repercussions, that would change the course of history, but that would, as a minor consequence, make Lindsey London, clotheshorse extraordinaire and superbitch, First Lady.

"I'm glad to hear that," Blake said. "But I didn't ask you to meet me to exchange pleasantries. I'm here to talk business."

London tried really hard to put on an intelligent face. Blake knew that he would report every word back to his campaign manager, Ed Dabny, so Ed could parse it for him. This would make Ed's day. Not to mention Ed's decade. Because when London won, Ed would be chief of staff.

Of the president of the United States.

"Business, eh?" London's face gloomed. Just a little sweat of anxiety. He knew perfectly well Blake was smarter than he was and he suspected some kind of double cross. "What kind of business?" London made a pathetic stab at keeping the worry out of his voice.

Blake plucked at the knife-sharp pleat in his Ermenegildo Zegna trousers. He hoisted his foot slightly to admire his Gucci loafer.

Lifting his head he met London's eyes. "Did you read the blog in *Area 8*?"

Area 8 was quickly becoming the most important political blog in the city, razor-sharp speculation coupled with deep hard news.

London dipped his head, suppressing a smile. "Sure."

Liar. London didn't read. Ed read for him. But Ed would have summarized this one. The article had pulled together a lot of other articles and had quoted interviews with some movers and shakers.

According to *Area 8*, Blake had decided to run. To pick up the mantle of Alex Delvaux and run on his pro-business but green platform. Scuttlebutt had it that Blake was going to ask London to be his veep, though London wasn't on the *Area 8* list.

London had already done the math. After the Massacre, Blake was a shoo-in for the nomination and would undoubtedly win the election. And after his two terms, London would still be under sixty and could run himself.

Eight years at Blair House and another eight at the White House. That was what was dancing through London's handsome but empty head.

"I read it. And I watched *Meet the Press* last Sunday, too. Interesting times, eh?" London was watching him avidly.

Blake sipped his tea. "Everyone's talking about possible VP selections. Fraser, Monti. And Kristen Nash. She's a woman. That hasn't been done yet, except on TV. A female veep. What do you think?"

"Nash. She was a firebrand DA when she was young. Some of her prosecutions might come back to bite her in the ass. Though it is a fine one." London smiled smugly, knowing he could say things like this in the Voyagers Club and no one would object. Blake sure wouldn't. Kristen Nash did have a world-class ass.

"It is indeed." Blake tilted his head. "So, that's *Area 8*'s list of possible VP candidates. The next president is going to have a hell of a lot on his plate."

"Or hers."

Blake bowed his head. "Good point. Or hers. So—after the Washington Massacre things have become more difficult. The military has still not stepped down from DEFCON 3. Costs us a billion a day."

London put on his policy face, the one he put on several times a week when going on news shows. His handsome head had been seen everywhere in the past couple of months. "Not to mention the market losses and economic downturn. The next report from the OBM will say that unemployment is at a ten-year high. We're going to need a strong hand on the tiller. And whoever is president is going to need a really good team, starting with the veep."

This was a little piece of red meat thrown out to Blake, the presumed strongest candidate. London was telling him that he expected Blake to be the candidate and win the election and that he wanted to be in the cabinet. Or even better, to be veep.

Blake gave a deep sigh. Looked down at the carpet in contemplation. "In all confidence, John—"

"Yes?" London leaned forward.

"I've been given assurances that the party will swing behind me. Armstrong and Macy want a whack at it, and DeLuca wants another try, but the party feels that if a strong front-runner is established early on, it won't be torn apart during the primaries. I was told that if I declare now, I can sail through New Hampshire and Iowa. Now that is a lot to take on. A lot depends as well on coming up with a viable and valuable veep candidate."

London scrunched his face into a thoughtful frown. "That's true. It's a lot to have on your plate. Especially right now."

His cue. Blake leaned forward, lowered his voice.

"Well, John, that's the thing. Party analysts are clear that I have a really good shot at winning and taking with me a lot of politicians riding on my coattails. But—"

London leaned forward, too, face a little perplexed. "But?"

Blake sighed. He'd done some deepwater fishing and at least the fish fought back. London was like a farm fish, way too easy to reel in. He pulled a long, sad face.

"But—I find myself unable to get past the Massacre. Alex was my best friend. We'd been best friends since childhood. The Delvauxes were like family to me. And, to tell the truth, I'm still a little shell-shocked by that night. I should have died along with the others. It is a miracle I'm still alive. I'm having a lot of trouble processing the attack. I'm having stress flashbacks."

Blake put a little tremolo in his voice.

London placed a sympathetic hand on his shoulder, no doubt mind spinning to know where Blake was going with this. "I'm so sorry, Blake. Anything I can do—anything at all. All you have to do is ask."

Blake managed not to smile. London wouldn't piss on him if he was on fire.

He briefly touched London's hand on his shoulder.

"You don't know how much I appreciate this, John. And, as a matter of fact, there is something you can do for me. Something big."

Surprise flared in London's eyes. His expression of help had been purely rote. But he knew how the game was played and gave a faint smile, meant to be encouraging. "You name it, Hector, and it's yours."

Starting to reel in the fish…

Blake took in a deep breath, as if bracing himself for something portentous. He looked London straight in the eye and saw him repress a flinch.

"I haven't spoken with anyone about this yet, John. I wanted to sound you out first. I've thought about this long and hard and prayed on it, too. You know better than anyone my sense of duty and love of this country, so the decision has been very painful. But the fact of the matter is, John…at this moment, I am unable to face a primary campaign. I lost too many people in the Massacre and I haven't finished grieving. The loss has simply been too great." He leaned over and clasped London's knee. "So that is why I am asking you to make the sacrifice for me. With your permission, I'd like to go back to the party and throw my weight behind your candidacy."

Hand on knee, Blake could feel the jolt of excitement run through London. He'd just been handed the keys to the kingdom and it was Christmas and a thousand birth days all rolled into one. This election was special. The Massacre was fresh on everyone's mind. The country was still traumatized and longed for a leader to rally round. The mantle of the Delvauxes was supposed to be Blake's, but he was passing it on to London.

More a coronation than an election.

London was trying to repress his emotions, but the skin around his nostrils grew pale. A pulse beat in a vein along his throat. He laid a hand over his heart and Blake had no doubt that it was a genuine gesture, not a studied one. His heart was probably jackhammering.

London's fondest dream, handed to him *on a plate*. Something he would never have been able to gain on his own, and it was going to be given to him.

"There's more." Blake gazed deep into London's eyes. "I have some very powerful and wealthy people behind me, John beyond the party itself. You have no idea the resources that we will make available to you. If you don't sleep with an underage punk rocker or get caught with cocaine up your nose or strangle a staffer, the job is yours. The *position* will be yours." He bowed his head, keeping all irony at bay. "Mr. President."

London huffed out an excited breath. "Oh, my God. Believe me, Hector, when I say I will do my utmost to be worthy—"

Blake cut him off before he started sounding like a campaign ad. "However," he said sternly. "There are a few promises you'll have to make to me. To us. To the people who will be backing you."

"Anything," London promised fervently. And Blake had no doubt he was telling the truth. He'd do anything, anything at all. Good.

"The people behind me have incredible resources which they will place at your disposal. But they are going to want certain things. Certain favors. Nothing that could harm the country, of course. Just things that will ease their business dealings. You need to make a commitment to me that on the rare occasions I ask, you will follow my suggestions."

"Absolutely. Anything you want." London's head was bobbing enthusiastically. He'd sell his firstborn to sex traffickers to be president. He thought he was agreeing to getting a few trade treaties passed or moving legislation that would cut business taxes. He had no idea.

Because phase two was not becoming president. Phase two was controlling the president. And Blake had just secured that.

Blake couldn't move if he was kept under 24/7 surveillance by the Secret Service. But he certainly could as a private citizen with untold wealth. Because beyond phase two were phases three, four and five.

After which America as he knew it would be gone.

Excellent.

FOUR

Portland

ISABEL DELVAUX?

Well, fuck.

The Delvauxes were American aristocracy. Joe knew about them but not enough to know individual members. He knew that the family was political, with many members involved in environmentalism. Another couple of kids were involved in movies. The older generation was powerful. Alex Delvaux—Isabel's *father*—had been talked about as the next president of the United States.

"Fuck me," he said. "She's rich and powerful."

"No," Felicity said. "Not anymore. Not the woman I saw. She's been reduced to rubble."

Felicity walked back into the kitchen to the big pan she'd set on the counter. Some amazing smells were coming from it. Joe lifted the aluminum and took a deep breath. "Wow. Big spaghetti."

"Baked ziti, you barbarian," Metal answered affectionately. "Are we going to get to eat this, too? I mean, after the boeuf bourguignon this seems almost too much." He closed his eyes and took in the amazing aroma, too. "Ah, a woman who cooks." Felicity shot an elbow to his ribs. "What? This is amazing stuff."

"I cook," Felicity protested.

Wisely, Metal kept his mouth shut. His fiancée was

beautiful and supersmart and scary good with IT. Her few stabs at cooking had practically landed them in the hospital. The only thing she cooked well was takeout.

"Isabel said to put this in the freezer, take it out an hour before you want to serve it and put it in the oven at 375 degrees for forty minutes and let it set for about a quarter of an hour before your guests arrive. I can't believe you get to eat like this."

"Hey." Metal cocked his head. "I cook."

She smiled smugly. "Not like this you don't." She turned to look at Joe. He probably still looked stunned.

Isabel, a Delvaux.

He'd been thinking that when she got better they could go out. Well, actually he'd been thinking more along the lines of when she got better they could have sex. A lot.

That seemed pretty foolish now. What would a Delvaux want with a beat-up former soldier?

"She's rich and famous," he said again. No use beating around the bush with Metal and Felicity. Metal knew him way too well and Felicity...well, she'd become one of the guys.

"No," Felicity said crisply. "She's not. I told you that. She's a woman alone. Sit down."

Joe raised his eyebrows.

"I've learned to just obey her," Metal said. "Makes things easier."

Joe sat down.

"So, Joe, what do you know about the Washington Massacre?" Felicity asked. "It happened while you were in the hospital between your third and fourth surgery so I imagine you read about it after the fact."

"The Washington Massacre." Joe lifted his eyes to

the ceiling. "Okay. When it happened I was in ICU. I didn't even hear about it until a couple of weeks after. Still, I think I know what everyone knows. Terrorist attack. Killed almost a thousand people. The electricity grid was attacked too so there was a three-day blackout."

"Those people who were killed included Isabel's entire family. Parents, brothers, aunts, uncles, cousins. It was a close-knit extended family by all accounts, and they were wiped out."

"Shit." Joe turned to Metal. "Al Qaeda was responsible, right? It was another 9/11, on a slightly smaller scale."

"Nobody really knows who was responsible." Metal bounced a fist off his knee. "There were very few survivors. Isabel was one, though I never thought to make the connection. Word was she was in a coma for a while and as far as I know, was never interviewed afterward."

"It was bad for us, wasn't it?" he asked Metal.

"The worst." Metal held up a hand and ticked off the points on his fingers. "First—this was an attack on a gathering of the president's political party, meeting at the hotel closest to the White House. Practically on the White House's doorstep. The attack occurred during an event celebrating the announcement of a presidential run by a scion of one of America's top political families. In effect, it took out the man who would probably have been president in a year and a half. The closest thing possible to a presidential assassination without being a presidential assassination. And it took out a good section of the nation's political elite. There were a lot of undersecretaries and heads of agencies and political journalists. And then the blackout. That scared the shit out of everybody. Images of a dark Washington, DC, in the moonlight spooked the entire country. Looked like what would happen after the zombie apocalypse."

"You think they calculated that? The photo op?"

Metal shot him a shrewd glance. "Yeah. One photo especially was seen all over the world."

The sounds of tapping and Felicity turned her monitor toward him. It was striking and one he'd never seen before. The iconic view of the Mall and the Washington Monument, in total darkness, a full moon rising behind the monument. The top third of the Monument was sheared off. In the background, shades of red as a section of the city was on fire.

Metal was right. "Looks like a snapshot of the apocalypse," Joe said quietly.

"It nearly was." Metal clenched his jaw. "The city went dark, all the cell phones in the area were jammed. The president was hustled into Marine Force One and taken to an undisclosed location. The VP was in the bunker. For about half an hour we were at DEFCON 2."

DEFCON 2. DEFCON 1 was imminent nuclear attack. The last time the country had been at DEFCON 2 had been during the Cuban Missile Crisis. Even 9/11 had been DEFCON 3.

"And I slept through that." Joe shook his head.

"You were blown up. You'd died a couple of times. You're excused."

"So… Al Qaeda, huh? They've regrouped?"

Metal shrugged. "That's the story. Some obscure group based in Yemen no one has heard of claimed it. JIAP. Jihad in the Arabian Peninsula. Loosely connected to AQAP."

"We bomb anyone?"

"Yeah. In Yemen. I think mostly we reduced boulders to rocks."

Felicity cleared her voice delicately. "Not everyone believes it was JIAP. Or even AQAP. Some believe it was closer to home."

Metal sighed and glanced at Joe. "She's Russian. She sees conspiracies everywhere. It's in her blood."

They'd clearly had this discussion before because Felicity didn't bat an eyelash. "Did you know that the next day over three trillion dollars disappeared from the American economy?"

"What? No." Metal raised his eyebrows, a big reaction for him.

"Oh, yes. Someone—and we have no idea who—made a killing in the market. Sold a ton of shares short. The darknet talks of nothing else."

"Christ." This was the first Joe had heard of it, too. He'd learned about the Massacre weeks after the fact, when the lights were back on in Washington and the funerals were over and it had been shoved off the talking head shows in favor of Russia invading Ukraine. "Is there a way to read up on that?"

Her fingers blurred again. "I'll send you stuff, but I'll send it encrypted and leave you the encryption code. Delete everything you read. I mean it, Joe. Get rid of this stuff from your laptop because some of this stuff is incendiary. There's a whole meme on the CIA being behind the Massacre."

"Fuck," Metal breathed.

"Yeah." Joe shook himself. "I just got shivers down my spine and I don't scare easy." He met Metal's eyes. "Let's hope it's not true because otherwise..." His voice trailed off.

"Otherwise we're fucked," Metal said. "Big-time."

"Okay." Felicity stood. "Now that I've given you nightmares about your foremost intel gathering institution actively plotting murder and mayhem, I'll leave. I've got some work to do at home."

Metal rose with her and Joe walked them to the door.

Felicity turned to kiss him on the cheek. "Read that stuff I sent you on the Massacre. Isabel's been through a lot. Be kind to her."

"No need to worry, honey." Metal put a hand on her shoulder. "I don't think there's any way Joe would hurt her." Metal met Joe's eyes. Felicity had taken Isabel under her wing and anything that bothered Felicity bothered Metal.

Joe met his gaze steadily. Fuck no, he wasn't going to hurt Isabel. He was going to protect her, just as the anonymous emailer asked.

It was dark when Metal and Felicity left and he closed up the house for the night. He wasn't going out, he wasn't going anywhere until he'd read every single word of the Massacre reports and the darknet conspiracy theories.

He carefully put the ziti—though it still looked like overgrown spaghetti to him—in the freezer and heated up the beef stew that was left. He mopped up the sauce with some bread Isabel had made that had olives and sunflower seeds in it and drank a beer.

Then he opened his laptop and started reading.

It was fascinating stuff. He looked at the attack from a specops point of view. If he was going to attack the country's best and finest in a fancy hotel across the street from the White House, how would he go about it?

Well, more or less exactly as the terrorists had done,

except they used some tech tricks that weren't in his arsenal. 9/11 had been low-tech, the flyers counting on the fact that no one could even remotely imagine people would fly fuel-laden jets into office towers. But it hadn't been a precision attack, based on special intel or weaponry. Basically it had taken box cutters and men willing to die and take thousands of other people with them.

This had the stink of a specops operation all over it. Starting from knowing where all the security cameras were and blanking them out before the massacre.

Whoever had planned it had the right event. After Alex Delvaux had declared his candidacy, he would have been surrounded by secret service agents. They weren't the best of the best, in Joe's book. They weren't as hardened as SEALs but that was because they operated mainly in the USA and not in hellholes the way SEALs did. But they would have certainly supplied better security than had been on hand at the Burrard Hotel.

Which had been, essentially, zilch. It wasn't stated specifically but Joe knew how to read after-action reports. There had been the hotel security, which was pitiful, and ten agents from a private company. Joe checked the company out and he'd never heard of it. He'd heard of more or less every single important security company in the US and most operating throughout the world. The fact that he hadn't heard of the outfit meant that it was either a superelite one or rank amateurs. Joe opted for door number two.

There was no way to interview any of the security force—whether the hotel's or the private company's—because they'd all died in the attack. Not one man from the security detail survived.

Very few survived, in fact, so there weren't many

eyewitness accounts. Maybe forty people including a congressional aide so traumatized he'd had to be sedated and was still in a psychiatric hospital.

Reading carefully, Joe was able to piece together a bare-bones timeline. He started with the recordings. Several major news networks and an even bigger number of bloggers with cell phones were recording the proceedings.

7:20 p.m. Big hullabaloo in the hotel ballroom, thousands of excited people. Canned music in the background. A buffet against the wall with waiters standing behind it, white-gloved hands clasped in front of them, staring off in the distance, as if the goings-on at the podium had nothing to do with them.

About thirty people on the podium, including Alex Delvaux. His wife was there and two young boys. Isabel was on the sidelines, smiling, talking to someone in the audience. The older brother was missing. Jack, his name was, Joe remembered reading. He didn't recognize many of the others on the crowded podium. Then a woman stepped away and Joe recognized a face in the second row. Hector Something. Hector… Blake. He'd been around for as long as Joe remembered. Had even been a Secretary of Something. A Senator, too. Maybe twice.

He saw Isabel frown, look around, step off the podium with a cell phone to her ear.

The crowd was chanting, "Del-vaux, Del-vaux, Delvaux!" Alex Delvaux stepped to the microphone, smiling, hands up, patting the air. Calming people down. It took him a quarter of an hour as they kept getting revved up, over and over again.

Finally, there was a little quiet. Delvaux bent his head

down to the podium mike. There was a feedback whine and Delvaux stepped back quickly. The whine stopped and he stepped forward again. “Ladies and gentlemen, welcome! Thank you for joining us on this historic evening. We’re going to shake things up!”

The crowd went wild, jumping up and down, most of them holding up cell phones to capture the moment.

Delvaux held back a moment, grinning, letting the crowd have its moment.

Joe rarely paid attention to politics and politicians. He considered it all a rigged game, like pro wrestling, only less fun. He had to admit, though, there was real excitement in the air. He leaned forward to study Delvaux. Handsome but not too handsome. The lines in his face showed that he smiled more than he frowned. Charisma came off the man in waves.

So this was Isabel’s father.

“I know some of you are thinking of the excellent buffet tables behind you—” Raucous laughter. “But first there are some things we have to say, about us as a people and about our country. We feel—”

The lights went out. Gasps, a few snickers, as if this was planned. There was light coming from the cells, a little forest of them held high in invisible hands. Some people started shouting.

And then the cells blinked to black and the camera feed cut out.

The screen showed nothing—a blank black.

There were no recordings of the Massacre, at least none that had come to light. When police and CSI units came after the shooting and killing was done, after the explosives had been set off, after the attackers fled and disappeared completely from the earth, they found candles that had been lit by staff still burning and a few flashlights, so there had been some light.

The killers had had night vision. They had to have had night vision. You didn't set out to do mass murder by first killing the lights, without being able to see.

A few eyewitness reports had leaked out from what was still an ongoing police investigation. They all reported that the attackers had been dressed in shiny black head to foot and had worn balaclavas. They had shouted *'Allahu Akbar!'* Over and over.

Jihadists changing the course of American history, killing another Kennedy. Another vigorous young leader who embodied hope and energy.

Joe was going to ask for the CSI photos and if he didn't get them through his friend Nick Mancino, a former teammate and now in the FBI's elite HRT, the Hostage Rescue Team, he'd get Felicity to hack into the FBI files. He wanted to see the results of the Massacre firsthand.

He wanted to see what Isabel had survived.

She was mentioned in the reports. She'd been interviewed several times, the first time after she woke up from surgery having suffered a broken clavicle and cracked hip bone and a very bad concussion in the explosion. And many times after that. She remembered nothing. Retrograde amnesia.

Ah, honey, Joe thought in sorrow. He hadn't been bugged by anyone after he'd woken up from surgery. Metal and Jacko had taken turns sitting by his bedside and then had arranged to have him flown out to Portland on an ASI private jet.

He hadn't had any worries other than getting better.

He hadn't been given the news upon waking that his entire family was dead.

How horrible it must have been for her. Even worse than horrible because of the concussion and amnesia. The phone call had saved her life. Apparently the explosion had tossed her into a section of the ballroom just past the area that had totally collapsed.

Amnesia. So she couldn't even remember what had happened. All she knew was that she woke up severely injured and her entire family was gone.

Joe put to one side the news reports on Isabel and continued studying the attack itself. He got up to make himself a pot of coffee and ate the last of the beef stew, then attacked the rest of the files with a notepad at his side. He took copious notes. There was a lot of stuff that made no sense to him.

Part of that might have been the journalists who got things wrong. Part of it was also likely classified as top secret, since this was the biggest terrorist attack on US soil since 9/11. So he made notes regarding what he thought would require further study and moved on.

He read every news report he could find, and read newspapers from around the world on the day of the Massacre and for a few days after that, putting everything through Google Translate. It was enough to get a feeling for which countries were truly sorrowful and which thought that the US had somehow brought this attack down on itself. After exhausting journalists' articles, he went on to those forensic reports that were publicly available.

Then he moved on to the blogs, all across the political spectrum. About 90 percent of what was written was speculative bullshit, but he waded through everything. What wasn't bullshit was the opinions of several specops blog sites he had read regularly before being blown apart himself. They had a lot of questions about what actually went down during the Massacre.

It was midnight and he'd been reading steadily for six hours. He stood, stretched, thought about another beer when his heart nearly stopped.

Isabel, screaming.

JOE'S FRIEND FELICITY had been interesting. First of all, she'd made it clear that she was Joe's friend but not his *friend* friend. That would be her fiancé Sean O'Brien, known as Metal. One of the endless number of former soldiers and current security guys who trooped in and out of Joe's house on a regular basis. He'd treated her knee when she'd hurt it and he'd been kind and very efficient. He visited Joe often.

God, her own home was so barren in comparison.

There had always been guests at the Delvauxes', open house. People coming and going, always guests at mealtimes. Her parents had had the gift of hospitality and friendship. Isabel remembered thinking her first week in the college dorm that her house had been more fun.

Now look at her.

Felicity, however, hadn't seemed to notice anything. She'd brought over the clean pot, sat down without asking and started chatting. It wasn't until well into the conversation that Isabel paused and realized she'd entertained her first guest, except for Joe. And Joe came over to help her with stuff.

When she'd paused, Felicity had looked at her kindly and said, "You're Isabel Delvaux, aren't you?"

Yes.

Such a relief! She changed her name because she'd felt attacked by the attention of others. Some wanted to smother her in commiseration, watching her face with sick fascination, when the last thing she needed was to be reminded of her loss. And others wanted her to get "past it" and come out and play.

For some reason, all her friends simply disappeared. Gone, into thin air. Maybe because they didn't know how to deal with her losing her entire family, being wounded, whatever. The fact was, no friends came around. So her only human communication was with people who wanted to feed off her grief or get bragging rights because they'd talked to the notorious Isabel Delvaux.

Going away and changing her name had been her only recourse.

But Felicity had been so friendly, face so open and candid, that she couldn't take offense.

And they'd talked. And talked. And talked.

"You know," Felicity had said thoughtfully, "you're lucky to have a neighbor like Joe. Joe is a real good guy."

"I know," she'd answered. That he was a good guy was apparent from the moment they met. He'd done nothing but help her. But Isabel would die before she admitted that she also found him wildly attractive.

"Of course," Felicity added, watching her carefully, "the fact that he's hot doesn't hurt."

And Isabel had turned bright beet red, the curse of the fair-skinned.

Felicity'd laughed and changed the subject.

They never spoke of the Massacre. Somehow, in

some unspoken way, Isabel got it that Felicity had known tragedy in her life, too.

It wasn't until Felicity stood up and put on her coat to go back to Joe's that the kicker came.

"You might know that Joe hosts poker games," she said casually.

"I know. I can hear them. Sounds like fun." She'd tried to keep a wistful note from entering her voice.

"It is fun. Though I don't know what the guys see in it, really, because Joe always wins."

Isabel's eyes widened. "He does?"

Felicity's grin was wicked. "Oh, yeah. He's a demon poker player. Card shark, in fact. What fun is it when he takes all your money? So anyway, I was thinking that if the guys are having so much fun losing money to Joe, maybe we could get together, too. There's me and there's Jacko's girlfriend, Lauren. She's really nice and a lot of fun. Why don't we get together?"

A girls' night out! For a second, a flash of a moment, Isabel was back in her old life, where a girls' night out was a frequent treat. Felicity was watching her out of her pretty, light blue eyes and all Isabel could see was intelligence and friendliness.

"I'd love it," she blurted out. And then, before she could stop herself, "Why don't you and Lauren come over here while the men are losing money to Joe in his house?"

"Well…" Felicity's eyes narrowed as a crafty look crept over her face. "Will you cook?"

And Isabel laughed. "Oh, yeah. I'll cook. As a matter of fact…" She went into the kitchen and passed Felicity a big pan covered in tinfoil. Felicity peeked under the tinfoil, widened her eyes and sniffed in delight.

"Oh, man. Smells delicious."

Isabel wagged her finger in a fake scolding tone. "Remember. That's for Joe. Tell him to put it uncovered in an oven that's been preheated to 375 degrees and to bake it for about forty minutes if it's for tomorrow night. Otherwise tell him to put it in the freezer."

"Joe is very lucky I like him," Felicity said. "Because I'm really tempted to steal this. So, see you tomorrow night?"

"Absolutely. Don't bother bringing anything, I'll take care of the food."

"Deal. I'm a lousy cook anyway. Metal takes care of that in our household. But I'll bring some wine."

"Deal," Isabel said. Felicity had held out her hand, shook hers firmly and disappeared into the night.

So.

Tomorrow night Isabel was going to have guests. Felicity, who was definitely friendly and not inquisitive. And this Lauren, who was her friend. So presumably she'd be relaxed and friendly and not inquisitive.

The invitation had come out of nowhere but it felt really right. It was her isolation these past months that felt wrong. It wasn't her. She'd always been social, enjoyed company. Only now that the clouds had parted just a little did Isabel realize the price all this isolation had exacted. She felt like she'd lost her soul along with her family.

The thing was, her family had died but she hadn't.

For the very first time since the Massacre, Isabel felt almost…normal.

Portland had been a good pick. She'd been right to relocate. She was anonymous here. And even if someone found out her real identity, like Felicity, maybe they wouldn't care. Washington had been full of memories, jaggedly painful ones. The Delvaux family name had become a burden, not a point of pride.

Here was a good place to start over.

Starting over.

Her deep melancholy was so wrong. It dishonored her family. They'd loved life so much. Her parents would be saddened to know she was willing to throw her life away.

And…life was good, after all.

Maybe.

Portland was pretty and friendly. She was enjoying cooking again, just a little. Not as much as before but maybe that passion could come back. Maybe. Felicity was nice. It was entirely possible that Lauren was nice, too.

And Joe was…well. Whew.

Up until now she'd ruled out an affair with him. She had a steady stock of excuses. She wasn't ready. He was a neighbor. What happened if the affair went sour and she had to see him every day? Better to keep things on a friendly neighbor basis.

The truth? She was scared out of her wits. She was frightened to death that she no longer had anything in her to give. That he would find her cold and dried out because that was exactly the way she felt.

But suppose…suppose that wasn't true? Suppose she had some spark of womanhood and juice left inside her? That she wasn't completely dried up?

Joe as a lover…she shivered. Wow.

He'd kept his physical distance, had always been a perfect gentleman, but every once in a while she'd seen something in his dark eyes. She hadn't been ready for that but now, maybe. Who knew?

Perhaps a new lover, certainly new friends. Maybe she could piece together a semblance of her old career, though she had to think about the spotlight. Her mind skittered away from that.

Time enough for that later, if she wanted it. For the moment she was happy to cook for Joe, and now for his friends. And the future, well. That would come soon enough.

As she cleaned up after making the baked ziti, Isabel looked deep inside herself. She liked cleaning up, she liked creating order where before there had been the mess of cooking. She liked every aspect of it.

But now there was another element creeping its way back into her life. Hope. It felt so faint, so delicate. Like tendrils of smoke. It was hard to take it out and look at it, it was so incredibly fragile.

Hope that maybe she was coming back to life. That life could hold pleasure again. Guests, tomorrow night. Seeing Joe again. Maybe going over to watch a hand of poker, see how he won all the time. SEALs were known for being tough and laconic, right? It must take someone really tough to bluff them.

She smiled at the thought and a second later realized—she'd smiled!

Isabel stood in the middle of her kitchen, holding a washcloth, frozen in place. She hadn't spontaneously smiled since—since then.

Since the Massacre, she thought. *Say it to yourself.*

And she did. She hadn't really smiled since the Massacre. Thinking the word *massacre* had been like a sharp punch to the heart, every single time.

The punch was less sharp. She rolled that idea around in her mind. The Massacre was horrible, tragic, she had lost her entire family. But, they were gone. No tears, no despair would ever bring them back. If tears and despair and heartbreak could bring people back, her family would be here with her.

Nothing would bring them back. They were gone.

But *she* was here. Right here, right now, she was alive in her house in Portland, Oregon. She could feel the hardwood floor beneath her bare feet. She could feel the softness of her sweats against her skin. She could feel her heart beating in her chest, slow and steady. She could still feel hope and joy, though for the longest time she'd thought they had fled her life forever. She could still have feelings for other people.

Like Felicity and maybe her friend.

Like Joe.

She stood back, looking at her gleaming kitchen, taking as always keen pleasure in order. Tomorrow she'd mess it up again cooking for her new friends. The thought gave her enormous pleasure.

A meal for chicks, unlike the cooking she'd been doing for Joe and his friends.

Grilled zucchini dressed with a balsamic vinegar reduction, orange and fennel salad, mini lentil burgers, slices of provolone with wine jelly, baked radicchio with grated parmesan cheese.

Yes.

For dessert, raspberry white chocolate mousse. And, if they were to join the guys, she could make chocolate-espresso cheesecake. Or a big pan of apple crumble, with brandy butter. It was one of her favorite party dishes and could make grown men weep.

Well, maybe not Navy SEALs, probably a little brandy butter wouldn't make them weep, but still. It would be fun to watch them put that first bite in their mouths.

She had brandy, didn't she? In some cupboard somewhere. The cupboards of this house were deep, so she went to get the powerful flashlight Joe insisted she keep handy. He'd chosen it for her and the light could probably be seen from the moon.

The brandy was under the sink, hidden in the back. The trusty super flashlight lit it up as if it was on stage. So, okay, there was the bottle of brandy. Brandy butter tomorrow night.

Tomorrow night would be fun.

Fun.

She rolled that idea around in her head. Having fun. It felt odd even saying the word in her head.

The girls over. Then going over to join the guys. Laughing at the grumpy ones who'd lost to Joe. Maybe they could go over in time to see the last couple of hands. She'd really like to see that. Watch Joe's face, watch his hands holding the cards.

His hands. Joe had the most beautiful hands she had ever seen, totally unlike the hands of any man she'd ever known. Her dad had always had his hands manicured. She smiled gently. He'd been such a dandy, her father. They'd teased him about it. His suits were always well cut, he sometimes changed his shirt during the day. Shoes always polished, hair barbered twice monthly by the best guy in town.

He'd said once that he considered it a sign of respect for people but she also knew he liked being well turned-out.

Joe was the exact opposite. Everything he wore was clean, but well used and rarely ironed. Presumably when he started working that would change, but maybe not. His buddies Jacko and Metal wore work clothes, not suits.

Joe's hair was getting shaggy and his hands definitely did not have manicured nails.

Those hands were strong, though. The strongest, most fascinating hands she'd ever seen. Enormous, callused, even rough. With large raised veins on the back that ran up his muscled forearms. Hard, tough hands. But delicate. When he fixed things or assembled them he had an incredibly delicate touch, gentle and steady.

Isabel went into her bedroom thinking about Joe's hands. She'd never really thought about men's hands before, but his fascinated her. Several times, watching him carefully repair something, she'd flashed on those big strong hands touching her. And she'd have one of those heat flashes that should have belonged to menopause but didn't. They belonged to Joe.

Isabel set the flashlight on her bedside table and undressed by the light in the corridor. She liked the half-light. The room seemed mysterious yet cozy, her small collection of silver frames gleaming in the penumbra.

She undressed and folded her clothes neatly on the small button back nursing chair that had belonged to her great-great-grandmother back in France. Naked, she padded to the chest of drawers and took out her favorite nightgown—a full-length long-sleeved pale pink cashmere nightgown that had been a present from her mother. It was soft and warm and pretty and she loved it.

She hadn't worn it since the Massacre. Almost as if wearing it was too great a pleasure for her, inhabiting the world of the half-dead. Something dark and cloudy had lifted inside her head and she saw the truth. Her mother would have wanted her to wear the nightgown. It had been given with love. Why had it lain in the back of her drawer all these months?

It was time, time to step once more into the land of the living.

The nightgown was voluminous and fell in soft folds to her feet. She hadn't worn it in so long she'd almost forgotten about it. Isabel gave an experimental twirl, loving how it belled around her ankles.

How did it look? She wanted to see it by the light, but was too lazy to cross the room. The flashlight had more candlepower than the ceiling light. She picked it up, turned it on, bringing it around to the mirror and—

There was a monster at the window!

Black-faced, with insectoid eyes. So grotesque it took her a second to believe her eyes, like a devil that the earth had just spawned.

She screamed and screamed, dropping the flashlight, turning to run and bumping into the chest of drawers. Her heart pounded in her chest—it felt like it was bouncing off her rib cage. For a second, she couldn't breathe through the panic and her chest squeezed.

"Isabel!" Joe's deep voice at the front door. He pounded on it so hard she felt the vibrations in the floor. "Isabel, open up!"

Joe! Isabel ran to the front door, fumbling to punch in the security alarm, pull back the bolt. The instant the door was free Joe pushed into the room. He was bare-chested, in sweats, barefoot. A big black gun was in his right hand.

"Isabel!" He grabbed her shoulders, looked her up and down. "What happened? What's wrong?"

Her heart hammered and it took her long seconds to get enough breath to speak. "A man—" She wheezed in breath. "A man at my bedroom window!"

Joe picked her up, placed her against the door, one hand to her shoulder. "Stay here," he said in a low voice. "Don't move and don't open to anyone but me."

She nodded, swallowing convulsively.

"Isabel?"

"Stay here," she whispered, throat raw. "Don't open to anyone but you."

"Good girl," he growled and slipped out the door.

Isabel felt bereft the instant he was gone. It was crazy, he was just outside but she felt completely alone. Whatever Joe was doing, he was doing it silently. There was no noise at all, the silence so deep her pants as she tried to breathe sounded loud in the dark living room. She was still shaking so hard she put her arms around her midriff to hold herself together, otherwise she felt like she'd fly apart in a million pieces.

Joe was out there, searching for…searching for what? What had she seen? Instinctively she'd said she'd seen a man but actually all she'd seen was smooth darkness and insectoid eyes. Glasses but steampunk-like glasses.

Isabel closed her eyes, trying to fix what she'd seen in her memory. In her treacherous, treacherous memory. She couldn't remember the event that shaped her life, how could she trust her own memory?

But she'd seen someone! Or something. It had been an instant, less than a second. By the time she'd drawn a deep shocked breath to scream, he—or it—had been gone.

Why would someone be at her window? She couldn't think straight. Her system had gone into overdrive when she'd seen that—that *thing.* Staring at her.

Think, think! she told herself. Joe would want to hear what happened. Unless he'd caught the thing and dragged it inside. But if he didn't, he'd want to know why she screamed.

Because she'd seen a monster.

Only kids saw monsters. And usually they saw them under the bed, not outside the window. And she'd only seen it for a fraction of a second.

Had her eyes been playing tricks on her?

Was she crazy?

Had she seen her own reflection and her sick, muddled mind had projected a monster onto the windowpane? An outward manifestation of the chaos and pain inside?

A soft knock that she felt through the skin of her back, pressed against her front door.

"Isabel?" Joe said. "It's me. Let me in."

Shaking, Isabel turned and opened the door. Joe slipped inside and she closed it behind him. In the moment it was open, she could feel the cold air. It was freezing outside but you wouldn't know it from him. Shirtless and barefoot, he wasn't shaking and he wasn't shivering.

Unlike her.

Joe looked her over carefully, head to toe, the way a doctor would check for injuries.

Oh, God, no. Please. When putting on her oh-so-pretty nightgown she'd flashed on an image of Joe seeing her in it. She imagined how he'd react. His dark eyes would flare with sexual desire and he'd reach for her.

His eyes weren't flaring with sexual desire, he was watching her the way you would watch a wounded person. And he was reaching for her because she was shaking so hard she thought she would fall apart.

"D-d-did you f-f-find—" Her teeth were chattering so hard she couldn't speak.

Joe wrapped his arms around her, just to stop her from flying apart, she was shaking so hard.

But oh! It felt so good! He was warm and hard and solid, something to cling to while she felt her entire world rock on its foundations.

"Did you—" She wheezed. Her lungs weren't working.

"Did I find someone?" Joe was holding her tight, head bent over hers. She heard his words through his chest more than from his lips. "No."

She jolted. No, he hadn't found him. It.

Maybe there hadn't been anyone there. How many monsters could be out roaming around on a cold Portland evening?

"But—but—I did see someone. Something."

Joe's arms tightened around her, his cheek resting on top of her head. He was curling himself around her as if he could protect her from all sides, including from the ceiling should a monster decide to drop down like a bat.

"I checked carefully, but couldn't find anything," he finally said. "But the ground is hard and wouldn't leave imprints. I checked your lawn and the bushes to see if someone passing changed the dew patterns, but I didn't see anything. Maybe tomorrow morning something will show up in the sunlight."

It would never occur to her, not in a million years, to check for dew prints. She sighed, burrowed her face in his shoulder. This was awful. At some deep level, she was expecting him to find something, some sign of a human being's passing.

But Joe hadn't seen anything and he was the kind of man who'd find some kind of sign of a monster's passing, if it was there to be found at all.

She whimpered, huddled in his arms.

There hadn't been anyone there.

No one.

Just a figment of her scared and crazy subconscious. No one there but the monsters in her own head.

Her shaking intensified and her head swam, as if she was in a centrifuge, a place where there was no stable footing, everything spinning out of control.

"I saw him. It," she whispered, more to hear the sound of her own voice than anything else. But her voice shook and she barely had the breath to form the words.

Joe's arms tightened again and suddenly her legs left the ground. For an instant she thought she was falling to pieces physically and not just mentally. But something strong was holding her. Joe. He was carrying her to the sofa where he sat down with her in his arms.

She wound up sitting in his lap, arms around his shoulders, face buried against his neck. Though he was bare-chested he was amazingly warm, like a steel furnace. One big strong arm was around her waist, the other cradling her head and she felt like he was the only thing holding her together. Without him she would fly apart.

Words were forming but they didn't make much sense. One big hand rubbed her scalp beneath her hair in a soothing caress. Maybe not caress. Maybe it was more trying to calm the lunatic. Isabel closed her eyes tightly but a single tear escaped.

This was worse than her worst nightmare. Someone seeing her rendered down to bedrock, afraid of everything. So far she'd managed to keep her craziness away from everyone, but here this man, this man she admired and liked and even had sexy thoughts about—this man was seeing her at her most desperate.

Another tear ran down her cheek. Even her dignity was being taken away from her. A long finger tipped her chin up so she had to look Joe in the eyes.

They stared at each other. He was studying every feature, his gaze going from her eyes to her mouth, where his gaze lingered. Then he lifted his gaze to look into her eyes again.

"I saw something," she said miserably. "I did."

Joe blinked. "I know you did," he said. "Did you think I didn't believe you?"

She nodded, never taking her eyes from his.

Joe bent his head, his nose nudging a lock of hair away from her temple. He bent down to speak directly into her ear, voice low and deep. "I believe you. I'll always believe you."

The words made hot tears spring to her eyes and she had to blink them away. How could he say that when she hardly believed herself?

It wasn't just his words that were having a big effect. His body was, too. Being so close to all that strength and power and heat.

She had a big effect on him, too. Big *big* effect. When she shifted in his lap her thigh came up against an erection. Not a half-assed one, either. Full-blown, hard as steel. Like sitting next to a section of pipe. With a large diameter.

For a second she'd wondered what it was, then a flash of heat ran through her like a hot wind.

This was a surprise. She'd have thought that her crazy behavior would be a turnoff for him. Who wanted a hysterical woman? Joe was handsome, built, had a good job waiting for him. Stable, handsome, built bachelors didn't grow on trees. He probably had his pick of women, what would he want with her?

His body didn't seem to care that she'd just sent him on a wild-goose chase because what she felt against her hip was arousal. Big-time arousal.

Joe didn't seem disturbed in any way. He wasn't thrusting it at her, he wasn't denying it. But it had the effect of clearing her mind. When she met his eyes she could tell he knew she was past her panic and fully in the moment.

He was still holding the back of her head in a strong grip and their faces were inches apart, noses nearly touching.

"You okay?" he asked quietly.

She nodded her head jerkily.

"Can you tell me exactly what you saw?"

She nodded again. Sighed. "You're going to think I'm crazy."

"No." Joe's voice was firm. "I'm not."

Okay.

"I was, um, planning tomorrow night's menu. Having fun with it. You know Felicity and Lauren are coming over tomorrow night while you guys play poker?"

A corner of his mouth lifted. "No, I didn't. Sounds

great. Then you come over to my house with dessert, right?"

"Something like that. Maybe. Though it appears you take everyone's money."

Joe nodded. "They keep coming back for more of it, though. I'm really glad you'll be spending time with Felicity and Lauren. They're great."

"Well, I liked Felicity and she likes Lauren so it looks good. Anyway, I went into the bedroom to change into my nightgown and go to bed."

Joe looked down at her nightgown, fingered the material. "It's a really pretty nightgown, too." When he looked back up at her there was heat in his dark eyes. Exactly what she'd hoped for when putting it on. The skin over his cheekbones tightened and the steel tube next to her hip came alive and surged.

She blushed. Crazy. Sex had never been a big problem for her, but by the same token had never been really that big a deal, either. She realized now that she hadn't truly desired her former lovers because she hadn't felt anything for them like what she was feeling now.

She *desired* Joe. A lot. Heat filled her down to her fingertips. Her womb contracted when she felt his penis move, exactly as if he had been inside her instead of her sitting on his lap separated by layers of clothing.

His jaw muscles clenched. They both knew what was happening.

"Go on," he said. "I need to know what you saw."

She'd been studying his face, all the minute changes in it as he went from fierce protector to man. Absolutely fascinating. He seemed to be more self-disciplined than she was, though, because it took her a second to realize what he said.

All this heat had served an important function. Isabel didn't feel so lost and alone and crazy. Joe's physical presence gave weight and heft to her memory, grounding her.

Isabel sat up straighter, brushing his penis again. His hand had gone from cupping the back of her head to cupping her neck and she tilted her head slightly.

"I was looking for something using that flashlight you gave me. It's really bright."

"It's supposed to be," Joe said.

"I went into the bedroom. I needed something and instead of turning on the bedside lamp or the ceiling light, I used the flashlight. It crossed the window and that's when I saw him. It."

"Why do you say *it*? You couldn't tell the sex?"

Isabel took her time. This was important, if he was going to believe her. "*It* because it didn't quite look human. Now that I think of it, it was probably a ski mask, but in that moment, that split second, it was like this—this *thing* outside my window had no human features. No nose, no mouth, just black blankness, and those eyes."

Joe frowned. "What about the eyes? What was wrong with them?"

This was the tricky part. "They, um. They weren't human eyes. That's what went through my mind. The immediate overall effect was alien." She shuddered. "That's when I thought I was losing it. But they weren't alien eyes. It or he or she was wearing some funny kind of goggles. Like steampunk goggles."

Joe looked blank. "Steampunk?"

"Yeah." She ventured half a smile. "It's a literary genre. Sort of Victoriana with a steam engine vibe. It's also a look. A style. Men in fancy Edwardian waistcoats and women with leather bustiers." Joe seemed more and more lost. "Think *The Golden Compass*. And the goggles, the eyepieces, look like those goggles the Arctic explorers wore in all those old photographs."

"Goggles." Joe had been looking up and to the right to envision what she was saying but suddenly his gaze dropped and locked with hers. He let out a harsh breath. His body was tight with tension. Every muscle was taut, delineated. She felt his shoulder muscles under her hands flex and harden. "Fuck," he breathed.

"Pardon?"

"That bastard was wearing night vision goggles!"

"What?"

"You didn't see a monster. You saw a guy in a ski mask with night vision. They are special eyepieces that magnify any ambient light and allow soldiers to see in the dark. It's military hardware. It shouldn't be in the hands of civilians. Did you strip naked?" he asked, mouth a thin grim line.

"Yes." She shivered. "The room was dark but I guess he saw…everything."

"Do you always keep the lights off in your bedroom?"

"No. I have a small reading light on my bedside table. I have a ceiling light—" She stopped, fingers digging into the hard muscles of his shoulders. "But you know all about my ceiling light because you put it up."

"Yeah. Do you use it much at night?"

Isabel looked up, thought. "No. I mostly have my bedside light on."

"So if someone's been looking in on you, watching you, he expects the room to be dimly lit. If he's been watching you, he'd expect you to be absolutely unaware of his existence. He can watch everything you do even in the dimmest light. Even in the dark. You went into your room and kept it dark and then used a flashlight that picked him out. And, by the way, that flashlight would have blinded him with night vision gear. It would have been like looking at the sun for him."

Isabel stared at Joe, disturbed and queasy. "So…you think someone has been…watching me?" She swallowed bile. The idea was horrible.

Joe didn't answer right away. When he spoke, his voice was firm. "Motion sensors are going up all around your house and you will have monitors. No one will ever sneak up on you again, guaranteed."

"Thank you," she whispered.

He nodded. "There's something else you need to know, honey."

The endearment just slipped out of him. Isabel didn't think he even noticed. But she did. It didn't feel like one of those words players used as a placeholder for a name. Joe knew her name. That *honey* had come out of his subconscious.

She watched his eyes. They were dark brown, with striations of a slightly lighter brown and they seemed to absorb the light. They were eyes that saw everything and betrayed a keen intelligence.

"What do I need to know?"

He studied her face for a moment longer and Isabel became uneasy. This was bad news coming and she'd had a lifetime's worth of bad news lately.

"I got an email about you today."

It felt like a punch to the stomach. All the wind went out of her. Her mouth fell open. "You got an email about *me*?" The bottom dropped out of her world. Nothing made any sense anymore. "What—what did it say?"

Was it a journalist looking for dirt? Was someone trying to ruin what was left of her life? But whoever had sent the email had sent it to *Joe*. Not to her. After the Massacre, Isabel had received all kinds of hate mail. There'd also been lots of condolence emails but also tons of political hate mail, to the effect that her godless family had gotten its just reward. Trolls crawling out of the woodwork to tear her down at her lowest point. She changed her email address and that was when she decided to move to Portland and change her name.

She'd known, beyond a shadow of a doubt, that if the hate mail continued, it was going kill her. She'd been half-dead and this wall of hatred, of vitriol was going to finish her off.

So she braced herself for whatever Joe was going to say. Somehow someone had latched on to the fact that Joe was being kind to her. And they wanted to destroy that. Leave her as alone as before.

She was ready for anything. For Joe to say that the email called her a whore, a bitch, a girl-child of privilege. That she wasn't fit for decent folk.

That had been the baseline of the emails she'd received. An avalanche of them, happy that her father would never be president.

She held her breath.

"The email was simple," he said. "It said protect Isabel."

Her heart stuttered and her breath blew out in a whoosh. "It said *what?*"

"Protect Isabel. Two words. And we were unable to find the source. Not even Felicity was able to find the source and Felicity is the atom bomb of IT. Someone seriously does not want to be found. But that someone also wants me to protect you. To keep you from harm."

Isabel watched his eyes and saw the truth of what he was saying. "I don't understand. I can't understand. There's no one left in the world who cares what happens to me."

Joe's face turned even grimmer as he took her chin and turned her head to fully face him. "That's not true, Isabel. Not anymore. I care what happens to you."

And he kissed her.

FUCK FUCK *FUCK!*

The bitch made him! Kearns stumbled his way back to his vehicle at a fast walk, still half-blinded. Luckily, training kicked in.

He knew how to walk without calling attention to himself. He knew exactly how to go in a mile-eating stride that looked normal but was about 30 percent faster than a normal walk. He knew how to unobtrusively avoid sources of light. He knew how to obscure his face when the odd car drove by this late at night in this residential neighborhood.

He knew it all. He'd been trained to observe strict surveillance rules. He knew how it was done. He'd worked for the CIA's National Clandestine Service for five years before being cashiered for some stupid anti-corruption rule. They'd trained him well. But the government didn't pay well. What did they care if he accepted money on the side? It had nothing to do with his mission. The discharge still burned.

No one had ever made him before. Ever. Kearns was furious with himself that he'd been made by a freaking untrained girl. A cook, for fuck's sake. A woman who'd had a nervous breakdown. He'd read the psych eval. Someone in her state was barely aware of her surroundings and here she'd caught him.

But goddamn. What betrayed him was that she was a freaking looker. He had a weakness for the ladies. Isabel Delvaux was a little on the scrawny side but fuck. Big eyes, big pouty mouth. Surprisingly large boobs for a thin chick. A guy'd have to be dead not to notice. Kearns wasn't dead. Not even close. And his cock worked just fine.

He had a low-level contract to keep an eye on the Delvaux woman who'd changed her name and moved to Portland. It was boring work because the chick never did anything. And the pay wasn't good because it was goddamned scut work. Nothing a half-assed snot-nosed newbie couldn't hack.

Watching a clueless woman was demeaning work. Kearns had taken it only because he was working his way up this new hierarchy he'd sensed was doing big-time stuff. Big-time stuff meant big-time money and he needed it. He'd blown the money from his last big contract in Vegas. He was flat-out broke and he wanted in on whatever it was that was happening. He'd put out the word that he was available and he'd gotten a bite within forty-eight hours.

He hadn't expected to watch a chick day after day, doing nothing but taking slow walks in the mornings and cooking and reading in the afternoons, from what he could see.

Another guy followed her at times, walked slowly with her at others. Her next-door neighbor. Kearns checked the name, and when he checked in military databases the hairs rose on the back of his neck when he saw the guy was a former SEAL. Those guys didn't fuck around and Kearns was no match for him in a fight unless he took him from behind.

And even then. The guy had been wounded—he had scars and he'd walked with a cane for a few days then threw it away. Wounded or not, though, he had that situational awareness the specops guys were born with and then had the gift pounded into them.

You didn't take SEALs by surprise.

He stopped day surveillance when he read that Joe Harris was a SEAL. Kearns didn't report that the Delvaux bitch had a SEAL living next door. Either he'd lose the gig altogether or he'd be replaced, and though it wasn't much money it was easy money.

So he didn't follow her around anymore in the daytime beyond the occasional drive-by. He checked in on her at night. Easier, simpler.

And got a real perk. Shit yeah. She looked scrawny when dressed but when she walked around naked, oh yeah. Everything a woman needed, she had. Instead of bony, she was delicate with perfect tits.

She wasn't sleeping with the SEAL. She was alone at night. Though Kearns did wonder what the SEAL was thinking not fucking a babe like her. Shit, the SEAL was following her around like some goddamned puppy, why not bone her?

Whatever.

The SEAL wasn't boning her so she was always alone at night with no one watching. So Kearns developed a routine, two, three times a week. He had a Tyvek oversuit in his car, special boots that left no prints, latex gloves, a mask and night vision gear. He knew the outside of the house like his own hand. There was a walkway that went past her bedroom. The Tyvek suit would leave no cloth samples, not even a thread and there was no possibility of DNA should he get caught on a bush. The mask covered his face. And the NV gave him a view he wouldn't forget in a hurry.

The big problem was not jerking off in the bushes. *That* would leave DNA. It was really hard, about as hard as his cock when he watched her coming out of the shower toweling her hair dry.

The NV gave everything a greenish glow so he couldn't see the color of her muff but it was light-colored, like her nipples. Mmm.

So Kearns spent a couple of nights a week looking into her house at night then going back to his miserable cheap motel room to jerk off. And he sent reports on her behavior—a whole lot of nothing, which was what his employer wanted to hear.

Kearns got it loud and clear that the more Isabel Delvaux stayed away from the world, the better it was. Kearns also got it that his reports were making someone happy.

So the last Delvaux was supposed to stay sick and sad and under the radar. Not stir up any waves. Fine.

The only thing she stirred up was his dick.

It was a disaster that he'd been made. Kearns realized he'd strayed a little from the walkway to get a better look. Who could blame him? She was a wet dream. And a Delvaux. They were like the Kennedys, only better-looking.

He was absolutely certain he'd left nothing behind, but that big guy next door had come running to the bitch's door when she screamed. He was barefoot but amazingly fast. And he came out again fast, but by that time, Kearns's Tyvek suit was off and he was in sweats and a hoodie, opening his car door. He drove by the house slowly and the big guy was checking the ground with a flashlight. A Maglite that lit everything up.

A sheen of sweat blossomed all over Kearns. The SEAL was looking very closely. Kearns had been careful. Hadn't he? A trickle of sweat rolled down the side of his face because—who the fuck remembered? He'd been enjoying the bitch's little show that had seemed designed for him. He'd been avidly soaking up every single goddamn detail because she was going to feature large that night in his bed.

Man, he'd never had a piece that fine. Long legs, long pale neck. A mouth made to go down on a guy. On him. Oh, yeah, he could imagine it so easily. All that dark honey hair swirling around his hands as he held her in place, pumping in and out of that mouth.

That moment—when he could almost feel her lips around his cock—that was the exact moment her flashlight picked him out. He was jerked harshly out of the fantasy that had been so real he had major wood. His hand been reaching for his groin when the white light had blinded him. He'd snatched the NV goggles off his face but it was too late. He'd lost his sight, temporarily.

Good thing he knew his way around the yard so well his feet carried him out of there without having to think.

But he didn't remember much between the moment he'd been blinded and when he stumbled out onto the street, tearing off his ski mask and unzipping the suit. He fell into his SUV and pulled out too fast and then, heart still beating, decided to go around the block and see what was happening.

That was when he saw the SEAL searching the ground and for the first time it occurred to him that he could be busted. That's when his heart started trip-hammering because he knew the guy he worked for wasn't warm and fuzzy. Wasn't the forgiving type.

He didn't dare make another turn of the block so he drove back to the motel from hell, sweating and swearing, slamming the steering wheel in frustration. And still hard, goddamn it.

Reason kicked in. This Isabel babe was unstable. And a Delvaux. Rich high-born assholes, all of them. Never done an honest day's job in their lives. Not like him.

And Isabel? A flake. She could've done anything she wanted but what did she want to do? Fucking cook. Like his mom. She didn't do her cooking in a diner that smelled of rancid grease and old socks with the toilets smelling of sex and shit, sure, but cooking was cooking.

She'd survived the Massacre but turned loony. So who was going to believe that she saw someone outside her window? The SEAL would look and look, but wouldn't find anything, no footprints, no stray threads caught in the bushes, nothing disturbed. That banshee scream was a hysterical woman who saw monsters under the bed.

As a matter of fact, Kearns was so sure he hadn't been seen by anyone but a hysterical woman, he wasn't going to report this. No, sir. Why should he? His reports had been coming in regularly, a guy who was doing his duty, watching her movements. She did absolutely nothing suspicious or even interesting.

So right now he'd be crazy to report the truth. *I get tired of watching her do fuckall so I watch her at night when she gets naked, then go to the crap motel to jerk off. And tonight I might have gotten caught. By her neighbor. Who's a fucking Navy SEAL.*

Nope. Not going to happen.

He'd report that Isabel Delvaux, now Isabel Lawton, was continuing her boring routine. Going for walks and cooking. Cooking and going for walks.

Nothing to see here, folks, just move right along.

FIVE

Joe hadn't kissed a woman in—shit. Two years? Three? The last one had been—he blanked. Oh, yeah, the lawyer from hell. It had been a one-night stand because she'd scared the shit out of him with her aggression. He'd crept out the next morning with his balls crawling up into his groin out of fear.

He'd been in the freaking Sandbox so long, operating out of remote FOBs with no women but the poor souls covered head to toe in blankets, he'd almost forgotten women existed. Sex was with his fist and that got real old, real fast. So he concentrated on staying alive and he almost didn't manage it. And man, after being blown up, whoa. That was when sex disappeared from his life.

The only women he'd seen with any regularity were the nurses who wiped his butt and the surgeon. He'd seen her exactly twice. Everyone said she was a miracle worker and his bones could attest to that. But she was fifty with a bun of gray hair and was not dream material.

So he'd sort of forgotten how great women were. Soft everywhere. Soft mouth, soft breasts, soft skin. And Isabel—he couldn't remember a woman as enticing as Isabel.

He touched his mouth to Isabel's, his first kiss in two or three years, and he nearly came. He tightened his ass cheeks because coming on the couch, wetting his thin sweatpants, would be super uncool.

Isabel could feel everything he was feeling. He slept commando so when he'd heard her scream he'd grabbed his gun first and then hopped into his sweatpants in less than a second and ran out the door. Barefoot, bare chested, thinking only to get to her as fast as humanly possible.

So now he was on her couch, cradling Isabel in his arms and she could feel every single thing about him, particularly the hard-on. Which was the hardest hard-on he could ever remember having.

And the kiss was the very best he could ever remember sharing. She was so soft all over, including her mouth. He lost himself in it, forgetting everything, just diving into her, feeling her warm and open in his arms.

When he finally lifted his head, he nearly lost it at the sight of her. So amazingly beautiful, hair mussed from his hands, mouth swollen from his mouth.

"I care what happens to you," he said. He didn't want her to think of herself for even a second more as being completely alone in the world.

"I know," she whispered, watching his eyes. She could watch his eyes all she wanted, she'd see nothing but the truth. She cupped his jaw and lifted her face to him again. This time the kiss was deeper, hotter and control slipped a little from his hands.

Control.

She was fragile, breakable. Joe had to have control and he usually did, damn it. Except now, when he needed it most.

He was trying to map out a strategy to get her to the bedroom, though his thoughts were cloudy. Kiss her some more. Maybe ask if she wanted him to stay the night, maybe sleep on her couch, though that would be sheer hell. Sleeping on a couch while the woman he desired more than his next breath slept a room away.

But he was a SEAL. He could do that. Stay over to-morrow night, too, and the night after that. And then maybe he could convince her to…

"Take me to bed, Joe," she murmured and it was like a lightning bolt shot through his system. He rose with her in his arms and went into her bedroom, fast.

When he set her on her feet the first thing she did was pull the curtains closed. Then she stepped into his arms.

He tried to undress them both between long kisses, hands fumbling. Isabel took pity on him finally and stepped back. Watching his eyes she pulled that soft nightgown over her head and let it drop, then stepped out of her panties.

She seemed uncertain as she watched him carefully and Joe couldn't understand that. She was perfection itself. Long slender neck, delicate collarbones, full breasts, tiny waist, long slender legs.

"God." He reached out a hand and hesitated a sec-ond. He had such rough hands, callused hands. Was he going to scratch that delicate skin? She took hold of his hand and placed it on her left breast. He smoothed his hand gently over that incredibly satiny skin and felt her heartbeat pounding.

She was excited. God, so was he.

A heartbeat. She was alive, in this room, with him, when she should have been in the ground these past six months. His own living miracle.

"Now you," Isabel said, looking at his sweatpants.

God yes. He shucked them without taking his eyes off hers.

Isabel placed her palm at the top of his chest and ran it slowly down him. "You're so beautiful," she whispered and he'd have laughed if he could have.

He blew out a breath. "I don't have condoms, Isabel." He could have slapped himself but it wouldn't have made any difference. He didn't have condoms with him and he didn't have them in his house, either. And he wasn't about to get dressed and cruise town for an open drugstore. No, sir.

He could lie and say that he had tons of self-control and would pull out in time and in the past that would have been true. But right now he knew he had very little self-control.

He opened his mouth to say something, anything but she surprised him. She stepped forward, right into his arms, breast to chest. She burned him all along his front.

"I was put on the pill," she said, watching his face. "There's been no one for quite a while and I've had every blood test known to man."

Joe froze then huffed out a strong breath. *Bareback.*

"I haven't had sex in at least two years," he answered. "And ditto the blood tests. Don't even have high cholesterol."

She smiled but he didn't smile back.

The idea of entering Isabel bare was making him shake. He was so excited he thought his heart would hammer its way out of his chest.

He was…dangerous. He had to be really, really careful here. He had strong hands, he had to be gentle and he didn't know how to do that so he did the only thing he could. He walked to her bed and lay down on his back, hand out.

"Come to me, Isabel," he whispered. If she was on top she could maintain some control.

She took his hand and moved to him. He caught one knee and gently lifted it over him. Isabel moved over him, braced herself on her hands, bent her head to his, her hair a soft curtain that closed them off in a private magic kingdom.

Joe stared into her eyes, hands roaming up and down that satiny back.

"I'm not going to last at all the first time," he whispered. "Just so you know."

She smiled faintly, bent down farther and kissed him.

Joe pulled his cock away from his belly, positioned it against her opening, wanting so badly to go slow, knowing he wasn't going to manage it.

"Now, Joe," Isabel said into his mouth and he thrust upward, hard, spilling as he entered her, his entire body shaking and sweating, coming as hard as a freight train. He jerked and trembled and kissed her and held her tight, completely out of control.

It ended, finally. He gentled his hands, pressed his head back against the pillow, completely ashamed of himself. "I'm sorry, Isabel," he said, laying a forearm against his eyes. He couldn't stand to look at her.

"Whoa." Isabel peeled his forearm away. Smiled into his eyes. "I came, too, didn't you feel it?"

God no, he'd been too busy living through his own personal earthquake. But he thrust a little in her and she was very wet. Maybe not just from him.

"You did?" His voice was hoarse. She smiled and nodded.

Thank you, God. That was an orgasm he didn't deserve. Someone up there loved beat-up soldiers.

She was smiling and she wasn't mad. Another miracle.

Joe was still rock hard. He hadn't even taken the edge off.

He rolled over, taking her with him and smiled down into her eyes. He moved in her a little, knowing he'd have better control this time.

"And now," he said, "for my next trick…"

ISABEL WOKE UP SMILING. No nightmares. None. Of course Joe had kept her awake most of the night so she hadn't had time for any REM sleep. Whatever, she felt rested and…happy.

Wow. Happy.

She was lying on a strong, broad chest with a nap of rough curly chest hair. This guy didn't manscape like everyone she knew. No, it was like resting on a soft carpet over a hard floor. Her ear rested against his chest and she could hear the steady heartbeat. Sixty beats a minute. A beat a second. So steady it felt like a machine that could go on forever.

Well, last night it hadn't been that steady. After that first wrenching orgasm, Joe had been breathing like a bull and she could see the fast heartbeats throbbing in the veins of his neck. Fast and hard.

Her lips curled at the memory.

Joe's hand was cupping the back of her head and his hand tightened briefly. "I can hear that smile."

His voice was so deep, a low rumble in his chest.

The idea of hearing her smile charmed her. "Can you? You have very keen hearing."

"You have no idea." He gently pulled her head up until they were staring at each other. "Good morning."

This morning his face was sheer sex appeal. All of him was, actually. From the sexy smile in a stubbled face, the wide shoulders, the lean muscles, the red-hot heat in his dark eyes, it all spelled sex. Writ large all over him.

Isabel blushed all over as she remembered last night and his eyes grew even darker as he saw her blush. His mouth tilted up on one side. "I love it when you do that."

Isabel blew her bangs out of her eyes. "What, blush? I should be way beyond blushing. It's embarrassing."

She was propping herself up on his chest with one forearm. Next to her thigh, his penis started hardening. Which was amazing, considering last night. She'd had a banker boyfriend who'd had fewer erections in six months of dating.

"I like making you blush," he stated and his eyes dropped to her mouth. Isabel knew she looked like a woman who'd had sex all night. Her hair was a tangle of curls that would take a brush with stiff bristles to tame. She was sure she had beard burn all over her face, neck and, um, breasts and probably had a few hickeys, too. She hadn't had a hickey since the early years of high school. Her mouth felt swollen. Everything felt swollen, including the tender tissues of her sex.

She blushed even harder.

Without any visible effort, Joe placed his big hands under her arms and lifted her fully over him. They were laying face-to-face, breast to chest, groin to groin. And he was now fully erect. Again. His penis was like a warm steel tube against her belly, growing warmer and harder by the second.

"You are, um…" she whispered.

"Yeah. Hell yeah." His voice was hoarse, eyes burning into hers. He squinted, as if she were a thousand miles away and he had to see every nuance of her expression. "You up with that?"

Was she up with that? She'd had more sex last night than in the past year. And the past six months after the Massacre had been like an historical period, the Era of No Sex. 400-300 BC. It was hard to remember, it felt like eons ago. At the time, she couldn't imagine anyone touching her or wanting to be touched. Her entire body had been dead to sex, lifeless and dry. She wasn't lifeless and dry now.

Isabel pressed down with her belly just as he pressed upward and her entire body just bloomed with heat. It opened up, happy to be here in bed with Joe. Knowing for a certainty that good things were about to happen.

"Yes." Her voice sounded strangled. She coughed to loosen it up. "Yes, it appears that, um, though my head says 'enough is enough', my body seems to have other ideas."

His face was sober now, tense, white lines bracketing his mouth. Thin nostrils flared as they took in more oxygen. "Let's see," he said suddenly.

What did he mean—oh. A big hand smoothed over her bottom, farther down, slid a finger inside her. She was wet, ready. Her body knew that before her head did.

Joe lifted his head and kissed her, one of those melting kisses where she had to close her eyes because they couldn't stay open. His entire body was kissing hers. Wiry chest hairs rubbing against her erect nipples, hard belly rubbing against hers, rough-haired thighs opening hers. His hand cupped a breast, callused thumb circling her nipple, an electric arousal. Oh, God, it felt like her skin was crackling, like some painless fire was burning her alive, only it wasn't killing her, it was bringing her back to life.

His mouth moved to her ear, giving it a little nip that brought goose bumps. He kissed it, whispered, "Lift up."

Isabel could hardly breathe from the excitement. She had to consciously expand her lungs and pull in breath.

"Lift," he growled.

She lifted, coming up on her knees. Still watching her carefully, Joe fit himself to her and slowly, slowly guided her down on him, holding her hips.

The pleasure was so intense it felt electric. "God," she gasped.

"Tell me about it." His face was tense, rigid. Everything about him was rigid, tightly holding on to control. When he was completely inside her, he stopped, lifting up to kiss her.

As if she needed more stimulation.

Isabel angled her head, licked her tongue in his mouth and felt the answering surge of his penis inside her. Her body answered the only way it knew how, clenching tightly. They gasped in each other's mouths.

Isabel licked his lips, moved her mouth over that strong, stubbled jaw, licked his ear, bit his earlobe. With each movement of her mouth, his movements grew stronger, faster. She bit his mouth and he jolted, lifting his hips off the bed, moving incredibly deep inside her.

Isabel moaned and Joe wrapped his arms around her so tightly she could feel every movement he made inside her and out. As he started thrusting hard, she was riding him with her body, her belly feeling his rock-hard belly against her, the hair on his thighs abrading the insides of hers, his hands holding her to him as he thrust inside her. Every single inch of her felt possessed by him, touched by him, her body as an extension of his, their excitement rising together, identical, until with a hoarse groan that felt wrenched from him, he started spilling inside her just as she rose over the top. With him.

Spent, Isabel fell bonelessly forward, lying on Joe's hard, muscled body, breathing heavily. She felt like she'd run a marathon at the spa. Exhausted, yet jazzed. Her body was humming but her mind was completely empty.

When she moved, he slipped out of her and she was sorry but the rest of his body was exciting enough. There was no sexual energy left in her, all fizzled out, though she was still able to appreciate the perfect specimen beneath her. Her hands came to rest on the balls of his shoulders, the muscle there so hard she couldn't dent it with her fingers.

"Wow," she murmured, eyes closed. A little nap right about now sounded just great. Vast physical effort, blinding pleasure, a little nap. Perfect sequence of events.

She could feel Joe pushing his chin down to look at her. All he'd be seeing was the top of her head. Her tangled bed-hair head.

"Not so fast, Sleeping Beauty." He tensed beneath her.

Another round? God no. She couldn't possibly. The newly awakened sexual part of her brain consulted her body for a second, but nope. Not happening. This was the time of lax muscles and that little nap. Besides, he wasn't growing erect. If he had he'd have been a wonder of nature or else he'd swallowed about ten little blue pills.

"We're not sleeping."

"We're not?" she asked, not really caring what he said. She wasn't getting up for anything or anybody. "Yes we are. At least I am. I'm staying right here."

"Nope, honey. I'm really sorry to contradict you, but we're getting up."

In your dreams. With difficulty she dragged her hand out from under the warm covers where it had been perfectly happy to clutch his shoulder. In comparison to the warm cozy space under the covers, the air felt cold. She held out her index finger and wagged it back and forth in the universal "no" sign, then put her hand back under the warm covers against his hot skin, where it belonged.

He grabbed her hand, kissed it and sighed. "We gotta get up, honey. Sorry." And the beast threw the covers off!

Without opening her eyes, she reached down blindly to grab them, pull them up and huddle deeper in the warm blankets. Then, in an act of incredible cruelty, he pulled them away again.

She sat up, indignant. Joe smiled into her eyes and tapped her mouth. The one he'd kissed all night. "God, you've got a sexy pout."

"I'm not pouting," she huffed.

"World-class pout. A real champ. I'd love to let you sleep, but I can't, because in about an hour's time Metal and Jacko are coming over and I don't think you want to find yourself opening the door in your nightgown." His smile was pure sex, eyes narrowed as he glanced at her nightgown on the floor, where she'd tossed it. He could have no idea that in her pre-Joe stage, a nightgown of hers would *never* be on the floor. Ever. Apparently fabulous sex made you lower your housekeeping standards.

"Wait." She frowned. "I thought they were coming over in the afternoon to play poker in your house. What are they coming here for this morning?"

"We'll play poker all right. Later." Joe's face went from pure male sensuality to sober soldier in an instant. "This morning we're all going to work to make your place more secure than Fort Knox. Remember I said that last night? No one is ever going to creep up close to your house and look in your bedroom window." He gave a short, sharp nod. "You can take that to the bank."

Something loosened inside her, something she hadn't realized was twisted tight. "You really believe me then. That there was someone here last night." It mattered. He wouldn't have called in his friends and colleagues if he thought she'd conjured up an intruder in her sick mind.

Joe's face pulled tight. "Of course I believe you. The fact that I couldn't find evidence doesn't mean anything. The ground was too cold to bear prints and I imagine he wouldn't be foolish enough to smoke a cigarette and throw the butt on the ground. But someone was here. And he had night vision. That's not ever going to happen again."

"Thank you," Isabel said quietly. She was wide-awake now. Joe and his friends were going way out of their way to help her. She knew only one way to pay them back. "I'll fix lunch for all of us and then snacks for the poker players and then dinner for Felicity and Lauren. It's the least I can do."

"Breakfast, too? Or is that pushing it?"

Pushing it? After the best night of her life, after he was going to spend his morning and afternoon making sure she was going to be safe, breakfast, lunch, snacks and dinner were definitely not pushing it. His friends were going to dedicate at least a half day to her safety. And Felicity and Lauren? She was starved for female company. She was going to take enormous pleasure in preparing a light dinner. It used to be her specialty—chick food.

This was going to be fun.

Isabel rolled that idea around in her head, tasting it, savoring it.

Fun.

Something that had fled her life six months ago.

She cupped Joe's bristly, square jaw. His skin was hot, the unshaven beard rough. She hoped he never grew a beard, fashionable as they were nowadays. It would hide the crisp clear lines of his jaw.

Isabel smiled into his eyes. "Breakfast coming right up. And if your friends are going to help me make this house more secure, I am more than happy to feed them. Particularly since, according to local gossip, they're going to lose their pants to you at poker. Consider lunch and snacks their consolation prize."

SIX

Washington, DC

THE RALLY WAS held in the Sentinel Hotel, two blocks from the Burrard, which was still being restored. Party leaders would have wanted the rally to be in the Burrard itself, but the reconstruction work kept getting bogged down in setbacks.

Which, of course, Blake was organizing. A broken, burned-down Burrard, still in ruins, was a potent symbol of failure. Of an inability to pick up, restore and move on.

Exactly what he wanted and what his team of men orchestrated. Every night a team of men went in quietly and undid the repair work and set little traps guaranteed to slow work the next day.

The consortium of owners had gone through three construction companies and was about to fire the fourth. Of course nobody knew he held a majority share through lawyers. That was how he'd gotten the blueprints to set the explosives.

The Burrard was gone and would never come back. Hector Blake would make sure of it. And in a year or two, when the plan was complete, it wouldn't be just the Burrard that would be a smoking ruin. Half the country would be a wreck.

So today's rally was in the Sentinel, old and staid

and not giving off the vibe the Burrard, all sleek glass and steel, would have.

After their talk at the Voyagers Club, Blake hadn't contacted London in any way. Neither had any member of his staff been in touch. London would be puzzled. He might even wonder if he'd imagined their meeting, imagined Blake handing him the nomination on a plate.

Because this was Blake's event, no question. His face was on a thousand posters, on banners held high in sweating fists, on screens set throughout the huge ballroom. The crowd spilled out from the hotel, lining the sidewalk. His handlers had herded them out here so that the journalists could shoot him emerging from his limo walking straight into a warm bath of wildly enthusiastic supporters.

The car parked smoothly by the sidewalk and his driver emerged to open his door. As soon as the door was open and he was visible, the dark afternoon lit up with the strobe lights as reporters used their flashbulbs. It was half-and-half. Half old-style reporters working for the dailies, holding out boom mikes, half bloggers with messy hair, sloppy jeans and cells held up.

"Senator Blake, Senator Blake! Who will you choose to be your veep candidate?"

The question was asked—shouted—by a young journo. Or maybe blogger? Hmm. Very pretty. Auburn hair cut short, green eyes accentuated by smoky eye shadow. Slim, great tits. Blake's eyes fell to the lanyard around her neck. *Area 8*, an up-and-coming political blog.

There was something familiar about the blogger. Maybe Blake had seen her on TV. He was good with faces and he never forgot a pretty one. So it was strange to find that face familiar but not know where he'd seen her before.

Never mind. She was as good a place to start as anywhere.

He stopped right in front of her, clearly ready to answer questions. But instead of gratitude, the minx, she looked up at him, eyes narrowed. Not intimidated, not grateful.

"Senator Blake, word on the street has it that you might not be running after all. That you might endorse someone else. What do you say to that?"

Shit! *Did that fuckhead London talk?* If that preening, empty-headed moron spilled the beans, Blake would have his balls on a plate. But London wouldn't have talked. Too much depended on discretion. The presidency, no less.

Blake's heart beat hard in his chest and he had to school his face to blandness. He smiled down into the reporter's eyes, momentarily nonplussed to find them so familiar. And intelligent. This was a sharp one and he had to tread carefully. She was getting info from somewhere.

Blake smiled. His patented you're-not-getting-anything-from-me smile. "Why, where would you get that idea?"

She didn't smile back, simply held her cell up. "Rumors swirl in this city, Senator. You know that better than anyone."

The little bitch. Blake wasn't going to play this game. He held up his hand and turned his head slightly. When played back, the viewer would see a palm and a one-quarter profile. Of no interest for a podcast.

"This country doesn't run on rumors, it runs on

facts," he said flatly and moved away. He motioned to his chief of staff and assistant. They came in fast and spearheaded his way through the crowd as he moved forward in a babble of voices.

Hands reached out to touch him, heads swiveled to follow his progress along the walkway.

Thank God the plate glass entry doors were wide-open. His staff would have insisted on that, knowing he liked to get into buildings fast. He hated revolving doors, they made him feel trapped, shuffling slowly at everyone else's pace.

With each step, he realized he had made not only the smart move but also the right move. Politics at this level wasn't for him. He'd had to glad-hand thousands of Virginians to be elected senator but the presidency? A year and a half of touching thousands and thousands, maybe even millions of voters. A year and a half of bad meals, hotel rooms, smiling at crappy jokes, pretending to like the local pols who endorsed him.

No, very soon, within the hour, all this would be behind him and he himself would be behind the throne. London would obey him and he'd be Cardinal Richelieu, crafty and strong, to the weakling Louis XIII.

He, Hector Blake, was going to bring the country to its knees, and it was going to bow to him and the masters he served. But he would stay in the shadows, as real power must.

Suddenly, the clutching hands, anxious faces, fevered voices got to him. Years ago he'd perfected the art of moving fast without looking like he was hurrying. He couldn't wait to get this farce over with. He lengthened his stride and watched as his aides and chief of staff scrambled, startled, to keep up with him.

Blake was only a few yards from the big entry doors of the hotel when someone bumped into him, hard. He was knocked back a step and almost fell. A hard hand grasped his neck, steadied him.

A vet. A homeless vet, by the look of him. Matted filthy hair, long beard, dark round sunglasses, a BDU that looked like it had been slept in for weeks. And the smell. God. Blake barely kept from wrinkling his nose in distaste. The man smelled like a sewer, with an additional layer of stale beer breath.

"Don't forget the vets!" the man shouted, spewing saliva.

Blake closed his eyes and stepped back in instinctive horror. God only knew if the man was carrying a disease. He was shouting slogans, rambling phrases, as one of the security guards placed at the hotel's entrance rushed forward and wrestled him away from Blake. The man struggled but the guard was strong. Blake saw the back of his head, tangled dirty hair straggling over his shoulders.

Blake cricked his neck, a little ache coming from where the man had grasped him.

God, he hated people. And he particularly hated poor people. He could never have put up with the farce of a presidential campaign.

He moved ahead again, eager to get this over with. As he entered the huge ballroom, thousands of people shouted when they saw him. Those who weren't near the doors saw him enter the room on the huge monitors on the walls.

Unnerved by his encounter with the vet, Blake made his way forward, touching as few people as possible. Clearly expecting him to glad-hand his way slowly to the podium, his handlers and the security people behind scrambled to catch up as he walked up the short staircase to the podium.

The roar of the crowd intensified, grew deafening. Blake appeared to bask in it, head uplifted, smiling. Though it was a crowd of politicized people, mostly wealthy, he could smell sweat under the thick haze of perfume. Some women down under the podium were screaming and jumping up and down in a frenzy. Very close to what looked like an epileptic fit.

They weren't crazy for *him*, but for what he represented—the Delvauxes, who had been taken from America. He represented pre-Washington Massacre America. He represented the America that kicked ass, not the weakened giant everyone perceived but no one could say. The crowd wanted a Delvaux but if they couldn't have Alex, then they'd take his best friend.

Well, they weren't even going to get the surrogate Delvaux.

They were going to get a puppet and Blake's job now was to make sure they'd scream for that puppet.

The crowd swayed to the piped in beat of "Happy", waving banners with 3 x 5 posters of his head, as if he or any politician could make them happy. The song had been chosen by his PR team and would do for London, too. "Happy" was a perfectly fine anthem for unhappy times.

Blake stood at the podium, spotlights honed in on his smiling face, seemingly soaking in the adoration, taking in the frantic crowds, foot tapping to the music, arms up, embracing everything about the event.

The lights blinded him but he was able to pick out people he knew in the crowd nonetheless. But most of the screaming enthusiastic men and women were complete strangers who had no idea who he really was. They were screaming for an idea, not a man. And even the idea was nebulous. Bright, shiny future. Prosperity while saving the environment. Inclusion, as long as it wasn't of people *too* different from them. Helping the third world as long as it didn't affect their lifestyle.

That's what they were screaming for.

They were so ripe. This time next year or maybe the year after, they'd have overlords and he'd be one of them and all the confusion and panic of freedom would be gone forever. They'd be told what to do and when to do it and they'd be happier.

Finally, when he judged the peak of enthusiasm had passed, he held his hands up. He bent to the microphone, judging it would take three passes.

"Dear friends," he began, but they were still enthusiastically shouting and waving. Blake put an indulgent smile on his face and bent again. "Dear friends."

They started shushing each other as he waited, kindly smiling at them all.

He patted the air and finally there was silence in the great hall, an expectant hush.

"Dear friends." Blake looked out over the crowd once everyone had settled down. He'd perfected the paternal smile, a loving father surveying his beloved progeny. *Each and every one of you is precious to me,* that smile said. "This city, our country, suffered a grievous loss half a year ago." When the crowd understood that he was opening with the Massacre, even the rustling stopped and they listened reverently. "Our attackers hate us, hate what we represent. And the only way they know how to deal with that is to kill what they don't, and they can't, understand. Not only did we lose many of our best and brightest, including the man I believe from the bottom of my heart was to be our next president, but we lost something even deeper. Our hope for the future. But the enemy cannot be allowed to win. They didn't destroy our spirit!"

Spontaneous applause. He waited it out. The smiling politician was gone, replaced by the somber statesman.

"We need a special kind of person to lead us in these perilous times." Blake bowed his head and when he lifted it again, there was the sheen of tears in his eyes. He could see himself on a monitor to the side and he had to admit, he was good. He had a sad cast to his face, a man who'd known tragedy and had survived, but it had marked him forever. "I intended to be that man. I wanted to be that man with all my heart. But my soul is troubled. I must admit this to you, my dear friends. I am not the man I was. I have worked hard to be what I once was. I have talked to my friends and my pastor. I have prayed on it." Another head bow and he bit his lower lip. You could hear a pin drop in the room. Something unexpected was coming and everyone felt it.

Blake lifted his head, looked out over the crowd, everyone still, watching him.

"Dear friends." His voice was hoarse and he coughed to clear it. He drew a hand down his face, surreptitiously wiping his eyes. Every single person in the room took note. If possible, the crowd grew even more silent. All eyes on him. "Dear friends, fellow Americans, as I said, I have prayed hard over this decision. I have searched the depths of my soul and I find I must bear open my heart to you." He allowed his voice to wobble. "I am—I am not the man I was before the Massacre. Before—

before, I was willing to go all the way to support my friend, Alex Delvaux, in his voyage to the White House. I believed with all my heart that he is—" Blake stopped, put on a horrified expression as he corrected himself. "He *was* the right man for the job. The job of leading these great United States forward into the third decade of the twenty-first century. Alex Delvaux is—*was*—a man of the future who understood the values of the past. He was one of a kind, and we will not see his like again for generations."

Blake's voice broke and he conjured up a tear or two, enough to make his cheeks glisten in the glow of the spotlights. Flashes from journalists' cameras started up, creating a strobe effect.

Blake heaved a sigh. "I knew it would be hard to fill Alex's shoes. Almost impossible. He was a man with a strong vision for our country and with the strong hand necessary to make that vision come true. I knew Alex well. He was my best friend. His family was like my family, and I honestly thought, unworthy though I am, I could pick up the fallen torch. But—" He held up his hand. Utter silence in the room. Not even a rustling of clothes. "The Massacre broke something in me. I lost my best friend. I lost friends I've known since childhood. I cannot stop grieving and my heart is too full of sorrow to be an effective candidate. After much thought and prayer, I realize that I am not the man who can pick up that fallen torch. There is a better man than I for our party and for our country."

Blake stopped, looked heavenward. Actually he looked up at the lighting technician's bay. They'd arranged this and the technicians knew what to do.

Blake pointed his finger dramatically. "There he is!

This is the man who can carry this country forward into the future and keep us safe from further attacks!"

The lighting technician unerringly spotlit John London's distinguished face. Piped-in music blared. Nobody was clapping. Most of the morons in the room had their mouths open.

London had the idiotic look of the beauty contestant who'd just been declared Miss America. He all but burst into tears.

Fucker was ruining the moment.

Blake gave a prearranged signal and the lights focused on him again. He leaned forward, making his voice deep, serious, but excited. "Ladies and gentlemen, dear friends, let's hear it for the next president of these United States, John London!"

Portland

Isabel watched the events unfolding in the Sentinel Hotel ballroom. She'd been in the kitchen preparing a ton of food, happily humming. Three guys, two and maybe three women. Lunch and afternoon snacks and then dinner. Her head swirled with recipes and that gear she had, the one that told her unerringly what food paired well with what, had finally cranked to life after being dead for so long.

"Honey!" Joe'd called from the living room. "Come see this."

Isabel had walked into the living room, drying her hands on her apron, looking with indifference at the screen. Some kind of political rally. She couldn't care less.

Then she saw the chyron on the bottom, big red letters scrolling across the bottom of the screen. HECTOR BLAKE STEPS DOWN, APPOINTS JOHN LONDON AS PARTY STANDARD-BEARER.

What? She stood stock-still, shocked to the core.

John London was a joke! Those handsome looks hid a mediocre mind and dubious morals. Dad had hated him.

Joe put an arm around her. "I'm sorry, honey. That should have been your father."

"Yes, it should have been. Uncle Hector was a miserable replacement. But John London? He's not worthy in any way of this. He's a moron and a lech. I'm ashamed to have him mentioned in the same breath as Dad."

Joe looked at her curiously. "Yeah. I wasn't able to follow US politics too closely in the field, but London's been around a long time. No one has ever praised him for his smarts. But a lech?"

"Pinched me once so hard I was sore for days," Isabel said. "Tried to fondle my breasts when I was sixteen. He's a total creep. And he doesn't give a shit about the environment. How dare Uncle Hector choose him as if he were a natural successor to Dad!" She frowned up at him. "What?"

He'd gone all stiff, his hand biting into her shoulder.

"He pinched you? Fondled you?" Joe's voice sounded choked.

"Yes. He's a creep. What was Uncle Hector thinking?"

"I want to tear his throat out," Joe said.

So did she.

"I like your thinking, Joe." She sighed. "But it's not possible. He's going to be surrounded by Secret Service agents from now on. And I don't think pinching and fondling, however awful, are crimes that warrant having your throat torn out."

Though the idea *was* appealing.

John London as president of the United States was so wrong on so many different levels she felt sick. But he'd make it probably, if he could keep it in his pants and if they didn't let him talk too much. Other morons had made it. And there could never be a candidate like her dad. Certainly not Hector and *certainly* not London.

Her father had been smart and good and capable of fighting for what he believed in. He'd had solid old-fashioned values while being open and tolerant. And he truly believed in protecting the environment and would have fought—and fought hard—special interests. There was no one else like him on the political horizon.

And her mother's nightmare, the reason they'd fought so bitterly over his candidacy, had actually come true. He'd been assassinated.

And so had she.

"This must be disturbing for you." Joe kissed the top of her head. "Knowing your father and knowing him."

She looked up at him and for the first time saw something she should have seen before. He shared characteristics with her father, which hadn't occurred to her before. She'd thought they were polar opposites.

Her father had loved living large. He always dressed in expensive clothes, wore expensive shoes and had expensive tastes. She rarely saw Joe in anything but jeans and T-shirts. A jacket when he was really dressing up. Track shoes and boots. He didn't have three-hundred-dollar haircuts and manicured nails.

But he said what he meant and he meant what he said

and there didn't seem to be any bullshit in him at all, exactly like her father.

"It is. I hate the thought of a man like that representing my father in any way." She snaked her arm around Joe's lean waist and rested her head against his shoulder. "Nothing I can do about it, though."

Joe kissed her head again. "Nope. Maybe he'll lose. *Then* I rip his throat out when there aren't Secret Service agents around. How's that sound?"

Isabel smiled. "Perfect. So, who's coming today to turn my house into a fortress?"

"Jacko and Metal and maybe the Senior. One of my bosses. He didn't know if he could make it, but he'll try."

"The Senior? Is that his name?"

"No. His ranking. Former ranking, but we all just call him the Senior. He was a Senior Chief."

"Sounds serious."

"Man, that guy defines serious. You did not want to get on the wrong side of the Senior. Talk about ripping your throat out. He'd do worse when we were in the military, like ordering us to drop onto the grinder and pump out an extra hundred and fifty." Joe shook his head, smiling faintly though Isabel didn't see how pumping out a hundred and fifty push-ups could be a fond memory. "Then go for a ten-mile run in the freezing surf. That's if he found a wrinkle in your bed. If you missed a target on the range, then he'd get creative."

Isabel blinked. "He sounds—he sounds cruel." Did she want someone like that in her home?

"No, not cruel." Joe took her hands in his. His face had turned sober. "Not cruel at all. The Senior's job was to train us to complete the mission while staying alive. He was our worst nightmare, until we actually went into battle. Being kind and soft to us in training was the very best way to get us killed in the field. If you sweat in training you don't bleed in the field. That's what we lived by. Man, we sweated a lot."

"You bled," Isabel said softly. She'd felt his scars. He was covered in them.

"I did. And my training saved my life. We were given intense lessons on explosive devices and I recognized a detonator in a pile of old junk in the Sandbox. I jumped and that saved my life, otherwise I wouldn't be here, eating your food, holding your hand. The Senior designed the ED lessons and he was thorough. I missed two detonators in the classroom lessons and I ran an extra twenty miles that week and I got assigned a couple of circuses. Next time I identified every single detonator. Ten out of ten."

"Circuses?" Isabel was fascinated. It was a look into what made an elite warrior.

"Circuses are an extra two hours of calisthenics a day. And trust me when I say that the vanilla version is already pretty extreme. Or we'd be turned into sugar cookies. Made to roll in the sand on the beach at sunrise and stay sandy and uncomfortable all day."

"I don't think I'd make a Navy SEAL," she said primly. "I don't like that sandy feeling."

Joe laughed. "Maybe not. We were kept cold and exhausted and sandy but we were expected to keep up in class. But in the field I was hot and exhausted and still noticed the detonator and jumped and that saved my life. So the Senior is more than okay in my book. And everyone says he's a great boss." He fidgeted. "I've been on the payroll for three months. I can't wait to get to work."

"That's generous of the company. To keep you on the payroll while you're recovering."

He was visibly uncomfortable. He clenched his jaw. "I begged them not to put me on payroll. It feels...*wrong* to be paid for doing nothing."

"Maybe they think they are assuring your loyalty."

He looked down at her and shook his head. "They have that already. These are former teammates. They've built a great company and I'm honored to be part of it. They have my loyalty regardless."

"That's why you trained so hard to get back on your feet," Isabel said on a sudden insight. "You wanted to get to work as fast as you could."

It had been amazing, and humbling, to watch. She'd never seen anyone put themselves through the paces like Joe. She sure hadn't been able to do what Joe had done.

Shame filled her.

She'd been grieving. She'd been lost and lonely. But probably Joe had been grieving too. A lot of men died in Afghanistan and he'd surely lost friends. And perhaps he'd felt lost and lonely too. It hadn't stopped him the way it had stopped her.

Just knowing Joe made her feel better. And after sleeping with him, she felt *way* better.

Joe's mouth lifted in a half smile. "Some complicated thoughts are going on in that beautiful head of yours."

"First you hear smiles, now you read thoughts?"

He didn't say anything, but the smile was full-blown and smug now.

"Don't answer that. Now." She stepped away and clapped her hands. "If I'm going to be feeding hordes I'd better get started, don't you think? And I'll start with feeding us breakfast."

Isabel was hungry. *Hungry.* She couldn't remember the last time she'd felt hungry. Her appetite had fled from her world, together with desire and joy and hope. For the first time in forever she was looking forward to eating.

She made to turn away but Joe caught her hands in his huge, callused ones. He searched her eyes. "Is it too much? Too much work today? You're going to be feeding a lot of people. The guys have learned to come hungry if you're cooking so they're going to inhale the food. And then you're going to have Lauren and Felicity and maybe Suzanne—"

Isabel reached up to smooth away the frown lines on his forehead. He already had a lot of them, she didn't want to add any.

"I love cooking," she said simply. "Or at least I used to. Enjoying cooking is just one of the many things that was taken from me. I feel a little excited at the thought of cooking for people, seeing their reactions to what I've prepared. I know everyone is going to be friendly and if I don't burn things or add a ton of salt, they're predisposed to like it. I can't go wrong. I really want to do this, Joe. Trust me."

"I do." A crafty look stole over his face. "But before they come over, what's for breakfast?"

BREAKFAST WAS AMAZING. Fresh-made croissants—Joe didn't think he'd ever met anyone who could actually make them from scratch. Homemade bread, too, chewy and delicious. Three kinds of red jams she'd made.

She hadn't churned the butter. He asked.

And he could see that she was telling the truth when

she said that cooking made her happy. Made him happy, too, in a major way.

But for Isabel it was clearly satisfying on some deep level. Joe was grateful without understanding it. Cooking was something he had to do once in a while because even he knew eating breakfast, lunch and supper in diners or ordering takeout wasn't good for you. But he hated it. He could never figure out timing. The steaks were done while the baked potatoes were still raw. And though he tried, he couldn't like salad or sliced tomatoes. At least he hadn't until he'd tasted Isabel's salads. They were light and fresh. And she seemed to find something that was *called* a tomato but wasn't a mealy pink thing, but dark red and small and luscious.

She looked happy as she moved around in the kitchen. No, more than happy. She glowed. He hadn't seen her like this and it was a world away from the trembling, paper-white woman he'd met that first day.

She'd been beautiful back then, too, she'd still knocked him on his ass but this Isabel? She rocked his world. Last night had been a different kind of sex than he was used to. Sex had always been great. He'd started young and he'd bedded a lot of women and he'd never turned anyone down. But sex sure hadn't been world altering. He'd set himself on a course when he'd enrolled in the navy and he hadn't deviated one step. He hadn't been tempted by any woman to change the trajectory of his life.

One night with Isabel and he'd throw everything overboard to be with her.

Man was he lucky that he didn't have to do that. He wasn't going to have to sacrifice anything. She already lived close by and was fine with his job and—

God! It felt like he'd rolled heavenly dice and thrown a midnight.

Joe had always relied on his instincts. In the Teams, he'd studied damned hard, he'd played everything by the book but on the streets and in the field, he trusted his instincts. Right now, it felt like something huge had come into his life. If some blood had been left in his head last night instead of pooling in his dick, he'd have recognized it. He recognized it now.

Homecoming, for a man who'd never had a home.

He watched her moving around in her kitchen. She knew it the way he knew his kit. Perfectly. Everything positioned just so. Well organized and in perfect condition, ready for use.

Of course his kit was for whacking his country's enemies and hers was to stun people's taste buds, but still.

Imagine having this every day.

Imagine her in his house, every single fucking day. In his bed, every night. This beautiful creature, all grace and light, his.

He was getting ahead of himself. *Down boy.*

She was beautiful and smart and classy. And she was a Delvaux. No getting around that. No way would Joe ever be in a position to replicate for her what her family had given her. He loved his teammates, his bosses, his job. Or he would when he could finally do it.

But he couldn't pretend for a second that they were this country's elite. They were solid guys, none better. Men he'd trust with his life. But they'd never be bestselling authors or Supreme Court Justices or presidential candidates.

So what—

Joe stopped thinking when Isabel slid a plate in

front of him. Pointless thinking, really, when everything looked and smelled so amazing.

He glanced up at a smiling Isabel. "Waffles? Really? You made me waffles?"

"With baked raspberry jam. One of my specialties. And I make my waffles really light. Try them."

He cut into the stack of waffles, slightly crusty on the outside, soft on the inside and oh God, the *smell*. If there were awards for food smells, she'd nail it.

He kept himself from moaning by sheer grit because it wasn't like any waffle he'd ever eaten. Light as air, with the tangy taste of that incredible raspberry jam… did she say she'd baked the jam?

Never mind. He didn't want to analyze the magic. He finished in record time.

"That was fast," Isabel observed. She was barefoot, in pale blue sweats that reflected her eyes, dark honey hair a little messy, no makeup. She looked more delicious than the waffles. His heart kicked once beneath his ribs, hard. "Do you want any more?"

God yes.

"Come here." His voice sounded thick and strange even to his own ears.

She was carrying her own plate to the table when she stopped at the odd note in his voice. Then she looked him in the face, glanced down at his lap, looked up again and blushed. What he wanted was clear on his face, not to mention the huge boner nicely outlined by his thin sweats.

She walked slowly over to him. No hesitation whatsoever. If she'd hesitated, if he felt he was forcing her in any way, he'd stop.

He hoped.

She stood by his side, legs brushing his where he sat.

Sometimes Joe initiated sex like he went into battle. Deliberately, planning every move beforehand. Mapping out which items of clothing had to go first, deciding where to touch the woman and when.

Not now, oh fuck no.

Now he felt out of control, an unusual feeling and one he'd reject in any other context. Control was gone. Right now, all he wanted was to be inside Isabel, to feel her naked body against his. There was no planning, no mapping of his actions, he acted out of pure instinct and he moved as fast as he could.

First her. "These have to go," he whispered, clutching the hem of the sweatshirt. "Up with your hands." She stuck her hands up in the air as if he was a bank robber. He pulled the sweatshirt up and threw it off, so quickly her hair crackled with static electricity. No bra. Fantastic. His hands were shaking so he didn't know if he could deal with little hooks and things.

She was so incredibly beautiful in the light of day. All that smooth pale skin, the large breasts on her narrow rib cage. The real deal. He'd felt every inch of them last night.

Trying to be smooth and failing at it, Joe pulled down the sweatpants, taking an incredibly lacy pair of panties down with them. She was barefoot, so all she had to do was step out of the sweats and voilà.

Gorgeous, naked woman.

Now him.

He was easy. All he had on was the sweats. Joe lifted his ass, pulled the sweats down and he was naked too.

He cleared the table with his forearm and settled Isabel on the edge, stepping between her legs.

He kissed her neck and murmured, “Eating your waffles got me hot.”

She laughed and her breasts shivered across his chest. He smoothed his hand up her long, slim thigh to her sex and touched her. She shivered. “Did watching me eat your waffles make you hot?” he asked.

Isabel’s back arched and her head fell to one side. Her neck was an erogenous zone. Joe had figured that out last night. *Gotcha.* He nuzzled against her neck, waves of soft hair caressing his skin. God.

“Find out,” she whispered.

He was so taken with the taste of her skin, with the feel of her hair against his face it took him a minute to understand what she meant.

Find out if I’m turned on, was what she meant.

Oh yeah.

He licked the skin behind her ear while stroking her and…yes. Watching him eat her waffles got her very hot. She was like a little furnace there, hot and juicy. He stroked her gently, slowly, pulling back to watch her face in the early morning sunlight. She glowed, like a pearl.

Joe read her face like it was a book, a book he really needed to learn, like a survivor’s manual. As he touched her, entered her with his finger, he studied her expression to see what she liked.

Her head was tilted back, eyes closed, absurdly thick eyelashes fluttering. When her face tightened he knew he was getting it right. She liked to be touched here. And here. And *here.*

Isabel gasped.

And there, too.

“Joe,” she whispered.

"Right here," he whispered back.

So slick and hot, he entered her like a dream, lifting his lips from her neck to kiss her mouth, another source of warmth he could enter. Everything about her was purest magic, the feel of her smooth slim back against his hands, her soft thighs clutching his.

He moved forward, into her, kissing her deeply, his tongue imitating what he was doing to her lower body, soft and gentle.

They were making noises in the quiet of the kitchen, their bodies kissing everywhere. For a second Joe tore his mouth away from hers and looked down at where they were joined, watched himself as he pulled out then slid back into her. She looked down too. His skin was darker, rougher. Watching their bodies writhe together was the most erotic sight he'd ever seen.

They both looked up, eyes meeting, faces sober. It felt like an incredibly solemn moment, as if the very air was hesitant, expectant.

This was serious stuff. Joe felt like it was not only his dick in her, but his heart, too, beating right next to hers.

She smiled, lifted a hand to his jaw, leaned forward to kiss him with a tenderness he'd never received from anyone. His chest hurt and the only thing that could help was kissing her again, moving more deeply in her, faster, until he erupted inside her and felt her clinging to him with her arms and her mouth and her legs and her sex. Clenching hard around him as he emptied himself inside her and held her tightly afterward, almost afraid to let her go.

She was his.

THERE WERE THREE men making her place as secure at Fort Knox, just as Joe had said. It was amazing watching them work together. Clearly they'd worked together before. Well…yeah. They'd gone on missions where they put their lives at risk together, which is probably where they learned to work as a unit.

Exactly like a well-run kitchen with dedicated staff, only going to war instead of preparing food.

They didn't speak much to each other as they worked, they didn't have to. They all knew exactly what to do.

When Metal and Jacko arrived they were both carrying duffel bags and Isabel thought that they'd brought tools. But they hadn't, they'd brought equipment. Lots of it, shiny and brand-new, high-tech and very expensive-looking.

"Ah, guys?" she said as both of them started unloading high-end electronics and stacking everything neatly according to criteria only they could see onto her coffee table. "This stuff looks expensive. You need to give me the bill so I can—"

"Nah," Metal said. He was fitting together highly machined pieces and his hands didn't stop. "ASI gets a professional discount, a big one, a lot of this stuff is being road tested so it's at cost, and besides Joe—"

Joe sent him a fulminating look and Metal shut up. You could practically hear his jaw clacking shut.

Isabel rounded on Joe. "You are not paying for this! I am!"

His hands didn't stop either, as he fitted one highly polished doodad onto another highly polished thingamajig. "It's all going around both our houses, honey. And I've already eaten more than the equivalent of your share so it's all good."

The meals she'd prepared for him wouldn't cover

one high-tech knob, let alone all this equipment. "No, I can't accept—"

He laid a long finger across her lips. His face was tight, brackets lining his mouth. "I'm putting a wall of security around both our houses. We're talking about your safety here and I'm responsible for that. It isn't open for discussion."

The man she'd made love with an hour ago, the man who'd melted into her body was gone. This man was all steel and resolve.

Isabel blinked. No one had ever said anything remotely like that to her in her life. Not open for discussion? She drew in a deep, outraged breath, ready to let loose, when Jacko spoke.

He rarely spoke, so it was sort of an occasion.

"Joe's right. He's keeping you safe. I do the same for Lauren. No one's going to touch her, hurt her, I make sure of that." Jacko's voice was even deeper than Joe's. It was more a low rumble than human speech. His dark eyes met hers and his gaze was hard.

"Ditto," Metal said. "This is even better than what I've got at my place to protect Felicity and me. As a matter of fact, you're doing us all a favor. We're testing a lot of stuff, and we'll probably be adding it to our places, too."

His default expression was friendly, unlike Jacko's. But Isabel saw the exact same seriousness and absolute firmness of purpose.

Three serious male faces were turned to hers, Joe's a little pissed off.

Okay. They believed in what they were doing and weren't going to stop because of her scruples. So she'd just resolve to feed them a billion meals.

"Right," she said. "Is there anything I can do to help you?"

There were thousands and thousands of dollars' worth of expensive electronics on the coffee table. The three men froze as they tried to disguise their horror at the thought of her messing with any of it. Presumably Felicity understood this stuff, she was an electronics genius, but Isabel…

"No," three male voices said at once.

"But thanks, honey," Joe said. He smiled at her but his eyes drifted down to what he had in his hands. They all looked enraptured, slightly punch-drunk. It must be really cutting-edge stuff to put that look in their eyes.

They were three huge guys, martial arts experts, superb shots, and they looked like dazzled nerds who'd just been handed the demo of the latest version of Grand Theft Auto.

Well. She'd leave them to their manly stuff and go do something womanly in the kitchen.

"A FLY CAN'T fart without us knowing about it," Joe said proudly three hours later.

It was true. Her house and Joe's were surrounded by a series of hidden sensors that would sound an audio alarm if anything crossed over into their yards. The guys were talking about delivering mild electric shocks when she vetoed that in horror. Suppose some of the neighborhood kids were playing and fell into the hedges or against the fences!

They also selected out false alarms by animals. The alarms were sounded only by living entities that weighed above thirty pounds, though Isabel had no idea how that worked.

Her front door opened by her thumbprint or Joe's pressed against a security pad, followed by a code number entered within ten seconds.

Video cameras were hidden in the eaves and in what looked like water sprinklers and they showed her that the cameras covered every square inch of her property. They fed into monitors in the kitchen and the bedroom. The kitchen monitor was on at all times, the bedroom monitor switched on when movement was detected, preceded by a soft alarm.

Joe had leaned over and whispered that he'd hear the alarm if she didn't. He was assuming that he'd be sleeping over each night. She'd blushed. Metal's and Jacko's gazes moved over her face but neither said anything.

Should she be miffed that Joe simply assumed he'd be staying nights? In theory of course, yes. No man should assume anything like that. It should come after a long tryout period and after careful pondering.

But…

This was Joe. Whose presence in her bed guaranteed not only hot sex but the most reassuring presence she could imagine. If she had nightmares, she wouldn't wake up alone and frightened in the dark. She'd wake up to Joe beside her.

She didn't say no. Didn't really even contemplate it. Joe in her bed every night was the best thing she could imagine.

Then—the windows. Some strange film had been applied to every window in her house and in Joe's. It didn't in any way affect sunlight streaming in. And from outside, it didn't look as if there was distorting film over her windows. It's just that it was impossible to see what was happening inside. As a matter of fact, you couldn't even tell if the lights were on.

Amazing.

Isabel made the rounds of the house outside, while either Joe or Metal or Jacko stood right behind the windows with a flashlight.

She couldn't see anything. Anything at all.

When she came back around the front, a big man was getting out of an enormous SUV.

A big *big* man. As tall as Joe and Metal. As broad as Jacko. With a rough, dangerous look about him.

Terrifying, actually.

Isabel was about to call Joe, trying not to reveal her panic, when Joe walked out the front door, followed by Metal and Jacko. Joe met the guy and thumped him hard on the shoulder.

"Senior!" he bellowed. "Good to see you!" Joe turned to Isabel, smiling, and introduced him.

"Isabel, this is former Senior Chief Douglas Kowalski. The guy I told you about. He'd be my boss if I were actually working."

"Joe…" the man growled. His voice was scary deep. His expression was ferocious. She glanced up at Joe for reassurance and saw only affection and respect. Ditto for Metal and Jacko.

Okay.

Scary-looking guy was dangerous but not, apparently, to her.

"How do you do?" Isabel did the most courageous thing she could imagine. She offered her hand to the man. "I'm Isabel Lawton."

Though if the grapevine worked in Portland the way it worked in DC, he knew her real name.

"Ms. Lawton." That rough deep voice turned gentle. He took her hand in his huge one, carefully squeezed, then let it go.

She'd half expected not to be able to use it for a day or two, but no. It was fine.

Well, he seemed like a perfectly normal citizen, even if he looked terrifying. Her manners, drummed into her by her mother, rose to the fore. "Would you like to come inside? I have coffee and I made some muffins."

A smile crossed that frightening face and it didn't really humanize him. It just made him look even more scary. He had a huge scar along his jawline that pulled when he smiled. It looked exactly like a knife scar.

"Thank you, but no. I wanted to come over with my guys and help lock down your place, but I was called away. But I knew Joe, Metal and Jacko would do a perfect job. I hear you had some trouble last night. You won't have trouble again."

He believed her. Believed there'd been someone there. Just as Joe believed her. And if he believed her, Metal and Jacko did too.

And he'd used his company's influence to get huge discounts.

"Thank you so much, Mr. Kowalski—"

A pained look passed over that rough face. "Douglas, please."

"Douglas. Thank you for all the help your company provided. I understand you essentially footed the bill." She gave a pointed glance at Joe. "One I am not allowed to reimburse."

Something warm and heavy settled around her shoulders. Joe's arm.

Douglas's head jerked back in astonishment. "Good

God, fu—er…there's no question of that. Joe's just making sure you're safe. I know I'd make sure no one can look in on my wife, make sure she's safe. The same for Metal and Jacko."

"Fuck yeah," Jacko muttered. He didn't have Douglas's aversion to the f-bomb in front of a lady. "No one's getting near Lauren. Told you that."

Douglas's gaze sharpened as his deep rough voice softened. He took one of her hands in his. His hands were large, callused. Not a businessman's hands. "I understand you're one of the few to survive the Washington Massacre, Isabel. That's more violence than anyone should have to live through in a lifetime. All Joe wants—and now that we know you, all anyone wants—is to make sure you're safe. And while I'm at it, I want to say how sorry I am about the loss of your family."

Isabel blinked furiously to hide the sudden spurt of tears. "Thank you," she whispered.

Joe's big arm around her shoulders, Metal and Jacko watching her, Douglas holding her hand gently. They were all trying to say the same thing. Somehow, through Joe, Isabel had come under the protection of some remarkable men. Douglas made that clear. He was treating her as if she were a family member, not a casual acquaintance of one of his employees.

All four men were letting her know, as clearly as possible, that they were on her side.

No one had been on her side since the Massacre.

She was a hair away from breaking down and bawling.

"Oh!" Douglas let go of her hand and dug into his coat pocket. "I almost forgot these!" He held out two slender rectangles of paper to her.

Isabel's eyes opened wide and her heart rate kicked up a notch in her chest. "Oh. my gosh! These are tickets to the concert next week by Allegra! She's one of my favorite singers." She checked the seat numbers. "And front row seats! How'd you score these? I called and the show is all sold-out."

Joe snickered.

Douglas smiled, his scar pulling. "Let's say I have connections." He pointed a long finger at Metal and Jacko. "Four tickets for you guys are in the office. I left them with Maddie."

They nodded. Joe bent down to Isabel's ear. "Allegra is Douglas's wife."

Isabel froze. Allegra was Douglas Kowalski's *wife?* She was a noted singer and harpist and the fact that she was beautiful hadn't hurt her career at all. She had a fey, Celtic beauty and played the harp beautifully and had the voice of an angel.

She glanced up at Douglas's face. Tough, ugly, scarred. Like his body.

Allegra's husband.

He stood, smiling slightly, while she processed this. Clearly something he'd done many times before.

He nodded at her. "Ma'am. Gents." This with a faint smile at Joe, Metal and Jacko. "See you all at the office." He pointed at Joe who had a big grin on his face. "Not you, soldier. You're coming in when bones tells you can, and not a day sooner."

And he turned around and walked back to his SUV.

Isabel clutched the tickets happily. Allegra in concert! Joe in her bed! New friends! Life was really looking up.

KEARNS BROKE INTO a beat-up pickup. He was wearing gloves and anyway he had every intention of bringing the piece of shit right back to its owner. He'd never know it was gone. All Kearns wanted to do was drive around the block. This was his third drive-by in as many hours. He'd used a different vehicle and wore a different hat each time.

It should be okay. Though nothing else was okay.

There were two men helping Joe Harris make Isabel Delvaux's house secure and they were doing a good job of it.

Kearns drove as slowly as he dared and on each drive-by he was alarmed at what he was seeing. Motion sensors, all around her house and Harris's. Spotlights. Keypads at the door. Some kind of film on the windowpanes that made them opaque.

Fuck. How the hell was he supposed to know if she was even home?

And if Joe Harris was a former SEAL, chances were the other two guys were, too. Kearns remembered the Special Forces fucks who waltzed in and out of bases. They didn't salute and they dressed as civilians and they carried whatever the fuck they wanted as firepower.

And they stuck together.

So now Kearns was dealing not with one isolated and weak chick he could jerk off to. He was dealing with a chick who was fucking surrounded by SEALs and whose house was now a fortress.

How the hell was he going to tell Blake that? Blake wanted weekly reports and Kearns could fake it but it was dangerous. There was no question now of sneaking into her backyard in the evening and watching her. He couldn't do too many drive-bys because there were now four vidcams on the front of the house and at least one of them would cover the street.

Blake would have the connections to have the house watched by a drone or even by a Key Hole Satellite but Kearns didn't dare ask. That's what he was here for. It was a cushy gig and there was more on the horizon and Kearns didn't want to mess it up. This Joe Harris had pushed the panic button and he and his buddies put the bitch in lockdown.

So he'd go buy himself a small GoPro camera and stick it in the grass in the lawn across from her and monitor the vidcam. It was the only thing he could do.

Besides lie to Blake.

So she was fucking a SEAL. So what? She was still shaky on her feet, still the same woman. What could she possibly do that would endanger Blake?

Nothing. Kearns had had a setback, that was all. Setbacks were normal. He was coping. No need to report anything to Blake. He'd just continue his Portland existence like before and pad the reports.

"I REALLY WANT to thank you guys again," Isabel said for the billionth time as she put something else amazing on the table. What was it? Joe leaned over to pull in the smells. Something stuffed with stuff and covered with stuff. "I really appreciate what you did for me today."

Silence except for chewing.

Joe swallowed and touched her arm. She looked so anxious, as if she had this huge debt to pay down. It hurt him to see her like that. The truth was that the three of them had had fun setting up the gear. A lot of it was bleeding edge that they'd be using again.

He pointed to Metal and Jacko with his fork. "They're

not answering because they're too busy stuffing their faces."

"Oh, man." Metal speared something small and brown. "What is this?"

Isabel smiled. "Warm gorgonzola-filled dates."

Metal's eyebrows shot up. "Whoa." He speared another four of them, put them in his mouth and moaned. "I want the recipe for everything on this table."

"Sure. I have everything on file. I'll email them to you."

"Metal cooks," Joe offered.

Metal shook his head. "Not like this, I don't. Man." He rolled his eyes. "This is like another kind of activity. Not cooking. Something else. Magic, maybe."

She giggled then covered her mouth. Yes. That's how Joe wanted to see her. Exactly like that. Blushing with pleasure.

For a second he was blindsided by a sudden intensely sensory memory of Isabel blushing during a climax. He remembered his face buried in her hair, her hands clutching his shoulders, her sex pulsing around his dick. It punched him, hard. He froze, barely breathing while his dick, which didn't need oxygen, stiffened.

Not here. Not now.

Joe was pretty good at compartmentalizing. He could put lust where it belonged, in the box labeled Off Duty. He controlled his dick, it didn't control him. Except right now, in front of his teammates.

But fuck. Just look at her! So amazingly beautiful, creating magic in the kitchen. Metal was right. She was magic herself. The way she moved, the way she spoke, the way she freaking breathed.

All the sounds in the room faded. He couldn't hear

Metal or Jacko or Isabel, he couldn't hear the cooking sounds coming from the kitchen. It was like one of those movie scenes where the sound cuts out and everything goes into slo-mo.

And Isabel simply glowed, no other word for it.

Metal said something, and the sound of his voice came from very far away.

"What?" Joe said.

Metal frowned. Joe wasn't known for being slow. "I said Isabel should continue her blog, it was fascinating."

This time Joe frowned. "You had a blog?" he asked Isabel.

Caught off guard, her face froze. "Yes," she mumbled. "It feels like a long time ago."

"It was famous." Metal forked up a bite of a chorizo omelet that was fluffy, incredibly light, amazingly tasty. "An old high school buddy of mine ended up a chef. When I went back home a couple of years ago, he showed it to me. The blog that day was part one of the history of bread and damned if it wasn't interesting. I read the blog off and on ever since." He pointed his fork at Isabel. "You really should continue it. It had a huge following."

"How big a following?" Joe asked.

Isabel ducked her head, as if embarrassed. "A million and a half."

A million and a half? "Journalists at the *New York Times* don't have that many readers."

Metal nodded. "If you were in any way interested in food, you read her blog."

"What was it called?"

"Foodways.com." Isabel sighed. "It's gone now. I haven't even looked at it since the Massacre."

"When does the domain name expire?" Jacko spoke so seldom, everyone paid attention. Three pairs of eyes turned to him.

"Yeah." Joe was intrigued. "If the domain name is still active you can continue. Just pick the blog up where you left off."

"But—but, the readers are gone."

Joe could tell the idea intrigued her, though. For a food blog to have that many readers meant that she had managed it really well. Must have worked at it hard. And she definitely knew her stuff. He attested to that every time he put a bite of her food in his mouth.

"Not necessarily, honey," Joe said gently. She'd put down a platter of something warm and creamy that smelled like sin, and had placed a hand next to it. Joe took her hand, brought it to his mouth.

Metal and Jacko looked at each other. Let them look. They had their own goddamned women. Both of them beautiful and smart. And now by some wild chance—the gods playing dice with his life—he had his own beautiful, smart woman. Incredibly talented, too.

She was his. He didn't mind who knew it.

"You can build a readership back up."

"Yeah." Isabel looked uncertain. "I suppose I could."

Man, he was so freaking lucky. He had good friends who'd helped him put his life back together again. A good job waiting at the other end. Metal and Jacko had worked right along with the rehab doc and had spent countless hours with him in the gym. Joe had cursed them and called them sadists and they'd got him walking again at least three months earlier than the docs had predicted.

Who'd helped Isabel put her life back together again?

No one, from what he could see. Her family wiped out, she'd moved across the country to get away from the fallout of the Massacre, and she'd been putting herself together completely on her own.

But she wasn't on her own now. Besides the fact that she had him, Joe recognized the Senior's appearance as a statement. *You're one of us, now.*

Joe didn't know if Isabel picked up on that, but he sure had. And he was relieved. As always, he had his team and now Isabel did, too.

The doorbell rang. Isabel rose, frowning. "Felicity and Lauren aren't due to arrive until after four. Who could that be? I don't know anyone else in town."

Joe rose, too, wondering whether he should have his piece in his hand. Metal and Jacko had stopped eating and were rising, as well. Joe pushed the button at the side of the small monitor beside the front door and relaxed at what he saw.

Isabel rose on tiptoe to whisper in his ear. "I don't know that lady. She doesn't look like a saleswoman, though."

Fuck no.

"My other boss's wife, Suzanne," he whispered back and opened the door.

Suzanne Huntington, Midnight's wife, swept in, cool and elegant as always, leaving behind a faint hint of expensive perfume, as always.

She was smiling as she held her hand out. "Isabel? My name is Suzanne Huntington and my husband is John Huntington. He works with Joe, Metal and Jacko."

Isabel took her hand. "From what I understand, he's their boss."

"He is. Though as a company, there isn't that much

hierarchy. I wanted to join Felicity and Lauren this afternoon, but unfortunately I have a meeting I can't put off. But I did want to swing around to invite you to an event we're hosting very soon. A friend of mine is opening a big lodge in the foothills of Mount Hood. I designed the hotel and restaurant and a colleague designed the spa. We're going to test-run it before the real inauguration in a month. We're inviting everyone from the company and my coworkers, too. And their plus ones."

That was going to be fun. Midnight's company was made up of former SEALs. Plus Felicity and a few admin staff, but mainly SEALs. Suzanne was a gifted designer and her friends were all on the arty side. Real arty. It made for interesting mixes.

Suzanne caught Isabel's other hand. "So…do you think you can make it?" She glanced at Joe. "You're invited, too, by the way."

Gee thanks, Joe thought wryly. But he was pleased. He didn't care if she was the one invited and he was the plus one. It was going to be a great day. He put his arm around Isabel, though, just to make sure Suzanne remembered him.

Isabel smiled. "That sounds great. We're just finishing up lunch, Suzanne. You're welcome to join us. You might know that Joe, Metal and Jacko have helped me, um, make the house more secure."

"I wish I could stay." Suzanne's beautiful face tightened. "And yes, I heard you had a Peeping Tom. This should keep any Peeping Toms away."

Wow. Women really did have some sort of underground intel network that put the CIA to shame.

Isabel smiled. "We're about to have coffee. Can you join us for that?"

Suzanne hesitated, checked her watch, finally sighed. “Oh, I would love to! But I’m going to be late for my appointment as it is.”

“Biscotti,” Isabel said coaxingly. “My special recipe.”

Suzanne closed her eyes briefly. “Don’t tempt me. But I’ll take a rain check, if I may.”

“Anytime,” Isabel said simply and they smiled at each other.

Suzanne Huntington was the classiest woman Joe had ever seen. There was just something about her that couldn’t be explained and couldn’t be quantified and yet was absolutely real. She was, as usual, dressed in an elegant tailored suit in a light color—she had an endless stock of them—and she looked like a million dollars. Not a hair out of place.

Isabel’s hair was mussed, she was dressed in a tracksuit, she had a touch of flour on her cheek, and she looked like a million dollars, too. They both had looks that had nothing to do with makeup or clothes or a hair salon. They were naturally beautiful and naturally classy.

Suzanne smiled. “The invitation to the lodge is real but I’ve also come to ask a favor and I have nothing to bribe you with.”

Isabel tilted her head in confusion. “Bribe me? Everyone has been so kind, you certainly don’t have to bribe me for a favor. I’ll do anything I can.”

“Good.” Suzanne was holding a pair of soft purple leather gloves and she slapped them against her other hand. “So. My friend who is setting up this resort lodge on Mount Hood was supposed to have a chef from San Francisco arriving but he broke a leg. So she has a kitchen staff that is very competent but no one to plan out a menu. I'm wondering—"

"Oh!" Isabel's eyes rounded. "If you think I'm up to it, I'd love to help!"

Suzanne gave an unladylike snort. "If you're up to it? I used to read your blog all the time. You're more than up to it. There will be about fifty of us, half of them the men from ASI whose tastes are hardy and simple—" She glanced with amusement at Joe, Metal and Jacko. "And the other half are their plus ones and my side of the aisle, who have more, let's say, sophisticated tastes. A fun mix. My friend really needs help with the menu. Can I put the two of you together?"

"Sure." Isabel and Suzanne brought out their cells and exchanged numbers.

Suzanne gave a sigh. "I am really sorry to have to go. But before I do..." She placed an elegant hand on Isabel's shoulder. "Let me say how very sorry I am for your loss. The Massacre was a tragedy for our country and for all the people lost. I would have voted for your father. He was a good man."

"He was. Thank you," Isabel said simply, placing her hand over Suzanne's.

Suzanne bent forward and gave her a hug, surreptitiously wiping under her eye. "So, I'll be in touch about the menu," she said briskly when she pulled away. "I'm leaving you in excellent hands and say hello to Felicity and Lauren. If Allegra can make it, she said she'd pop in to say hello, too."

"I'm such a fangirl," Isabel said.

"I'll be sure to let her know. Douglas said he'd stop by with tickets for the concert. Did he?"

"Oh, yeah." Isabel pointed with pride at the two tickets on the coffee table.

Suzanne smiled. "One thing you'll learn about these guys—" She waved her arm to include Joe and Metal and Jacko, who had barely lifted his head from his plate. "They're really reliable. If they say they'll do something they'll do it."

"I know." Isabel smiled at Joe and it was like a punch to the stomach. "I've got a bank vault of a house to prove it."

"I'll be in touch." Suzanne looked at her watch again and winced. "Must go, bye!" She kissed the air and was gone in a cloud of perfume.

"You okay, honey?" Metal and Jacko were back to the food, really absorbed in what they were eating. Joe bent down and kissed Isabel's cheek, but really it was an excuse to touch her skin. He'd never felt skin that velvety before. Strands of her hair caught on his stubble. He fingered his chin. He had to shave or he'd rough up that smooth soft skin tonight.

And man, he didn't want to do that. He didn't want anything rough to touch her, ever again. He himself had big, rough hands but he took care to touch her gently. She was so soft all over, particularly that warm wet softness between her legs.

"Yes, I'm fine. Why?"

He shrugged. "Dunno. Maybe because you've got your house invaded by men who from the looks of it haven't eaten in a year. Then their women are coming over and you've promised to feed them. Then Suzanne comes over and asks for help in preparing for the big party up at the Lodge. Is it too much?"

She didn't even pretend not to understand what he

was saying. She'd led the most secluded life he'd ever seen for these past three months. Now that he knew her background, he understood why. Massive trauma, the terrible aftereffects of the Massacre. She'd fled here to Portland to hide away from the world.

Now the world had found her. Metal, Jacko, the Senior, Felicity, Lauren, Suzanne. And the party at the new lodge—the entire crew, fifty strong. Could she handle that?

"Growing up, our house was always filled with people," she said softly, looking him directly in the eyes. "I loved it. I think I needed these past months of solitude. I wasn't fit company for anyone. But now—"

"You were absolutely fit company!" Joe protested. "It's just that—"

"Hey, Isabel." They both turned to the table where Jacko was holding up a super clean plate. There wasn't even a molecule of food left. He was trying for pathetic. The waif who hadn't eaten in days. Even if he was a super buff two-hundred-forty-pound mass of muscle. "Any more of this stuff?"

SEVEN

ISABEL HAD NEVER seen a human face with no expression whatsoever on it before. Even blankness was an expression. But Joe betrayed absolutely nothing as he beat the pants off Metal and Jacko. Actually, if it had been strip poker instead of for money, they'd have both been naked right now and a fully dressed Joe would have had a pile of clothes on the table instead of a pile of chips.

They were sitting around the dining room table at her house instead of his and they weren't talking. The poker game was a form of warfare. Though the three men were clearly very good friends, and Joe had talked a lot about how they'd helped him through rehab, you wouldn't have known it from the game.

Isabel had offered alcohol. She had a bottle of brandy and a bottle of bourbon, but all three had turned it down, Metal and Jacko with expressions of horror.

"Bad enough playing Joe sober," Jacko said. So she'd served coffee. The cups steamed at their elbows as they snapped cards up and down.

She didn't really know the rules of this form of poker, so she wasn't following the game, she was following the players. It was fascinating. There were moments of tension, but they all came from Metal and from Jacko. Though they had poker faces, too, there were tiny signs of elation or despair. What she knew were called tells.

Metal's eyelid twitched a time or two, something

entirely autonomous. Jacko's index finger drummed against the hand of cards.

Joe had no tells. None. The skin around his eyes and mouth remained exactly the same. He had deep brackets around his mouth and the skin around his eyes was weather-beaten, but he had those all the time. Nothing at all changed. Not muscles, not his breathing, not his eye movements.

He only broke that utterly blank facade once, to wink at her. Then his face became a blank wall once more.

He'd won either twenty dollars or two hundred dollars—Isabel wasn't too sure how much money each chip represented—when the front doorbell rang.

"That's Lauren," Jacko said, folding with an expression of disgust. "She just texted me. Joe, if you weren't wearing a T-shirt, I swear I'd think you had an ace up your sleeve."

"Watch, children, and learn," Joe said, voice carefully neutral as he spread out his long arms and pulled in a ton of chips.

Metal and Jacko gave loud expressions of disgust just as Isabel opened her door.

Felicity and Lauren rushed in and laughed when they heard the two men groaning. "Joe's winning again," Felicity said.

"Winning big." Lauren shook her head. "That's real pain I'm hearing." She offered her hand. "I'm Lauren. I belong to that big sore loser over there—" She pointed at Jacko, who was scowling at his hand of cards. "He's usually not as sour as that, though he isn't much of a smiler, either."

"I heard that," Jacko grunted as he looked over.

Lauren gave him a sunny smile and, to Isabel's surprise, Jacko smiled back. It was genuine. He was happy to see her.

Lauren walked over and gave his shaved head a kiss. "Hello, darling, nice to see you, but I'm not here for you."

"Gotcha. You're here for the food."

Lauren laughed. "That, too. But most of all to meet Isabel."

"Who's going out with the Prince of Darkness here," Metal said.

"That's an interesting thought," Felicity said as Isabel took her coat and Lauren's. "Do you think Joe made a pact with the devil? Sold his soul?"

"I'm right here," Joe complained. "I was shot up but my hearing is just fine."

"It's more than possible he sold his soul," Metal said. "I want a kiss, too."

Felicity bent to kiss his cheek, whispered something in his ear. He met her eyes and smiled. A private joke.

Isabel's parents used to do that, all the time. Drove their kids nuts until they got old enough to appreciate the fact that their parents genuinely liked each other. Not many of her friends had parents who even spoke to each other.

Isabel's throat tightened, then she shook off the sadness. No sadness today, no. For the first time in a long time, her house was filled with people. Friendly people who showed in every single way that they liked her. She was feeding people, which she loved doing. And they were almost pathetically grateful for the food.

The sun had broken through the clouds and though from the outside nothing was visible, the bright light streamed into her living room and kitchen.

"Let's have tea in the kitchen," she said.

"Yes!" Lauren gave a little shiver of excitement. "I like you already, Isabel, but I've heard such great things about your cooking! I can't wait!" She frowned. "You'll feed us, right? I had a light lunch to leave room."

Isabel laughed. "Yes, I'm going to feed you. Later. But for now, I baked apple tarts and I made some panna cotta."

"Sounds great." Felicity linked arms with her. "I don't know what panna cotta is. I'm Russian by blood and we don't do good food. We brood. And I don't know how to cook, so anything that isn't poison is okay by me. But Metal says that your food is magic, and I am so up for this."

So was Isabel. She had laid a nice table at the breakfast nook. A lace tablecloth, her best china—a Limoges set her mother had bought as her graduation present—a small bouquet of wildflowers in a Rosenthal vase. Two pillar candles to be lit when it got darker. By a happy chance, the afternoon sun streamed in through the windows and bathed the table in a warm glow.

All three women stopped.

"Oh, my," Felicity said. "How lovely."

"Can I come over some afternoon and sketch your table?" Lauren was looking at the scene with her head cocked, studying it. Joe had told her Lauren was a gifted watercolorist.

"Of course," Isabel answered. "I can make cherry tarts, they're really colorful."

"Don't you dare not ask me," Felicity said in a mock serious tone. She put her arm around Isabel and gently squeezed.

"Of course not." Isabel hooked her arm around Felicity's waist for a second. The kettle whistled. "Okay, tea will be ready in a minute."

She had a special Lady Grey blend with orange peel that she ordered specially from London. Felicity and Lauren loved it. Loved the apple tarts. When Felicity put a spoonful of the panna cotta in her mouth she closed her eyes in delight.

"My new favorite sweet."

"They're all your favorites," Lauren objected.

"True, true. I am a dessert slut," Felicity cheerfully replied. "So." She put down her spoon and turned to Isabel. "Joe."

Isabel blinked. "Joe?"

Felicity and Lauren both leaned forward. "As in you're sleeping with Joe," Felicity said.

Lauren elbowed Felicity and rolled her eyes. "You'll have to forgive Felicity. She spends most of her time with computers and nerds. Luckily Metal is teaching her how to be human. What she *meant* to say was that you and Joe are…together?" She said that last word delicately.

"You mean are we sleeping together," Isabel said, amused.

"Exactly!" Felicity smiled in triumph at Lauren. "So, we want to know your intentions."

Isabel's eyebrows rose. "My *intentions?*"

"Yes." Lauren took over. They'd planned this in advance. They were playing off each other. "We want to know how serious you are about Joe. Because Joe's a good guy. And, in the eyes of many, you could be considered…well, out of his league."

Isabel thought about being angry. This was a major intrusion into her personal life, by two people she barely knew. At any other moment she'd have interrupted this, stood up and ushered the two women out.

But…

They cared for Joe. It was clear in their faces. They weren't curious about her and Joe, they were worried. Worried that she'd break his heart.

Isabel had grown up in a world where people cared about each other. Her family had never been reticent about intruding into each other's lives because it was done out of love. Right now, there wasn't anyone who cared enough about her to intrude, to be nosy, to nudge her this way or that.

She'd lived with nosy loving people and she'd lived in an emotional void. She knew which one she preferred.

"Okay." Isabel clasped her hands. "Let's look at the facts, here. Joe is a former Navy SEAL. I don't know much about that but I do know it is not easy to become a SEAL and they do hard, dangerous, necessary jobs. I know he was grievously wounded in the service of his country. I know he has a close-knit group of friends who love him and respect him and are helping him. I know that when I moved here three months ago, we were both physical wrecks. Only, Joe had the willpower to make himself over. I haven't. I don't have one-tenth of Joe's determination. So—" Isabel lifted her hands, making them scales. The right hand tipped way up. "On this side we have Joe Harris, valiant warrior, highly self-disciplined, who is upset because he is on his company's payroll without being able to do the work yet. He hates that. Further, since the day I moved in, he's done nothing but help me."

"And he's a demon in bed," Felicity added.

Isabel nodded and lifted her right hand higher. "And, yes, he is a god in bed."

Both women sighed and leaned back in their chairs.

Isabel glanced at her left hand, way down. "So now let's look at me. The one who is supposedly out of his league. I'm twenty-eight years old and I'm jobless. I have a talent for cooking, yes, but I haven't trained as a chef. I was blown up six months ago and I haven't put myself back together again at all, as Joe has done. I haven't got my strength back, I have dizzy spells. Sometimes I am afraid to go out for walks because I don't know if I'll make it back."

She looked Felicity and Lauren in the eyes. Their faces were now sober as they listened to her.

"I have nightmares. Every night. Last night, thanks to Joe, was the first time I didn't have a nightmare, but believe me, sleeping with someone who wakes up terrified isn't fun. I don't know if I'll ever be physically fit again. I lost my entire family and that's left a huge black hole punched in my chest and I can't be sure I'll ever be emotionally whole again. I miss my family every second of every day and I grieve for them. How attractive is that? To have a woman who isn't emotionally stable. Oh, and money. Everyone thinks I'm rich because I am a Delvaux, but I'm not. Our family was well-off, sure. But Dad put all the family assets in a blind trust when he decided to be a candidate. That blind trust was the Solem Group."

Both of them gasped and Isabel gave a sharp nod. The Solem Group had gone bankrupt two days after the Massacre, destroying thousands of family fortunes, including hers.

"I was left with huge debts. I sold off our house, paid

the debts and was left with enough to buy this place, but not much more. My savings will run out in a few months, and whether I'm physically fit or not, I'm going to have to look for a job."

She leaned forward and they did too. "After the Massacre, my life became a nightmare. The last of the Delvauxes, this wretched creature. I couldn't go out of the house without being accosted. There wasn't a tabloid that didn't catch me looking like a ghost. That was too much for my friends, who didn't want the Delvaux bad luck to jinx them. And of course, the kicker. I was dead broke. Even if I wanted to go out to dinner, to go to the Hamptons or Aruba, go clubbing, I couldn't. I didn't want to but my so-called friends assumed I couldn't afford to. A grieving, suffering woman who is also dead broke—who wants that?"

Isabel looked at her hands forming the scale. Joe up high, Isabel down low.

"So, ladies, if anything, Joe is out of my league. A strong and vibrant man, attractive and with a good job waiting for him. Surrounded by loving friends. And me. Alone and broke and not in good health. I wonder what he wants with me? Because he could sure do better."

Lauren and Felicity exchanged somber glances. "You're not alone, Isabel," Lauren said.

Felicity lowered Isabel's right hand, tipped up her left, until the scales were even. "You're surrounded by friends, too. And Joe's a really lucky guy."

JOE TRIED TO keep an ear out to hear what the women were saying in the kitchen, but their voices were too low. At first he'd heard Felicity and Lauren gushing about whatever miracles Isabel had baked. And then they started talking and he couldn't make anything out.

He also had to pay some attention to the game. He had a natural bent for card games and enjoyed the strategy and dealing with the element of chance. He could also count cards in his head.

He'd have gladly sacrificed a few hands to be able to listen in on the conversation in the kitchen but pride kept him in his seat.

One thing for sure, there was a friendly atmosphere.

Bless Lauren and Felicity. And bless Suzanne. He knew for a fact that once Isabel met Allegra and Claire, the wife of their homicide detective buddy, they'd become friends too.

She was lonely. He could read it in her face. She'd been through something so horrendous it was hard to fathom. Joe had been in battle, but he was trained and prepared. The Massacre had been horrible beyond belief, and Isabel had lost her entire family.

Joe knew that he was there for her. She was the one, the one he didn't know he'd been waiting for. But friends were important, too, and now Isabel was going to be surrounded by the finest women Joe had ever met.

She deserved it.

"Fuck, man." Jacko threw his cards down in disgust. "Who the hell are you bribing?"

"That's why they call it the luck of the draw." Joe gave a quick check of his chips. He'd won two hundred and twenty dollars. Jacko wasn't complaining about the money—he had plenty of money. He was complaining about losing, which he didn't do gracefully.

Tough shit. Joe smiled to himself but he knew absolutely nothing showed.

Time to make up for the losses. "I bought myself a sweet karambit. Wanna see it?"

It was a peace offering. Metal grinned. "How long?"

"Five inches. So, it's over at my place if you want to see it."

The two men were getting up. "Okay. The least you can do after taking all our money," Metal said.

Joe went into the kitchen, stopped at the threshold.

Isabel, Felicity, Lauren. Three beautiful women, smiling at each other. But though both Felicity and Lauren were good-looking women, they couldn't hold a candle to Isabel. It was like she had a special aura around her.

Felicity and Lauren stopped talking and Isabel turned around and saw him. And she smiled at him. It was almost staggering. Joe rubbed at his chest where his heart had thumped—hard—inside his rib cage.

He swallowed, hooked a thumb. "Going over to my place to show the guys something. We'll be back soon."

Lauren cocked her head. "I'm glad you're quitting early. Jacko and I want to take a vacation to Europe next summer and we won't if he keeps losing money to you."

Felicity, who understood her man, said, "What you're going to show the guys. How many bullets does it shoot?"

Joe smiled. "None."

"A knife, then. Don't be gone long, we have to stop by the Apple Store on our way back home." Felicity often stopped by the Apple Store where she had nerd friends who could use her help. Felicity was persona very grata there.

"You got it."

"Fixed or folding?" Jacko asked as Joe pressed his

thumb to his front door. He'd seen a movie where the security depended on the DNA contained in a drop of blood. Very cool. But not practical. The door gave a discreet click and he pushed it open. He would need to program it to recognize Metal, Jacko, maybe Midnight and the Senior. It already recognized Isabel.

They walked in. Joe had a really weird sensation walking into his own home. It felt…odd. Cold. It was clean because he was clean and neat—you couldn't be anything else in the navy—but there were no nice smells, just bleach and detergent. He hadn't paid any attention to decor, just shoved the pieces of furniture he needed against the walls. Unlike Isabel's house that smelled of spices and flowers, full of colors and pleasing shapes.

"Folding. Make yourselves at home. I'll go get it."

He'd left the karambit in its box, in the closet. He opened the closet door, pulled out the box, placed it on his desk—and froze.

"Guys." He kept his voice steady. "Get in here."

Metal and Jacko came. Whatever they'd heard in his voice made them move fast.

They both held weapons in their hands, coming in high low, Metal to the right, Jacko to the left, as if they'd rehearsed it. Which, of course, they had, in the Teams. Thousands of times.

When they saw what he was pointing to, both of them holstered their Glocks and came closer to his monitor.

Do you know anyone in the FBI you trust absolutely?

"Same guy?" Metal asked quietly.

"Yeah. I think so. But this is new. He just took over

my computer. Letters that appear on my desktop. Which means he really knows what he's doing."

Jacko was studying the monitor but beyond the words in caps, Arial 40, there was nothing to see. "We don't know when he sent this."

"Or she," Joe answered. "But no. I was at Isabel's all night. I came over at about nine to grab some fresh clothes and it wasn't here. It's seventeen hundred hours. It could have arrived at any time over the past eight hours."

"He didn't ping your cell. If he can do this, he can find your cell phone number."

"Absolutely." Joe nodded. "So I gotta go with the idea that he wants to communicate this way instead of texting me."

Metal cocked his head. "If you let me, I'll ask Felicity. But I get the sense that this is more private and less traceable than sending a text."

Joe grunted. This was someone who was connected to Isabel in some way. The first message had been to protect her. And now this.

"Dude." Jacko elbowed him. "You gonna answer?"

Joe sat down and typed:

Yes. Nick Mancino. Former SEAL. Now FBI HRT.

An old buddy and a real stand-up guy. He'd helped find and rescue Felicity's old mentor, retired FBI Special Agent Al Goodkind.

"He's answering." Metal's voice was quiet. He knew he owed Nick Mancino, big-time. They all did. Was Joe getting Nick into trouble?

Can't be bought off?

Whoa. Joe sat still. After a moment, he typed:

No. And neither can I.

A couple of minutes passed. None of them spoke. Whoever was at the other end had his own agenda. Joe had no idea whether he was a good guy or a bad guy. All he could do was wait and gather more intel.

Finally, words appeared on the screen.

Good. Call Nick and tell him to meet you in Portland.

Fuck this. Joe's answer was swift.

Why should I?

And the answer, when it came, was like a punch to the stomach.

The Washington Massacre was homegrown terrorism, directed by someone in the CIA. Our guys. They are going to strike again. We need to stop them.

"Fuck," Joe breathed.

"Can I talk to Felicity?" Metal asked. "She's got a higher clearance than any of us have anyway."

Felicity had done work for the FBI before joining ASI. And Felicity was of Russian blood and had grown up in the WITSEC program. She knew how to keep secrets.

"Yeah, man. Absolutely. We need all the help we can get."

This was serious stuff. If the Washington Massacre had really been carried out by CIA guys, and Isabel was one of the very few survivors, then she was an eyewitness to one of the greatest crimes in the country's history. And a real threat to the perpetrators. She didn't remember anything but memories were notoriously unstable.

Was there an immediate threat to her? Because that was the point of the first message from Mystery Man. PROTECT ISABEL. Had this guy been tipped off somehow that the Massacre wasn't carried out by jihadists?

Because, if the Massacre was organized by the CIA they were all in real trouble. Joe found it hard to believe it, but he knew that rogue elements existed everywhere. If there was a rogue team within the CIA's Clandestine Service, the country was in a shitload of trouble, because the Clandestine Service operated almost without oversight.

And they had sneak and peek powers jihadists didn't have.

"From now on we operate under opsec," Joe said.

Metal and Jacko nodded.

If this was a conspiracy run by people with access to NSA and Homeland Security assets, every word they spoke on the phone, every email they sent, could be tracked.

"Metal, buy us some burner phones. If this thing is true and it goes to the top, we need to be untraceable."

"Uh, Joe?"

"Yeah?"

Metal was looking uncomfortable.

"Felicity has, um, about two hundred untraceable burners, and they all have military-grade encryption and voice alteration software."

"Wow. I don't dare ask how she got them."

"Birthday present. From a hacker friend she, um, helped."

Joe did not want to know what Felicity did to help the hacker friend. He was just grateful that she'd done it and that they had access to those phones. "Great. I'll make sure Isabel has one too."

"Isabel..." Jacko said.

"Yeah." Joe met his sober dark eyes. "She's right in the crosshairs."

EIGHT

Washington, DC

THE PLAN. PHASE TWO STARTED.

Now phase three. And then four and five.

Hector Blake read the file on his computer avidly. It would erase itself in fifteen minutes but as a lawyer he was used to absorbing large amounts of data in short amounts of time. Here, he didn't have to memorize the details because he wasn't involved in three of the major events.

For the moment, he was just involved in the Washington Massacre and making sure an obedient weakling became the next president. Considering the target, it made sense to have him in the loop. The other events were described in general terms.

Someone in some ministry somewhere—he suspected China—had a very strong grasp of economics and mass psychology. Five events, maybe more that he wasn't privy to, guaranteed to bring the behemoth to its knees. The shadowy forces pushing the events were using America's strength against it, like a jujitsu master fighting a bloated overweight monster. Because many of America's strengths became weaknesses if you looked at them the right way.

America had very efficient, very fast financial markets and stock markets. They were able to squeeze value from stones, thanks to the quants. But by the same token, when overwhelmed, the system ate itself. The Massacre had tanked the economy, sucking several trillion dollars out of the system. On his way home from his office, Blake counted several soup kitchens, more appearing every week.

His own money was safely abroad. Two billion dollars that no one would ever see but him. He could even access some of it legally since he had an "advance" from a small publishing house no one had ever heard of for his memoirs. And then several million sales of the book would be arranged.

He was thinking of doing that again, just so he could have capital in-country he didn't have to account for. He'd already made discreet inquiries for a good ghostwriter.

Being rich while everyone else was poor was delicious. Power lay in contrasts. Poor people were obedient, subservient, biddable. Particularly those who had come down in the world. They were so desperate to come back up they never questioned why they'd fallen in the first place.

So step one—impoverish everyone—was done. Trillions of dollars had been sucked out of the economy and sent elsewhere. Blake imagined that there would be a couple of other economic shocks coming down the pipeline.

Then London as president. He'd do anything Blake told him to do.

The step after that, ah. Pure genius. The next step was blinding America and he now understood exactly what he'd been told to do while on the Senate Intelligence Committee and why. He now understood the value of the people he'd placed in strategic positions. He knew there were others, in the NSA, in the DIA, at the Pentagon. Not the FBI, though. The FBI was proving impenetrable and incorruptible.

It was something Blake couldn't understand. The base salary of a newly minted Special Agent was a little under forty four thousand dollars. Peanuts. It topped out at about a hundred and thirty thousand for the Director. What some people spent on clothes. How could it be so hard to recruit FBI Special Agents?

But the plan could go forward even without the FBI, who weren't tasked with foreign intel anyway. By the time anything came to the attention of the FBI, the US would be a giant on its knees. The FBI could even be disbanded. There was Homeland Security anyway—the FBI was a drain on resources America didn't have.

The file winked off and he knew he would never be able to find it again. But no matter. Blake understood that immensely resourceful and smart people were behind the project and that in five years' time, maybe less, the United States as he knew it would be gone.

Portland

They Skyped Nick. They could do that safely. Joe wasn't going to say anything overt anyway. Nick was a smart guy, he'd catch on fast.

There he was. Walking along a street in DC. Nick was dressed in civilian clothes, wasn't on duty. Not decked out in MultiCam camouflage, Kevlar helmet, armed with an HK416 assault rifle.

Metal took point. The two had recently worked together on an op that involved backpack nukes.

Nick smiled. His cell's camera caught him from below, showing a jutting jaw with a dark five-o'clock shadow though it was only fourteen hundred in DC. "Metal! My man! Wassup? How's Felicity? She hacked into the NSA yet?"

"Nah. She's working for us now and we keep her in check. Listen, Nick, we need your help." Metal turned Joe's monitor around so Nick could see Jacko and Joe.

"Jacko, Metal," Nick said nodding. He brought the cell closer to his face. "Is that Joe Harris? Hey, man."

Joe nodded his head and didn't smile. Nick was no dummy. His smile dropped off his face, too. "Sitrep," he said quietly.

"Not over an open line." Joe looked at the camera directly. "It would be nice—it would be *really* nice if you could make it to Portland."

Nick's black eyebrows drew together. "Soon?"

"Now."

Joe shifted the monitor so Nick could see both Metal and Jacko in close-up. He was glad he'd Skyped because the seriousness of the situation could be read in their faces.

"Now?"

"Now."

Both Metal and Jacko nodded.

Joe turned the monitor back. "Can you do it?"

Nick was checking his cell phone. "There's a flight leaving in five hours. A red-eye. I'll be there tomorrow morning."

"Come to the office," Joe said. "We'll have a briefing."

"I'll be there," Nick said and killed the connection.

"We need to tell Mystery Man." Metal and Jacko nodded.

Mystery Man seemed to be keyed into Joe's computer. Probably by malware. He'd been meaning to have Felicity secure his computer but hadn't managed to get around to it yet. That was good news and bad news. If bad guys had access, he was in a shitload of trouble. However—if Mystery Man had access, presumably he'd gone through his hard disk for signs of other intruders.

Taking a deep breath, Joe keyboarded:

Tomorrow we'll all be at ASI. Including FBI.

After two seconds, words formed on his monitor.

Mancino?

Joe looked at Metal and Jacko. Metal gave a thumbs-up. Okay, they were going all-in with this guy.

Yes.

He checks out.

Yeah, by any measure Nick Mancino checked out.

Yes.

Give me number of encrypted satphone.

Joe sat back while Metal input a number he took from his cell. Felicity would have made the number untraceable and she would make sure the encryption was strong.

Four bells.

Four bells was 10 a.m. nautical time. A reference to the fact that he knew Joe was navy. Was this guy navy? Former navy? What the hell was he?

Four bellsJoe confirmed and sat back in his chair.

SOMETHING HAPPENED when Joe and the guys went back to his house. They'd been laughing and teasing Joe about taking all their money when they left. When they came back, they were sober and quiet.

Felicity and Lauren picked up on it right away. The three of them had been laughing over the plot of the latest lame romcom, scarfing down the squares of double chocolate fudge Isabel had pulled from the freezer, when the guys walked in. Felicity and Lauren immediately quieted, watching their guys carefully. It was amazing to see. It wasn't as if they were watching Metal and Jacko out of fear of a mood change. No, it was more as if whatever their guys felt, they felt.

Nothing showed Isabel more than this that they were couples. Teams. Jacko walked directly up to Lauren and whispered in her ear and Metal made a beeline for Felicity and put his arms around her.

Couples.

She was contemplating that when Joe walked in a minute or two later, carrying a duffel bag. He walked straight to her, eyes glued to hers, as if there was nobody else in the room. He opened his arms and she walked straight into them.

A couple.

Crazily, yes, they were a couple. It was the sex, sure, because that had been spectacular. The best of her life. But it was more than that. She was attuned to him, dialed in to his frequency. She was aware of wherever he was in the room. She looked for him, constantly. Joe did the same. When he walked in, he didn't look anywhere but at her.

He felt it, too.

The embrace lasted a minute, the time it took to reacquaint herself with his smell, with the feel of him in her arms, to search out that specific spot where she nestled her head. His body was an extension of hers, part of hers.

It would have been frightening, this immediate connection, if it hadn't felt so right.

But because she was so attuned to him, she realized that something serious had happened while he was gone. He was holding her too tightly. His muscles were harder than usual, tense and stiff. That reassuring heartbeat, a beat per second, like a metronome, was speeded up. His breathing was speeded up, too.

She could ask when the others had left. Or she could wait for him to tell her what was wrong. Because intimacy ran both ways. She hadn't told him about the Massacre. About the hell she'd endured after.

It was still too painful to talk about, still jumbled up in her head. She had things she wasn't ready to discuss. Maybe he did, too. Maybe this was a business thing and it was confidential.

One thing she knew, though. She trusted him. If he felt it was necessary to talk it over with her, he would.

If he didn't, there was a good reason. Joe was a straight shooter. She felt that down to her bones.

By the time she lifted her head, both Lauren and Felicity had their coats on. So did Metal. Jacko seemed perfectly willing to brave the cold dusk with only a T-shirt on, a light denim jacket over his arm. Looking at that dark, impervious face, it was as if nothing affected him, except Lauren.

Metal had a hand to Felicity's back. He gave Joe and her a two-fingered salute off his forehead and Isabel had no problem seeing the soldier he'd been. "See you tomorrow morning," he said to Joe. "Felicity's going to do some research."

Felicity looked up at him. "I am? On what?"

"Conspiracies," Metal said darkly.

She smiled. "Love me a good conspiracy. I'll search the darknet. That's how I found out the aliens in Roswell are secretly vampires."

"You know," Jacko said as he walked Lauren out the door. "That doesn't sound too far-fetched."

Felicity stuck her head back in the door. "But we have a rain check on that dinner, right?"

"Right," Isabel answered. "Whenever you want."

She cupped Joe's jaw briefly when they were alone. "You want to tell me what this is about? Something happened over at your place, didn't it?"

Joe took her hand, brought it to his mouth. She felt his lips, warm and soft, against the palm of her hand.

"I'll tell you, yeah. Not right now, though. Not until I have more information. Do you trust me?"

She pulled her hand away, letting her fingers caress his cheek. Her faith in everything had been broken, shattered. The Massacre had poisoned her faith in everyone and everything. But to her vast surprise, she trusted him.

"Yes," she said softly.

The taut muscles of his face relaxed a little. He checked his wristwatch. "Do you know it's been almost six hours since you fed me?"

She smiled, rolled her eyes. "That long? You should call 911."

"I should." He kissed her hand again. "So what's on the menu for tonight?"

CHRIST, A FUCKING *army* coming out of the bitch's place!

Kearns was dressed in a tracksuit and had dumped some water over his face to look like he was soaking wet with sweat. With a watch cap, yellow wraparounds, scarf around his neck and lower face, he was sure he was unrecognizable.

Kearns had run three times past her house at half hour intervals. Couldn't even tell if there were people in her place. But there were three vehicles parked right outside the house on the street so she had people over.

He was walking slowly, pretending to have runner's cramps, when the front door opened and two big guys one tall, one not—came out with two lookers. The ones who had helped Harris put up security cams and monitors around Delvaux's house.

The men were operators. Kearns could tell by how they handled themselves, the way they looked around. It was pure luck that he was coming up on them as they walked down the little sidewalk and got into their vehicles. If he'd already passed them, and turned to look at them, they'd have made him. These guys observed everything.

Shit, this was getting impossible.

Level of protection the bitch had, he'd need at least a twenty-man team, and here he was in Portland, all alone with his ass hanging out.

Blake should be paying him ten times what he was for this.

His cell rang. One of the guys—the shorter one but still a big bruiser—glanced over briefly. At least Kearns had a reason to stop.

Jogger getting a business call. Or maybe a call from the little lady. *When are you going to finish that run? The food's getting cold.*

"Talk to me," Blake said. He wanted a report.

Kearns swore he could feel his spleen spurt bile. *You send me out here with zero resources, no backup at all, I'm supposed to keep tabs on a chick that has navy SEALs protecting her?*

He couldn't say that, though. Because then Blake would want to know how long the SEALs had been around and he'd have to start defending himself.

Blake himself wasn't scary. He was a politician and he was soft. Used to the good life. Had fucking drivers, probably had forgotten how to drive. Wouldn't know how to mow his own lawn or fix his own car. But he had operators around him and those operators were scary. He was surrounded by guys who'd carried out the Washington Massacre. Almost one thousand people gunned down and blown up, one thousand Americans, and they did the job in ten minutes then disappeared slicker'n snot. Not even DNA left behind.

If Blake snapped his fingers there would be no place on earth for Kearns to hide, because that was another thing. Blake seemed to have unending money. Rivers of it. Oceans. World-changing money.

So he said what he had to say.

"Nothing's changed. It looks like she hasn't even left the apartment today."

"It *looks like*?" Blake said, his voice icy.

Fuck.

"I'm alone here. I make the rounds every two hours, but I can't do more because someone is going to notice something. I haven't seen her go out. And last time she did go out she was shaky. Today's cold and there's ice on the sidewalks. I figure she won't go out when it's this cold."

"Next report, I want more facts. And make sure you brief me on any changes."

"Roger that," Kearns said evenly, keeping the resentment out of his voice.

No changes, asshole. Just a pack of navy SEALs. Nothing worth reporting.

DINNER WAS SOMETHING called spelt soup with onion and cheese bread. Joe didn't actually know what spelt was but learned all about it from Isabel. One of the oldest cereals known to man. Mentioned in the Bible, older than wheat. Isabel said that some specialty microbreweries made beer from spelt and promised to find some for him. She said it had a special nutty flavor.

God.

He'd never eaten like this in someone's home. Home for him meant takeout or something scrounged from someone else and put in the freezer for a rainy day. Lots of rainy days in Portland.

Metal was a decent cook and Joe loved eating over at his place, but it was nothing like this.

"So. You ran a food blog?" Joe pointed his spoon at Isabel.

She smiled sadly. "*Ran* is the operative word. I haven't posted anything since..." She swallowed, kept her voice even. "Since the Massacre. I haven't even looked at it since then. I'll have lost all my readers."

"How many readers did you say you had again?"

"About a million and a half."

Fuck. "Your readership was more than the number of active personnel in the US military. That's a lot. Literally an army of foodies."

She'd been tracing a pattern in the tablecloth with the tines of her fork and looked up. "Yeah. I guess so."

There was something in her voice.

"You ever think about starting it up again?"

Isabel sighed. "Off and on. And only in the past few weeks. But it would be like starting over and it took years of very hard work to get to where I was. I don't think I have that kind of energy anymore. And I did a lot of research and sometimes I traveled to get local recipes and pictures."

"I don't think you'd have to work that hard," Joe protested. "I mean these things go viral, don't they? As soon as word gets around that you're starting up again, readers will flock back."

"Maybe."

"And, well, if you can hold off for when I'm free, I'll accompany you on your trips. We could do it on weekends. Don't know anything about food but I can carry your bags for you. Prime bag-carrier, top tier. And I work cheap. For food."

That brought a smile to her face, a little less sad. "Yeah?"

"Oh, yeah." Joe put certainty in his voice. Very aware of the fact that this was the first time any kind of future was mentioned between them. It was going to keep cropping up because he had no intention of leaving her side. Did she want to go to Tallahassee to research chitlins? Joe was right there. "Is it still online?"

Isabel's eyes widened. "Do you know—I don't know. Isn't that crazy? I haven't looked at it once sincc…since the Massacre. It probably is."

It wasn't crazy. Joe was firmly of the suck-it-up-and-move-on school. Her life had come to a standstill and she'd just dropped everything. But Isabel loved what she did. It had given her joy and maybe it could give her joy again.

"Lately, even before the Massacre, I'd eased up because I had another project."

Her eyes had gone back down to the tablecloth.

"Which was?"

"Well, I was taking notes for a book. I wanted it to be a big book, full of beautiful illustrations. Full of information and recipes. A celebration of food. A book you can dip into and always find something interesting. An agent was interested."

Joe put his hand over hers. "That sounds fantastic. I'm sure it would be a great book, a bestseller. Do you still have those notes?"

"Oh, yes," she breathed. Joe looked into those beautiful eyes and saw something that made his heart thump hard in his chest.

Hope.

Isabel had hope again. She was coming back and

she would be stronger than before, because that was the way it worked. If you were broken and came back, you were stronger in the broken places.

He squeezed her hand gently. "Sounds like writing a book is going to be in your immediate future. And picking up the blog again too. Can I see it?"

"The blog?" Isabel rose and Joe noticed that she seemed to be moving more easily, too. He was beginning to see the magnificent woman she must have been and would be again. Beautiful beyond words, graceful, smart, knowledgeable. Capable of moving millions of people with her own passion. "Sure. If it's still there."

She went to her desk and clicked a key to turn the monitor on. In a second she'd pulled up a home page. She turned the screen so Joe could see better. He pulled up a chair and sat down and was instantly lost.

The blog was beautiful to look at. Across the top a carousel of brightly colored photos floated from left to right. Aged, agile brown hands kneading bread, a smiling farmer holding a bushel of small intensely red apples, two women in hairnets pulling on mozzarella in a vat, making knots, another woman rolling rice inside a grape leaf…the images went on and on. The quality was exquisite, many of the images were in sunlight and all of them celebrated the joys of the products of the earth.

"You've got a great photographer."

She was watching the screen with him, the colors so intense they reflected off her pale skin. "Thanks. I took most of those."

Astounded, Joe watched more images march across the header. His first impression was right. The photographer was inspired. And the photographer was Isabel.

"These are incredible images. Makes you want to reach into the screen and pull something to eat out."

"Thanks. I've traveled a lot and I like to take photos. I had a whole bunch in my archive so when I started the blog I put together a slide show of some of the photos I'd taken. It was just a question of balancing out the color palette and making sure there was a flow from one photo to the next."

"Huh," Joe grunted. He'd never have thought of that for a blog header, not in a million years. The blogs he read had to do with geopolitics and gear. But now that he was paying attention, he saw that from photo to photo there was a slow continuity of color, an intensely pleasing sense of balance.

He scrolled down and saw that the blog was dated two days before the Massacre.

"I didn't have time to update the blog at all," Isabel said quietly. "My father was preparing to announce his candidacy and everything was in an uproar. My next blog was going to be a three-parter—celebratory foods throughout the world." She huffed out a breath. "Because I thought we'd all be celebrating."

No, they didn't celebrate. They were all dead.

Joe scrolled down, read the last entry. "The Humble Chickpea." He read for half an hour, fascinated. The history of the chickpea dating back to the Bronze Age, its nutritional value, the use of chickpea flour, different ways of making hummus. She'd even unearthed some poems praising the chickpea, translated from Lebanese Arabic. At the end of the post were four recipes arranged according to difficulty, which even he, ignorant as he was, saw was smart. The blog appealed to beginners and sophisticated cooks alike.

He scrolled quickly down and saw feature after feature on various foodstuffs, giving the history, interesting factoids, the same scale of recipes. All lavishly, beautifully illustrated.

He couldn't imagine the amount of work that went into it, the vast research behind the highly readable and entertaining articles. Toggling left, he saw that the archives could be accessed by foodstuff, by recipes, by ethnic cuisine.

"This is amazing, Isabel," he said seriously. Joe was ashamed of himself. When he'd heard Isabel had run a food blog he'd thought—*how cute*. This wasn't "cute". It was a very serious labor of love that a lot of people found useful. She was an expert in the very thing that kept humans alive. Food.

They had that in common. It just so happened that he was an expert, too, on one of the other things that kept humans alive. Weaponry.

"You need to bring this blog back to life. And you need to write your book. Promise me you'll at least think about it."

She looked him full in the eyes, this incredibly talented woman. This incredibly beautiful and talented woman who was *his*. The smile reached her eyes. "I promise."

She was coming back to life right in front of his eyes. Putting herself back together again, picking up her life where it had been blown up.

He knew all about that. He'd picked himself up, too. The difference was he'd had a lot of help along the way.

"It's late. Are you tired?" Startled, Isabel checked her wristwatch.

Joe didn't bother checking his watch, he had a perfectly functional one in his head. It was 10:35 p.m., give or take a minute. He didn't give a fuck what time it was, though. All he knew was that it was *time*.

"Because I'm tired," he said, rising. He cupped his hand under Isabel's elbow and she rose, too. "I think it's time for bed." Either he took her to bed or his dick was going to explode.

Right now Isabel was absolutely impossible to resist. The Isabel he'd met had been like a wounded bird. He'd wanted to touch her, kiss her, bed her, but also curl himself around her and protect her. But there was another Isabel inside, not wounded, a confident woman, talented and worldly. Incredibly sexy. Like she was the woman sex had been invented for.

Joe softened his hands. He wanted to hold her tight, kiss her hard, but he had big strong hands and he had to watch himself. To make sure he didn't clutch her too hard, he placed his open palm against her back and kept it open as he moved her toward the bedroom.

She looked up at him in amusement. "So, it's like that, is it?"

He wanted to smile but it was hard to do when he was shaking with lust, trying to control himself. "Exactly like that."

In the bedroom, Isabel immediately veered for the bathroom. Yeah. Okay. Chicks wanted to be all fresh before they had sex. Joe didn't need that. He'd want her if she just came off a marathon. He wouldn't care.

He sniffed his armpits just to see if they were rank, but they weren't. Let's hear it for twenty-first century deodorant. Inside of five seconds he was naked and under the covers. He was boiling hot but he had the blankets up over his crotch because his cock looked almost inflamed, and it felt harder than it had ever felt before.

It almost scared him and it was *his* cock. So he didn't want her to see it and run screaming. He wanted her to scream all right, but not that way.

He sat up against the headboard, hands behind his head, waiting. She was doing something in the bathroom. He heard running water, then silence. Oh, God, she was naked in there. He shut his eyes because his cock had given a painful pulse. He didn't think it could become harder than it already was, but it did.

Because Joe knew what she looked like naked. She was designed specifically to drive a man wild. Soft skin, full breasts with pretty pale pink nipples, only the very tips became cherry red when she was aroused. All that honey blonde hair—enough for six women—fluttering around her shoulders. Those long slender legs, a pale little cloud between them, groomed and neat, pink-and-red folds peeking through.

The folds glistened when she was excited.

Oh, yeah.

God, please make her come out now or he was going to spill all over her bed and wouldn't that be fucking embarrassing? The sheets were soft and crisp at the same time. He'd read somewhere that sheets were graded on a thread count, the higher the count the higher the quality. These sheets probably had a billion thread count. And covering the bed was a huge thick comforter patterned with rosebuds, feminine overkill.

It was certainly killing him.

He waited and waited and waited. Though the clock in his head said that about a quarter of an hour had gone by, it felt like days, weeks, months. He had to clench his abdomen a couple of times to keep from ejaculating. He recited the Ranger Creed in his head. He wasn't a Ranger but they had the coolest creed of all the armed services.

He was running through the driest of the SEAL exams—mechanical comprehension—when the bathroom door opened and all thoughts flew out of his head. Straight out of his head. He was reduced to a sack of oversensitive skin, an aching dick and a hammering heart.

Look at her. She didn't have on that pretty woolly nightgown that had been secretly sexy. Now she had on a nightgown that was openly sexy. Full-length. Cream-colored, thin straps, showing every outline of her body. The full breasts with the hard nipples, the tiny waist, the gently curving hips…

She wasn't wearing anything at all underneath.

Joe blew out a breath, hard.

She was swaying as she walked, eyes on his, smiling. She knew the effect she was having on him. Though she couldn't see his dick, he was sure it was sending out signals.

He held his hand up. "Stop."

She stopped, pretty feet gripping the floor. She cocked her head. "Joe?" Her voice was low and husky. She could see how worked up he was. Her stopping wasn't in the program.

"Pull your nightgown up." His voice was hoarse, strangled.

Her eyebrows shot up, but she obeyed, bunching that soft, creamy material in her fists and raising the hem to her shins.

Fuck. Those feet and ankles were so damn pretty.

He was going to suck her toes…his cock surged, grew slick. He couldn't afford to think of sucking her toes.

"Higher."

Isabel studied him, trying to figure out what his deal was.

Well, tell her.

"I'm…a little worked up. As you can probably tell." Joe manfully refrained from looking down at his lap. "So this is about the only foreplay you're going to get. You're going to have to do it yourself."

"DIY foreplay?"

"Yep." He was glad she seemed to have a sense of humor about this because it was actually not in the seduction playbook—to tell the lady that she wasn't going to get any foreplay, she was going to have to do it herself. But he didn't have a choice here. "When I get my hands on you it won't be slow and it won't be gentle."

Her eyes opened wider.

"So pull that nightgown up."

Isabel didn't feel his urgency, otherwise she would have pulled that fucking nightgown over her head in a flash and run to the bed. But she didn't. She was having fun. The hem of the gown inched up a little higher. Not much.

"More." Joe was reduced to words of one syllable.

Isabel smiled. Raised the hem another inch.

"More." Joe rubbed a hand over his chest. He was sweating slightly.

Another inch.

"More."

Isabel swayed slightly, tilting her head, studying him. She gave that Mona Lisa smile only beautiful women manage, because she had his number. He was dead meat here, fragged, bagged and tagged. She lifted her hem higher, to the tops of her long smooth thighs.

Ah, Jesus…

"What are you feeling?" He hoped against hope she felt a fraction of what he did. Like jumping out of his skin. Like being radioactive.

"Hot," she whispered, "In every sense."

"Show me." Joe's voice was urgent.

"What?"

"Show me you're hot. Show me you're ready. Show me *now.*"

Goddamn, why was he pushing this?

Because he was hanging on to control with two shaking hands and it was slipping from his grasp by the second.

With one hand, Isabel bunched the nightgown in her fist, lifting the folds of material up and to the side, baring her body from the waist down, pubic hair neatly shaped around her sex. The hair on her mound was a light ash brown, the same color as her eyebrows, a shade darker than the hair on her head. Her skin was so pale it looked silvery in the light from the bathroom.

She looked for a moment almost otherworldly, a dream of a woman instead of flesh and blood. Insubstantial, as if she could float right away at any moment. But she wasn't insubstantial. Joe had been inside her. He'd kissed almost every inch of her and if there were a few square inches left unkissed he had every intention of making up for it tonight.

"Show me," he said again, his voice insistent.

"How?"

He took in a deep breath. "Open your legs."

Watching him, she widened her stance. At some

point in her life she must have taken ballet lessons because she lifted one foot, pointed her toes, then gracefully placed it back on the ground.

"I know how to show you," she said, her voice a breathless whisper in the quiet darkness. With her free hand, she reached down and opened herself, to show how she glistened. She was wet. For him.

Reaching with her index finger, she slid it between the folds, then lifted it so he could see. Even in the semidarkness, he could see that her finger was coated with moisture.

The hand that held her bunched nightgown moved upward and she pulled the gown over her head and tossed it to one side. The gesture lifted her honey hair and it settled back down around her shoulders, crackling with electricity.

It was time. Isabel recognized that as she stepped to the bed. At the last minute, when she was ready to climb in beside him, Joe lifted her up and over him, settling her down on top of him.

He'd run out of time.

Feeling her against him nearly set him off. She smelled and felt so damned good. Instinctively she'd opened her legs, kneeling along his thighs, her sex open and hot over his cock.

Joe groaned. He brought her face down to his with a hand cupped over the back of her head and opened her up with the fingers of his other hand. Feeling himself at her rim was simply too much. He kissed her hard as he thrust up into her, seating himself fully inside her with a grunt.

He felt her cry against his mouth and pulled her head back half an inch. "Did I hurt you?" he said, his voice guttural. It seemed to come from his stomach instead of his throat.

Isabel opened her eyes, stared down into his. She was panting, her breath washing across his face in hot waves. Her face—he couldn't read that expression. It was pained, but not pain. All of a sudden it was as if she turned inward, frowning, her shoulders turned inward and he was about to pull out when she gave a cry and fell forward onto his chest, fingers digging in deep, writhing around him.

She was coming.

Her sex was milking him hard. There was absolutely nothing in him that could resist her. Lunging upward hard, he came, too, in long painful spurts so intense they almost made him black out. He didn't even thrust, just kept himself deep inside her as she moved against him, clutching him with her arms and thighs.

Finally, finally he stopped, completely wrung out, holding her tightly to him. He was breathing hard, bathed in sweat that plastered them together. Isabel's hair fell in tumbling curls over his shoulder, caught on his stubble, a lock crossed his forehead. He shifted it away, savoring the softness, that subtle smell of a sweet shampoo.

Was he hurting her? Was he holding on to her too tightly? Probably. He gave his arms the command to let go but there was a kind of communications breakdown and his arms remained tightly wound around her. He had to give himself orders, like an instructor to a trainee, a newb.

Right arm, pull away.

Except his right arm was comfortable and happy

where it was, arm crossing Isabel's back, hand resting lightly on her firm butt.

Right arm, pull away NOW!!

With a sigh, Joe obeyed himself. He didn't exactly pull it away so much as loosen his grip. Because not being in touch with all that soft satiny skin seemed insane. Why would he do that?

Because you might be hurting Isabel, fuckhead, was the reply.

He loosened his left arm, too, just a little. He was embracing her now, not clutching her. He wanted to be on her good side because, well…he tested her. Moving his dick in her gently, thrusting maybe an inch in and out.

Oh, man. His juices and hers. She was soft and completely welcoming. Oh, yeah. Because in a minute or two, Joe was going to be ready for round two. Or, considering that round one hadn't exactly been a masterwork of style, technique and stamina, round one and a half. At the thought of sex with her again, he hardened.

This was going to be better than the last time. She was a little less tight, softer, wetter. Joe nudged inside her again. Oh man…

But she wasn't responding. She was lying on him, breathing calmly. Joe couldn't breathe calmly, not while in Isabel. Then he heard a weird sound coming from her. He pulled his head back, swiped her hair away from her face and grinned.

She was fast asleep. Out cold, actually. Not even a flicker of those thick eyelashes. That luscious mouth was slightly open and a ladylike little snore escaped from it.

So. No more sex. Not right now, anyway. He couldn't

bear the thought of disturbing her sleep. She'd often said that she had trouble sleeping.

Carefully, carefully, Joe withdrew from her body, edged her gently over so she was nestled against him, head on his shoulder, and pulled the covers up over her shoulders.

He lay back and studied the dark ceiling, wondering how far gone he was when lying in bed next to a woman he wanted more than his next breath, with a hard-on that could hammer nails, developing blue balls—and just holding her was better than sex with any other woman.

An air of evil in the room, so strong it was almost a stench. People all around, happy, popping with joy, dancing to the celebratory music. Smiling, smiling. Couldn't they feel it? Couldn't they feel the darkness like smoke swirling around the room?

She looked around, trying to warn everyone. Most of them were familiar faces, though she couldn't put any names to them. They didn't stick around long enough for her to identify them. They'd dance close to her then twirl away. She'd reach out but they swirled out of her grasp the instant she opened her hand.

Everybody moving, moving. Only she stood stock-still in the room as the shadows in the corners filled it. Wisps of darkness coalescing, wrapping itself around the clueless partygoers.

She screamed and no one listened. They were having too good a time.

The music was so loud she couldn't hear herself think, couldn't make herself heard by anyone, not even those close by.

Someone danced close to her, grabbed her by the

waist, twirled her. It made her dizzy and unsteady. She had to watch her feet so she wouldn't fall over. When she lifted her eyes she saw HIM.

Always him, always watching her, always just out of reach.

She caught a glimpse of his face but then he disappeared again. He was somewhere in the room, elusive and mocking. A viper in human form and oh so dangerous. Why couldn't anyone else see it, feel it? She could feel him so vividly, though she couldn't see him.

She saw him every night in her dreams. In her nightmares. No matter how the dream started, it ended as a nightmare. Always lots of happy people, celebrating, with a hidden monster lurking at the edges. And yet nobody noticed, nobody cared.

Every night she struggled to make her voice heard above the noise, to warn the happy people what was coming.

Every night she failed.

She tried to scream but no sound came, a huffing of breath, no more. She clutched at jackets and dresses and they removed her hand and moved on.

Right now she could see the bare outlines of his face, staring at her from a podium. The light came from behind and his eyes were in utter darkness, only cheekbones, mouth and chin visible.

That skull-like head with no eyes, watching her.

And, just as she had known, monsters came out from the walls, an army of them. Bearing guns, swords, in a killing rage. They wore black masks and seemed inhuman as they shot and cut their way through the happy throng, happy no more. Trying to flee the monsters.

Men and women, shot and stabbed, dying.

And still no one heard her scream. The breath in her lungs wasn't enough. The black-suited minions continued killing and killing. And yet she was spared.

She looked again to the podium and he hadn't moved. Dark voids where his eyes should be but somehow she knew he was staring at her, watching her as all around her people died.

Then, he smiled. A horrible rictus of a grin, the empty holes where the eyes should be, the mouth lifting in an unnaturally wide smile, mouth another dark hole.

That horrendous face filled her horizon, coming closer, ready for the kill, closer, closer. Though he hadn't moved, she was suddenly shackled, immobilized. Utter prey as he came closer.

She tried to scream, scrabbled with her feet, fought for her life...

"JESUS, HONEY, calm down. It's a dream." A deep voice. Calm. She knew that voice. Her nightmares didn't have voices, nobody spoke. They were like silent movies from hell. No deep, calm voices. Something was stroking her face. "Open your eyes, honey. You were having a bad dream. See for yourself where you are."

Something that had shackled her released, just as she opened her eyes and saw she was in her bedroom. With Joe. Who was looking calm, but with deep brackets around his mouth. "It's okay," he said.

She hadn't been shackled. Joe had put his arms around her. They were still around her, only not so tightly.

"I'm going to let go of you." His dark eyes bored into hers. "Do you understand that you were having a nightmare?"

She nodded, throat too tight to talk.

"Good," he grunted, and stroked her hair.

She was with Joe, in her bedroom. She was safe. It was like something had been squeezing her, stopping her from breathing. Isabel took in a huge wheezing breath. Another.

"That's right," Joe said. "That's my girl. What were you having?"

"Nightmare," she gasped. "Not real."

But it had *felt* real. The evil, the killing, the man with empty eyes staring at her—it had all felt as real as anything. Her heart was still trip-hammering.

"No, not real," Joe said. "Here." She always kept a glass of water on her bedside table. He pressed it into her hand and she sipped. "See if you can get it all down," he urged and she did.

"Better?" Isabel started shaking her head no, when she stopped. Actually, she did feel better. She nodded.

But his face didn't clear, it still looked tight.

"You scared me." He closed his eyes, then opened them again. "Scared the shit out of me, as a matter of fact."

"You should have seen it from my point of view," she said and gave a little laugh that might have been hysteria.

"No, thanks." Joe put pillows behind him, sat up and coaxed her to sit between his legs, her back against his chest. He grunted with satisfaction when his arms went around her. She was surrounded by warm, hard man. Warm, hard, reassuring man. "It was bad enough being beside you. I couldn't get you to wake up. It sounded like someone was torturing you but you were gagged.

And your legs were running, like you wanted to run away."

This, *this* was the reason she hadn't slept with anyone since the Massacre. The nightmares. It wouldn't be any fun at all for a man to sleep with someone who went crazy every night. No wonder she hadn't had a love life. Too scary, too creepy.

"Sorry. I'm so sorry." Isabel pushed her hair out of her eyes. She felt washed-out, as if she'd run a thousand miles. Maybe she could convince Joe to go back to his house. And then avoid him until he got the message. It was too humiliating for words being exposed like this. What had she looked like while in the nightmare? Not pretty, that would be her guess. She hadn't been pretty since the Massacre but in the light of day she could at least put up a front. Or if not a brave front, she could at least put on lipstick. But at night, when having nightmares? The rawest part of her was exposed.

Luckily, she wasn't facing him. She didn't know if she could face him right now.

Joe's arms tightened briefly. "Good God, don't apologize! I was just terrified that I couldn't wake you up. What was the nightmare? Do you remember?"

"What it always is, the Massacre," she said wearily, looking down at her hands. He'd clasped them in his warm fists. Where she touched him—all along her back, along the sides of her thighs, her arms and hands—she was warm.

The rest of her was deathly cold.

"The Massacre? In detail?"

"No. And it's not really the Massacre itself, I shouldn't have said that. I have retrograde amnesia and my memory so far is not coming back. I don't have memories of much of anything beyond Friday afternoon, the day before the Massacre. What I'm dreaming of—what's in the nightmares—is more like—like a metaphor. A metaphor of the Massacre."

Joe rested his cheek against the top of her head. Her head was now warm, too. "Tell me," he said gently. "Tell me everything before you forget it. And do you have these nightmares often?"

"Every night," she blurted, then covered her mouth. She'd wanted to say *never* because only crazy people had constant nightmares. But the truth had simply fallen out of her mouth, like poison her body wanted to expel. "I have them every night. Except last night." She twisted her head briefly to see if that sparked a smug smile. Fabulous sex that kept the little lady from her nightmares. He could be proud of that.

"I'm glad." Joe didn't have a smug smile. He just looked worried. He nudged her with his shoulder. "So, tell me. Is it always the same nightmare?"

Isabel blew out a breath. "This is going to sound weird, possibly cowardly, but I am so terrified when I wake up that my only thought is to get the images out of my head as quickly as possible."

"That doesn't sound weird and it sure doesn't sound cowardly. Do you think you can make an exception now and try to remember instead of trying to forget?"

Now that Joe was with her, now that she was surrounded by him, now that she could feel his steady heartbeat against her back…yes. Having him here made all the difference. Before, all those nights and nights of waking up in terror, cold sweat covering her body, she'd felt absolutely alone. Not just alone in her house but *alone*. The last human in a dark universe populated by monsters.

"Okay."

Joe's hands tightened around hers and she realized her hands had been trembling. It gave her a spurt of warmth and energy. No one had held her hands during the night terrors.

"I can tell you about *this* nightmare. The one I just had. I'm in a room. A big room, a room I've never seen before. It is filled with people dressed up for an occasion and there is the air of a big party in process. The people are laughing, happy. Waiting for something big."

"That sounds like the ballroom the night of the Massacre. So you do remember it."

"No." Isabel frowned, trying to explain what she barely understood. "My memory of the Massacre, if it ever returns, will be different. Because I'm familiar with the Burrard and I knew a lot of the people there to celebrate—" Her voice wobbled. "To celebrate Dad's intent to run for the presidency. There would be a lot of the party activists I wouldn't necessarily know but I'd know a lot of people there, if only fleetingly. Dad's friends, reporters, donors. There wasn't anyone I recognized in my nightmare. And there was this air—"

She shivered, looking for the words to describe the horrible feeling of menace.

"Take your time," Joe murmured.

He was good. She'd been to two shrinks who had tried to lead her through her memories but she had felt pushed, prodded. Joe simply waited to hear what she would say. You'd think soldiers would be restless adrenaline junkies, but Joe was the opposite. He always gave off an air of infinite calm and right now of infinite patience.

"This air of menace. Of great evil. I know that sounds crazy—"

"Evil exists in the world," Joe said quietly. "I've seen it, touched it."

Yes, he would understand. He had been a soldier in terrible wars. He would understand evil.

"Dark, menacing. Horrible. *Triumphant.* As if it knew something we didn't. But all these people dancing and laughing and celebrating—they're clueless. Something truly horrible is about to happen and I am trying to warn everyone, but they're not listening. They can't hear me. I want to scream but I can't. I want to run around but I can't. I can't move. It's horrible."

"Sleep paralysis," Joe said. "Glycine and gamma-aminobutyric acid paralyzing the muscles during REM sleep. It's a self-defense mechanism of the body. Otherwise we'd kill people in our sleep."

"Awful. Just awful." Like being trapped. "So no one would listen to me, no one paid me any attention at all, though I knew something horrible was going to happen. They didn't even pay attention when something horrible *did* happen." She drew in a deep shuddering breath. "People started dying."

They were silent. Isabel couldn't go on and Joe simply wrapped himself more tightly around her, a wall of warm flesh acting as protection.

Finally, Isabel spoke again. The nightmare was starting to lose its contours, fade. She wanted to nail it while she could see some flashes of it. "I was told by police authorities that they used machine guns during the

Massacre. They even told me the make and the caliber, though I don't remember any of that."

"AK-47s," Joe said softly. "The weapon of choice of your discerning terrorist."

Isabel shook. AK-47s had killed her parents, her brothers. Her aunts, uncles, cousins. And hundreds more family friends and supporters of her dad's policies. She squeezed her eyes tight but one tear seeped out, ran down her cheek.

Joe wiped it away with his thumb. He didn't apologize for telling her the make of the weapons. Any website would tell her. She'd wiped it from her mind, but the reality didn't change.

"In my dream they had guns, of all types. And swords. They hacked at people. I saw limbs being sliced off. What I think was a shotgun nearly took off the head of a man standing next to me. I'd been holding his arm, trying to get his attention, when all of a sudden I was covered in blood and brains."

She twisted again to look at Joe. His face was expressionless but his dark eyes were warm. "None of this is real, though. From what I understand there were no swords. The lights went out immediately anyway and nobody could have seen anything. So it's a nightmare that comes from my subconscious and not my memory. Do you see the difference?"

He nodded his head slowly.

"And then there was...*him.*"

"Who, Isabel?"

There was only one possible answer to that. An answer that came straight from the bottom of her soul. "Evil. Pure evil. A—a man. On the podium, staring at me. Only I couldn't see his eyes, they were deep in shadow. And he had a huge mouth, full of teeth. It seemed like he had more teeth than a human should have…"

Isabel shut up. It sounded like she was describing a vampire, not a human. Some supernatural being. It was her subconscious ascribing monstrous qualities to him when the monstrosity was internal, not external.

"Sorry. He was…unsettling. And he smiled as his minions mowed people down. As if he were enjoying it. As if he were on the stage watching something that pleased him. None of the killers had a face, they were like devils, killing and killing. And yet some of the people in that big room still hadn't understood what was going on, were still laughing and chatting, while others were being killed in the most horrific ways. And I couldn't get them to listen, to pay attention. To run away. It was as if I were invisible. So I tried to get them to head for the exits but I couldn't, and I slipped in the blood that was flowing and I tried to run harder…" She buried her face in her heads.

"And then I woke you up," Joe said gently.

She nodded, her limbs shaking, a huge lump of something sharp in her throat.

Joe pulled the blankets up to cover her shoulders, rocking her gently, as you would a child.

At that moment, Isabel felt like a child. A child who'd seen the boogeyman and was terrified he'd come back.

Joe let her take her time putting herself back together again. He didn't say anything, he just held her, rocked her. Finally, when she was calm again, he leaned down and spoke in her ear.

"You know, Lauren is a great artist. Do you think

you could give her a description of this man, like you would to a police artist?"

Could she? "Maybe. But in my nightmare he was a monster. It wouldn't be of any use to anybody."

"You never know," he said, his voice neutral. "If nothing else, it might rob him of his power in your subconscious."

"Maybe." Isabel hadn't thought of it that way. She'd dreamed of the man almost every night, but when she woke up she could never remember what he looked like, only that he was cruel and evil. Brought darkness and violence in his wake. She'd fixed some elements of his face in her memory. She'd perhaps be able to talk Lauren through the drawing, even if the end result would probably look like a comic book villain. Manic and diabolical, like the Joker.

Joe nudged her gently with his shoulder again. "So we can plan that? Come to the office tomorrow morning and talk Lauren through the portrait?"

In the office. Talking about her nightmares in front of everyone. She suppressed a shudder. "I'd rather do it here." Not let all Joe's friends know about her craziness.

"I know, honey." Joe's voice was regretful. "But Felicity has her stuff there and we're going to try to get back into contact with the guy—or the person who contacted us about you. Remember?"

God, yes. How could she have forgotten? So much had happened. "How does he know about me? And how does he know I live here?"

"All questions we want answered," Joe replied, voice grim. "If I had to make a guess, I'd say he's CIA or ex-CIA. And I'd guess he knows something about the Massacre that doesn't fit the narrative."

Isabel felt her eyes grow wide. She turned again to look at him. "Something about the Massacre? Like what?"

"I don't know. But I think he thinks you have some kind of key or intel about it."

"Me?" Good God. "I don't have anything, least of all what you call 'intel'. I don't even remember it. Plus how did he track me down to Portland? That's creepy."

"It wouldn't be hard to track you down. You weren't on the run or anything. Did you file to change your name from Delvaux to Lawton?"

Isabel nodded.

"There you go. That would be in the public record. You weren't in hiding, you just wanted a fresh start. If this guy is CIA and is secretly investigating the Massacre, he'd start with the survivors. How many survivors were there?"

"I don't know. I don't know if anyone has done an official count. I don't know how many of the serving staff survived. Presumably some of them weren't in the part of the building that collapsed. I think about thirty or forty people who were in the ballroom survived. But I'm not positive."

"So maybe this guy is contacting them all."

"But how would he know to get in touch with *you*?"

"It wouldn't be that hard. Your new address is on record. He'd look at the other people on the street and I'd pop up. I'm a former SEAL, that's on the record and I am on the record as an employee at ASI, which is a well-known company. Very aboveboard. He'd add two and two. Even if I didn't know you well, it would make sense for him to contact me and ask me to keep you safe. Maybe he's making his quiet way down the list of survivors. We'll know soon enough. He's asked for someone from the FBI to be in the office tomorrow."

"The *FBI?*" This was getting more and more strange.

Joe slid down in the bed, taking her with him. She was on her side and he was curved around her.

He was also erect, but he wasn't prodding her with it, or asking for sex. He kissed her shoulder gently. "I think we'll be getting some answers tomorrow, but I also think you need to rest. It's 4:00 a.m. and we should get up around 7:00, so that only gives you three hours to sleep. See if you can manage it."

"I don't think I can," Isabel said, then yawned.

"Uh-huh." Joe kissed her shoulder again. She could see his face above her, smiling down at her. "Just try. Close your eyes for a minute."

Oh, man, he didn't know just how hard she tried to get back to sleep after a nightmare. It was impossible. She'd just lie awake, tense and frightened, until the sky outside her bedroom window started to lighten, and she'd get up to start another exhausting day.

"It doesn't work."

"Try," he coaxed. "Just for a minute. For me."

"Make me," she said, her voice suddenly low, suddenly husky. In a flash, a switch had been thrown. That massive male body surrounding her, that enormous erect penis against her back… All those intense emotions evoked by the nightmare morphed in an instant to desire. There had never been another mechanism for her to deal with the aftermath of the nightmares before. Just silence and the endless hours of the night. But now—now there was the world's greatest distraction wrapped around her.

"What?" Obviously Joe didn't operate like she did,

emotions flipping from one extreme to the other. He had to keep up.

Isabel turned her head to smile at the dark male face above hers. "I need help getting to sleep. So either you warm up some milk for me or make love to me. Your choice."

He closed his eyes briefly and when he opened them his gaze was fierce.

"Put like that," he said. "I don't have much of a choice, do I?"

He turned her gently on her back and mounted her. There was no other word for it. His hands were gentle. She could see the effort that gentleness was costing him in the taut tendons of his neck, but the movements were pure sex, pure animal. His thighs separated hers and he slid into her with an ease that astonished her. She was ready for him, though. Needed him, even, and her body knew that before her mind did.

And oh, God, when he entered her she was infused with heat and strength. Sex was this, too. Elemental, primal. Heat and power entering her as much as his body entering hers.

His mouth covered hers and he started moving and there was nothing but heat and blinding pleasure and the animal comfort of his body in hers.

NINE

"THIS DOESN'T LOOK like the right part of town for corporate headquarters," Isabel said as they cruised through the Pearl.

She was right. It was a funky part of town, formerly full of warehouses and railroad yards and now gentrified but artsy. No high-rises, no corporate buildings.

"Just wait," he said as he turned onto the street where the back entrance to ASI was. He didn't want to say anything because he wanted to see how she reacted to the business's premises.

"Okay."

Joe shot her a glance. She looked rested. Thank God. That nightmare had shaken him to the core. She'd been mewling and moaning, thrashing in the bed. It had been a monster nightmare. He'd kept calm but what she'd told him could only mean one thing. Her memories were returning in the form of dreams. Nightmares. And if Mystery Man was right, she was remembering something that was worse than a terrorist attack. Mystery Man wanted the FBI because he suspected homegrown terrorists. Worse. Homegrown terrorists who might be connected to the government. At least 9/11 had been carried out by foreigners.

And Isabel was smack in the middle of it. So Joe was not going to let her out of his sight until he had a clearer understanding of what the fuck this was all about.

He circled round a high redbrick wall until he came to a big gate and pressed the accelerator.

Isabel gave a half cry that was strangled as the gates slid open quickly. Every ASI operative had a special transponder installed in his or her vehicle. Joe loved it and loved that he was working for a cool company. Going to be working for a cool company.

"Magic." He grinned as he drove into a well-ordered compound with parking spaces and a large, attractive brick structure to the side.

It was only faced with brick. It was actually made of steel and concrete and was unbreachable. Inside was the ASI armory and a spectacular thing it was, too. Besides weapons, it also held the very latest in military-grade gear. It was like their very own playground only made of steel, not sand.

But ASI was not the only company in the compound. Midnight's wife, Suzanne, had a design company, too, so not only was the compound a gearhead's wet dream, it was also spectacularly beautiful. Joe was sure they were the only aesthetically pleasing security company in the country.

"Wow." Isabel looked around. "This is where you work?"

"Will work," Joe grunted as he parked the car. "When they give me the go-ahead. And you haven't seen anything yet."

"Well this is already fantastic. There's more?"

He just smiled as he exited the vehicle and helped her to the ground. He let her look around because it was worth it.

The vehicles and the armory were ASI, but everything else was Suzanne's. What had once been the loading dock for her grandparents' shoe factory was a carefully landscaped area neatly divided up by brick-lined sections of planters. There was a series of arches planted with climbing ivy, a small Zen garden, elaborate outdoor lighting, even a couple of stone benches around a little fountain.

Of course what the ordinary admirer wouldn't see was the motion sensors, the NV and infrared vidcams hid in the greenery, the outer wall that was built in a way that would mitigate debris even in the case of a perimeter breach explosion…

As a matter of fact, Midnight and Suzanne were working together to provide extreme high-tech security solutions that incorporated design elements, too. That business was starting to take off.

Joe touched a small key fob and the door to the building opened too.

He enjoyed Isabel's pleasure at the sight of the long corridor. Being a chick, she'd probably appreciate it better than he did. All Joe knew was that he loved entering the building, loved the physical premises. If you put a blowtorch to his bare feet, he'd also admit to loving his teammates and his bosses.

He was one lucky son of a bitch.

Joe held out his arm and Isabel took it with a smile. It was like she was made to walk these halls, her natural habitat. She was as classy as the decor.

When they walked into ASI's offices, Felicity and Lauren rose, smiling, and proceeded to make an enormous fuss over Isabel. The sounds of the women's voices filled the room as Metal gave an ironic one-fingered salute with his index finger and Jacko refrained from giving his usual one-fingered salute, only with a different finger.

Suzanne had two big thermoses of coffee and pretty mugs with roses waiting for them. The mugs were from her business, not Midnight's. ASI had *Game of Thrones* and "Assassin's Creed" and "Call of Duty" mugs.

Lauren and Isabel put their heads together. Isabel nodded and Lauren pulled out a big block of sketch pads. They sat in a corner talking quietly as Lauren started sketching.

Joe brought out his laptop and was setting it up when Nick Mancino walked in. He looked tired but alert, having flown across the country on the red-eye.

"Hey." They fist-bumped and Mancino slapped the backs of Metal and Jacko and shook Midnight's hand.

"Senior." He shook the Senior's hand. Joe and Mancino had gone through Hell Week together and the Senior had been the worst thing about it. He'd screamed in their faces constantly, seemed to live for giving them extra laps, had begged them to ring the bell signifying defeat, had been like Satan's spawn himself…and then had bought them all beers after they slept thirty-six hours straight upon completing Hell Week.

From being a living, walking, fire-breathing king of the sons of bitches, Kowalski turned out to be a pretty cool boss. Maybe he'd mellowed with marriage. To everyone's enormous surprise, he was a gigantic pussycat when his wife was around.

Go figure.

"Saw Kay Hudson the other day," the Senior said casually and Nick looked like someone had stuck a prod up his ass.

"Yeah?" He was trying for cool and it was a massive fail. A few beads of sweat sprouted along his dark hairline.

This was amazing. Nick was a former SEAL, just like Joe. Now he was on the FBI's Hostage Rescue Team and though they weren't the badasses SEALs were, they came pretty close. Nick's specialty was sniping. He was cool and calm, always. He'd even been cool and calm during Hell Week. Had even joked.

And a woman made him sweat?

Joe would give up one poker session's winnings to see that woman. She must be something.

"Yeah." The Senior had his own poker face on. Senior's poker face wasn't good enough to win against Joe in their sessions but for outsiders it served well enough. But Joe could easily see that Senior was hiding a huge grin. "She stopped by Portland on her way out, to say hello to Felicity and Metal."

Nick's eyes were wide, the whites showing like a pony's. "She say—she say where she was going?"

"Nope," Senior said cheerfully. "Not a fucking clue."

Nick made a strangled sound in his throat.

Enough of this. Ordinarily, the entertainment value of seeing Nick squirm in his boots would have been enough to stretch this stuff out, but he had Isabel to think of and it was time to get down to business.

"Nick," Joe said, voice hard and Nick shook himself and morphed back into the cold operator Joe knew.

"Yeah." Nick had himself under control now and looked at all of them, plus Felicity who was sitting at the keyboard of her Magical Mystery Computer. No one was allowed to touch it, no one was allowed to even breathe on it. It was a prototype—illegally smuggled out from some secret super computer lab somewhere in the world—and it reputedly cost fifty thousand dollars.

At that keyboard, Felicity became God.

"Gentlemen," Nick said. He nodded at Felicity. "Felicity." He turned to the guys. "So. I'm here. Flew all fucking night. What the fuck is this about?"

Joe switched on his computer and nodded at Isabel and Lauren. "The lady talking to Lauren is Isabel Lawton, who used to be Isabel Delvaux."

Nick's face changed. "Delvaux? Of *the* Delvauxes?"

Joe nodded. "Alex Delvaux's daughter."

"So she's one of the ones who survived the Massacre."

"Yeah. Barely. She has amnesia. She was badly concussed in the explosion and doesn't remember anything beyond the day before the Massacre."

Nick glanced behind him, where Isabel and Lauren were engrossed in the drawing flowing from Lauren's hand.

"So what's she doing here, way across the country, under another name? She on the run from someone?"

"No. Not on the run." Joe shook his head. "But the other day I got an anonymous message sent to my computer. We couldn't trace it. Not even Felicity could."

"That's true." Felicity shook her head. "Not for lack of trying. But he—and we're assuming it's a he because he's sneaky and manipulative—used an anonymizer and I think it was washed through three points. Totally untraceable without bringing monster crunching power to bear for a long time. Plus," she shrugged, looking at Joe. "I get the feeling he's—well, he's a good guy. Could be wrong but if he doesn't want to be identified, there's probably a reason."

"I think he's CIA," Joe said bluntly. "Which doesn't necessarily make him a good guy in my book. But he's stepping outside the CIA. Asked specifically for someone good, someone incorruptible from the FBI. So we called you."

Nick nodded.

"And we have a ten o'clock computer appointment." Joe checked his watch. It's ten now—"

Hello, Joe

appeared on his monitor.

Joe sat down at his laptop. Felicity scooted over in her office chair, pulling her laptop along. They were sitting side by side.

Hello, Joe typed.

Let's talk.

Joe looked around. Felicity was calm. The guys all leaned in.

Okay, he answered.

"Hello, Joe." A metallic affectless synthesized voice came from his speakers. Joe was familiar with the software. It washed out all identifying traits, including gender.

"Hi." He kept his voice neutral.

"So, introduce me to your friends."

Joe could feel his eyebrows climbing up. Felicity leaned forward. "If you've got eyes on us, we should have eyes on you. Switch on your camera."

A metallic laugh. *"Nice try. Maybe later. Not quite yet."*

"You have us at a disadvantage," Joe said evenly. "But I'll introduce everyone anyway. Felicity Ward is our computer expert. The guy to your left is Douglas Kowalski, then Sean O'Brien and Morton Jackman."

Jacko grimaced at hearing his real name.

"And the man on the right is Special Agent Nick Mancino, FBI. HRT. You asked to have him here and here he is."

"Special Agent Mancino. Nice to meet you. You any good with a computer?"

"I'm okay," Nick said evenly. He pointed to Felicity. "But we've got a genius here."

Felicity's face didn't change. She was a genius with a computer and she knew it.

"Mind letting us know what this is about?" Joe was getting impatient. "This is about the Massacre, isn't it?"

"What do you know about the Massacre?"

"I was in a coma when it happened. Battle injury, got on the wrong side of an IED. So I'll let Nick answer that. FBI were among the first responders."

"So, Special Agent. What do you know about the Massacre?"

Nick wasn't fazed. "Alex Delvaux was expected to announce his run for the presidency at around 7:30 p.m. at the Burrard Hotel. They were running a little late. There were about seven hundred people in the room and behind the scenes. The Delvaux family itself, the extended family. Friends of the Delvauxes. A lot of the party higher-ups because Delvaux was the party's leading light. And party activists. There were about a hundred and fifty members of the press who had received accreditation, but estimates are that there were also about fifty unaccredited bloggers who were allowed in. And then general supporters of the Delvaux campaign.

"The room was fifteen thousand square feet and it was packed. There was going to be a buffet reception later and there were a hundred and seventy people who were either part of the kitchen staff or waitstaff. A deejay who was on a podium at the end of the room. And ten armed guards. There were no Secret Service special agents since Delvaux hadn't actually declared his run yet. As of the next day, Secret Service protection would have begun."

"So if something were to happen it had to happen that night."

Nick met Joe's eyes then turned to the monitor as if it was a face. "Yeah. I guess you could say that. I mean the security that night was good but not Secret Service level."

"No. What next?"

"At 7:20 the lights went. At 7:21 cell phone coverage stopped. All cell phone coverage died. Everyone taking pictures, everyone Instagramming, uploading videos to YouTube—it all stopped at 7:27. All internet coverage stopped too."

Felicity stirred. "It was a powerful jammer."

"Yeah," Nick said.

"Not just the cells," the metallic voice said from the monitor. *"Power, the power backups, elevators, security vidcams, all switched off. All over the city, too."*

"Yeah, the power going out all over DC was crazy," said Nick. "It was all crazy. We were part of the rescue team that night after it was clear that it was a terrorist attack. We thought there would be hostages but there weren't. It was just wholesale slaughter." Nick clenched his fists. He'd been there that night, seen the carnage. For Joe it was all secondhand information, acquired after he'd woken up. No one had actually given him an overall recounting of the event and the first month after he'd woken up he'd been in pain and weak. The outside world had retreated to a far-off signal for him. And Isabel had no memory of it at all.

"So what's the official version of what happened that night in the ballroom of the Burrard?"

They all looked at each other uneasily at the mention of the term *official*. As if there were several versions.

"The few eyewitnesses who survived said that a group of men dressed in black, with black ski masks and goggles, stormed into the room shouting *'Allahu Akhbar.'* God is great. They were heavily armed and they opened fire immediately with automatic weapons. AK-47s. Police and the FBI were notified only at 7:32 that there was an attack at the Burrard, via landline. Since the hotel is so close to the White House, the Secret Service was notified and they hustled the president into the war room. By the time we scrambled and were on the scene, the explosives blew and half the building came down. Most of the few people who survived the massacre died in the rubble. There were very few survivors."

"And the terrorists. They all escaped."

"Correct."

"And the lights went out all over Washington."

"Correct."

From what Joe had read, it was the lights going out all over the nation's capital that had brought the situation briefly to DEFCON 3. Even the White House and the Pentagon and Congress had lost power. There had been talk of an invasion of the United States. Martial law had been declared and there was a nighttime curfew. Police officers shot three hundred and forty people who didn't obey the curfew.

"Flights were grounded. The president was subsequently taken to an undisclosed location where he addressed the nation. Wall Street closed for two days."

"That's all correct," Nick said steadily.

"The country lost three trillion dollars, almost overnight."

"I heard that." Nick leaned forward, as did the others.

"Your genius friend, Felicity. Ask her. She'll have details."

Felicity looked serious, sad. "That's right. It's not a figure that has been officially published. The country was just coming out of the tail end of a recession. But three trillion dollars were siphoned out of our economy. As much as we lost in the decade of war with Iraq and Afghanistan. It's all over the darknet but the mainstream media hasn't talked about it at all."

"Nor will it ever. But that three trillion dollars went somewhere. What does the darknet say, Felicity?"

Felicity looked uneasy. Metal said that Felicity, being Russian, thrived on conspiracy theories but this seemed to spook even her. "Darknet says a lot of things."

"But the thing it says most?" the metallic voice inquired.

"Well…" Felicity shifted in her chair and looked unhappy. "A lot of money was sucked out of the economy due to the Massacre and that money had to go somewhere, as you said."

"Yes. Does the darknet say where?"

"A handful of offshores."

"A handful of offshores suddenly gains three trillion dollars. And no one notices?"

Felicity's mouth set as her fingers blurred over the keyboard. "Here's who noticed. I'm sending you a list of websites naming the companies. But no one in the mainstream media even touched this." She huffed out a breath. "Like after 9/11. Like the collapse in 2008. No one talks about it except the conspiracy crazies."

"Not so crazy after all."

"No. So you seem to know a lot about this, too." Felicity glanced at Nick. "And if you want someone squeaky-clean from the FBI that means you don't trust the CIA, even if international terrorism is their thing."

There was a long silence.

Joe leaned forward. "Are you CIA?"

Another long silence. Then: *"Not anymore."*

The hairs on the back of Joe's neck rose. "You contacted me. About Isabel. What does Isabel have to do with this? Are you contacting the survivors?"

"Not all of them."

Goddamn. Isabel was in the middle of something really fucking serious. "Is there, is there a chance that someone from the *CIA* could be involved in this?"

Of course not. The CIA was full of liars and cheats—that was their bread and butter. But traitors? No.

"*Yes,*" the voice answered and Joe looked at Senior, Metal and Jacko in turn. They all looked grim.

Joe's hands were balled into fists. "Who?" Who in the CIA could turn traitor like this? "Not the entire agency, obviously. How many people do you think are involved? And can't they be reported?"

"I don't know how many people are involved. Probably not many, four or five I think. But they are stra-

tegically placed. And those who ask questions of the wrong guys end up dead."

A shudder went through Joe. He glanced at the corner where Isabel and Lauren were working hard on the image she saw in her nightmares. "No one is touching Isabel."

"No. Keep her alive."

Fuck yeah, he was keeping Isabel alive.

Nick shouldered Joe aside. "If any American citizens were involved in the Massacre, they're going down. Whoever is involved is guilty of high treason."

"And mass murder."

Joe was a warrior. He'd been in battle. He'd killed. But he had never encountered anything like this before. *From his own countrymen.* It was hard to wrap his head around this. Afghan warlords behaved like this, not members of the US government.

"Why?" His voice came out hoarse but no one seemed to notice. He felt rattled like never before. He knew the crazies out there. He'd fought them far away from the homeland never thinking that pure random evil on that scale could happen here.

"Money, for one," the metallic voice answered.

So—not pure random evil. This was worse.

"As Felicity said, those three trillion dollars went somewhere. Check what I'm sending."

On Joe's laptop files started appearing, data streams flowing vertically like something out of *The Matrix.*

"Stop," Felicity said, typing furiously. She picked up her laptop and showed her monitor to Joe's monitor. For a second it was like SkyNet had taken over the world and the monitors were talking to each other. "Send the info here. I'm showing you the IP. Joe's computer can't handle the data, mine can."

The men in the room looked at Joe to see if he'd taken offense. He hadn't. It wasn't like Felicity was challenging his manhood or his dick size. And anyway, hers *was* bigger than his.

The data stopped immediately on Joe's monitor and after a few seconds began flowing into Felicity's computer. It flowed like a curtain and as Felicity did her thing, the data started morphing into different patterns, sliding, forming shapes then flowing apart.

After ten minutes. Felicity froze her screen and lifted her fingers from the keyboard.

"Okay," she said. "Ex-CIA guy, are you still with us?"

"Oh yeah," the metallic voice answered.

Felicity shot them all a glance. "You guys ready for this?"

Isabel and Lauren were lost in their world in the corner but Joe's guys were all ready and waiting.

Felicity drew in a deep breath, let it out slowly. "So those three trillion dollars fled the country. And as you all would have noticed if this weren't such an incredibly well-run company—" she shot a quick glance at the Senior, "—you'd know how impoverished this country is now. Or perhaps you know it already. We had just begun climbing out of the post-2008 hole when the Massacre struck. Since the Massacre we've lost over two million jobs, unemployment is at its highest level since the Depression and the stock market has lost two thousand points. It's like the Massacre sucked out the economic backbone of the country, besides scaring the shit out of everybody. The darknet hasn't managed to actually trace the money that was lost, but this information is new.

"These tables—" she gestured to her monitor, "—courtesy of a former hedge fund manager via ex-CIA guy, show sudden spikes in income and asset creation of a number of offshore funds and tax haven banks. Ordinarily it would be impossible to figure out who the people behind those funds and banks are but we have a treasure trove of info in these charts. I had to data-dive and do some massive number crunching to start to understand who profited from the Massacre but we have some preliminary results."

Everyone leaned forward. Joe was sure that Metal Voice was leaning forward, too.

Felicity gave a dramatic pause.

"Well?" Joe nudged her shoulder. Ordinarily Metal wouldn't let him get away with that, nor would any of the other ASI guys because Felicity was untouchable, but they were burning to know, too.

"This doesn't make me happy," Felicity said. "Usually when I crack a difficult database the sheer challenge is enough to make me smile, but this doesn't make me smile at all. Not when you think how many people died in the Massacre. Not when you think how many people have lost their homes, their businesses, their jobs. How many people's lives have been ruined."

Metal put his hand on her shoulder and she reached up to put her pretty hand over his, never taking her eyes from the monitor.

"The best way to tell you is to show you." At each step, Felicity clicked a key, and a different screenshot came up. "That initial flow of data was several terabytes of bank account data and stock exchange movements and hedge fund quotations. The stock exchange now is run by quants running algorithms that operate with split-second timing and there are several million exchanges done every second of the day. It is almost unquantifiable. Almost."

The screen started slowing. Was less a flow and more a series of data sheets. The data sheets had elements highlighted and the highlighted elements were then put on another set of pages.

"I can go over this step-by-step if anyone wants, but my system analyzed the funds and bank accounts and they were all shell companies. But digging down there were a few names that jumped out. First of all, the top earner was the PRC."

Joe let out his breath slowly. The People's Republic of China was behind the Massacre? If this news got out, it would mean war. A big, big war that would dwarf anything that had happened in Iraq and Afghanistan, which had been limited wars. This would be a war fought on land, sea and air, the US against a billion and a half people and a military of over seven million people, including reservists. A war with a nuclear power that also had a fleet of submarines with nuclear warheads that could cross the Pacific. A cold shudder ran down his spine.

"But there were also individuals who earned big. And the one who earned the most—several billion dollars in fact—is a man who is very well-connected." She glanced up at Metal, then at Joe. "And he was on the Senate Intelligence Committee, too, so our ex-CIA guy is right to stay off the radar."

The screen was coalescing, thousands of lines scrolling down, slowing, until one name was on the screen.

Joe exhaled again. This was worse than anything anyone could have imagined because the name was a man who was supposed to have been Alex Delvaux's vice president. Hector Blake.

A cry came from the corner and Joe turned, goose bumps rising on his skin. Isabel. That was a cry of pain and shock. He whirled ready to run to her, reaching for the gun in his shoulder holster, ready to leap and throw his body over hers because Isabel in danger was his worst nightmare…

But she wasn't hurt, no one was attacking her. She stood and turned to him, her face utterly white. She swayed and he didn't even feel his feet as he shot across the room to her, putting his arm around her, not as a sign of affection but to hold her up.

Lauren was looking up at them, white-faced too. Jacko was by her side in a second.

"The man, Joe. The man in my dreams. The monster of the Massacre." Isabel pointed with a shaking hand at the drawing Lauren had made.

Joe looked at the drawing

"Hector Blake," she said. "Uncle Hector."

TEN

Isabel couldn't have done it without Lauren.

"I'm not very visual," she apologized when they sat down in a corner. "I never have been. Unless it's about food, I'm not very observant."

Lauren smiled and patted her hand. "My dear, who cares about being visual when you can produce food like that? No one cares. But I *am* visual so let's see if we can do something here. You want that, don't you?"

"Oh, God, yes!" Isabel said. A pang of anxiety pulsed in her chest. "More than anything. This man is in my nightmares, night after night after night. People don't usually repeat their dreams. I've done a lot of reading up on it. A repeat dream is rare and is always anchored in reality in some way. So this man, this man I call the Monster, somehow exists in some way. Even though I don't recognize his face and I never remember it when I wake up."

Lauren set herself up—a big pad over her knees, several different types of pencils, erasers, charcoal sticks. The tools of her trade just as knives and wooden spoons and pans were Isabel's. "That's where I come in. The human face is infinitely variable. Seven and a half billion people in the world and, except for twins, no two faces are alike. But there are also only so many variables. Face shape, cheekbone and chin shape, eyes, nose, mouth. So this is going to be a collaborative experience. You talk, and I listen. I've got a big pad because we're going to strike out a lot. That's the nature of the exercise. We'll get a lot of things wrong before getting them right."

"Like kissing a lot of frogs before finding—"

"A Joe?" Lauren asked, then laughed at the face she made. "Don't be embarrassed. Joe's worth kissing a lot of frogs for. He's a really good guy."

"Yes." Isabel sighed. "He is. In a way, he's the reason I'm doing this, trying to exorcise a face I see in my nightmares. I long to get all of this out of my system because he deserves a sane, whole woman. Right now I'm a mess."

Lauren was testing the consistency of the pencils on the top left-hand corner. "Don't worry about it," she said absently, cocking her head as she studied the results. "Joe will take you any way he can get you. He's crazy about you. Has been for months, I hear."

Isabel's eyes opened wide. When she'd arrived she'd been a massive wreck. "Really?"

Lauren looked up, studied her face. "You didn't know? We knew the week you moved in that something big was going on with Joe."

"He didn't make a move. He didn't say anything to me. Most guys—" She stopped for a second because she didn't want to sound boastful. But then Lauren was a beautiful woman. She'd have been hit on a billion times in her life. No one hit on Lauren *now*, not with big, bad Jacko glowering by her side, but before Jacko they must have, surely. She knew what that was like. Guys who were attracted usually weren't shy about saying so or doing something about it.

"He was in very bad shape," Lauren said, her voice

gentle. "You might not have noticed because he did his best to hide it, but Joe wasn't anywhere close to recovery when you moved in. He'd only just begun putting himself back together. Jacko told me Joe said he didn't have anything to offer a woman until he was in better shape. He had a good job right here at ASI but he fought them hard because he thought he didn't deserve the job and the salary until he could work as hard as everyone else. Jacko says Joe didn't dare make a move on you. But surely you noticed that your garden was in fabulous shape, he'd drive you anywhere if so much as a drop of rain fell and that your house was in a great state of repair."

"Yes, but—" Isabel's head whirled. And she felt ashamed. Joe hadn't wanted to make a play for her until he had more to offer? "Didn't he see what shape I was in?" She met Lauren's eyes, brimming with sympathy. "You have no idea what I was like. My head would spin for no reason and I had to sit down if I didn't want to faint. I spooked at loud noises, I didn't sleep at night but then sleepwalked my way through the day. I was constantly exhausted."

"You had and probably still have PTSD," Lauren said gently. "No one better than a soldier to understand that. They all saw horrible things in the war. And frankly, I don't think Joe cared that you were a mess. I think all he saw was that you're beautiful and fascinating." Lauren patted her hand.

Isabel felt like hanging her head. The first month or two she hadn't noticed much about Joe Harris other than the fact that he was an amazingly helpful neighbor and that she could count on him for just about anything. She'd been in a fog of grief and sadness. But Joe had had his own wounds that hadn't stopped him from helping her every way he could.

And while he had worked hard to put himself together, she'd just mourned and baked cookies.

"I want to be better," she said to Lauren. "I want to get myself together physically and mentally. I don't want Joe to consider me a basket case. I need to move on if we're to have a hope of being a couple."

Lauren straightened and held a draftsman's pencil over the paper. "I think we can make a good start if we can nail this face you see in your nightmares. That would be a really good first step."

It would.

Isabel struggled at first. She couldn't pin down the features. And when she did, a wave of dread washed over her. He was a creature of her nightmares but the horror bled into the daytime. She had to fight not to wipe him out of her mind.

Lauren walked her through it. "Shape of face?"

Just thinking of that shadowy form with darkness for eyes made her shiver. "What?"

"What was the shape of his face?"

Lauren's hand flew over the paper. Twelve face shapes appeared. "So, these are the basic shapes, barring major deformities. Which one?"

Without thinking, Isabel put a finger on one. "This shape." Long, narrow at the chin, broad in the temples. But she couldn't have described it. The face still danced just out of reach of her consciousness.

"Okay." Lauren lifted the sheet away and drew on a new one. "These are some shapes of a mouth." Full lips, thin lips, top lip fuller, bottom lip fuller, wide, narrow…

"Like that!" Isabel felt a pulse course through her

system, because those thin, narrow lips were exactly like those of the man in her nightmares. Again, she couldn't have verbalized it, but she recognized it.

On another sheet of paper, Lauren drew hair, once Isabel said that the man's hair was cropped short in an expensive cut and was salt and pepper. More salt than pepper.

Lauren fit the hair over the shape of the face Isabel had chosen and added the mouth. A prickle ran up her spine. They were getting there. And the man looked… she cocked her head. He looked somehow familiar.

Up to now she just thought the monster in her nightmares was some kind of composite representing the evil that had carried out the Massacre. Was the monster real?

"Nose," Lauren said, but before she could start drawing sample noses Isabel surprised herself.

"Long, narrow at the bridge, finely cut nostrils." Lauren looked up at her then her hands added…exactly the right nose.

Isabel couldn't breathe.

"Eyes?"

Isabel never saw the eyes in her nightmares but the answer came welling up from a dark place inside her.

"Deep-set, slightly uptilted." Though Lauren was drawing in black-and-white, she added, "Chocolate brown."

Because she knew who this was.

Something was cracking inside her, some carapace that had enveloped her since the Massacre. The cracking open *hurt.* Faster than she could follow, her brain was making connections, filling in the dots. Filling in the holes that had plagued her since that terrible day.

There was a connection between the monster in her

nightmares and the monsters that had taken away her life. All these months, her nightmares had been trying to talk to her and she'd been too scared to listen. She'd tucked them away in the back of her mind until they broke out of the walls.

Lauren's hand stopped moving and she turned her head this way and that, frowning at what her hand had created. "Doesn't he look..." She glanced up at Isabel. "Doesn't he look familiar?"

The walls had collapsed and the floods came. Isabel was frozen to the spot, head whirling. She felt dizzy and sick.

"Isabel?"

Lauren's voice was sharp with worry. She reached out to Isabel but Isabel stood up, swaying. The band around her chest grew tighter.

"Isabel, what's wrong?" Lauren put a hand on Isabel's shoulder.

"Hector Blake." Isabel's voice was low and raw. The words hurt.

"What?" Lauren glanced down at the drawing she'd made and blinked. "Oh. Yes. Wow. I've seen him on TV. It does look like him, doesn't it?"

But Isabel could barely hear Lauren above the buzzing in her head, so when she spoke, her voice was loud. The group huddled around Felicity's computer lifted their heads and looked at her.

"Hector Blake!" she shouted. "Uncle Hector."

Her head felt like it was splitting open.

Joe was right beside her. She hadn't even seen him cross the room. He opened his arms and she huddled against him because right now her skin wasn't enough to keep her together. She was shaking so hard she was going to fly apart in a million pieces.

Uncle Hector.

He'd always just…been there. Her parents had been social animals with hundreds of friends and she'd grown up surrounded by people, Uncle Hector included. He wasn't actually her blood uncle, but their families had been friends for generations and he'd grown up with her father.

She didn't really like him, never had. He'd always seemed so pompous and self-important, but then she didn't always like her parents' friends. She didn't have to. There were plenty of other people around to like.

She wasn't even too sure her dad liked him. Her mom certainly hadn't.

Hector Blake, Uncle Hector.

She was choking, shaking, trying to drag in air. Everyone was standing around her. Lauren and Felicity. Metal and Jacko and one of the two bosses. They were watching her as she fell apart.

No.

She stood straight, stepped back. Joe dropped his arms. He sensed she didn't want the support. She had to be strong here. When she was standing apart, she wrapped her own arms around herself because she was the only one who could support her. She was the only one who could do this.

Memories were flooding in, an unstoppable flow, that night now clear in her head, so clear it was as if she was reliving it.

"Hector Blake," she repeated, as if his name were some kind of horrible mantra. And she saw no surprise in anyone's eyes.

"Tell us, honey," Joe said.

"That night…" She stopped for a second, breathing heavily, breathing as if it was a job she had to do. No one shuffled their feet or coughed. No one betrayed any impatience whatsoever. They wanted to hear what she had to say and they were willing to wait for it, however long it took.

That gave her courage.

"It was about ten minutes to the time Dad was going to make his announcement. The evening looked completely spontaneous but three days of planning had gone into it, into the timing and what Dad was going to say. Everyone was excited. There was a lot of noise. People screaming, the piped-in music, it was like a wall of noise. But the planners knew that this would be the moment of maximum excitement before Dad made his announcement. And they knew there would be pandemonium when he finally threw his hat into the ring, officially. Dad's advisers were all smiling, really happy. I'd gone out a couple of times with one of Dad's press officers and I asked him if all this excitement was fake and he said no. He said a lot of people understood that they were on a trajectory that would take them straight to the Oval Office."

She'd shaken her head at that and decided then and there that there wouldn't be a third date. This thirst for power wasn't something she understood. She barely understood it in her own father, even though she knew that in him, it was mixed up with an idealistic sense of mission. For the aides and hangers-on of the new campaign, there was no mission, no ideals, just the whiff of power.

She met Joe's sober eyes, dark and steady. He was

with her as she stepped into the past, into an unimaginably painful and brutal past.

"All the family was up on the stage except for me and Jack. I think he'd gone to the bathroom. I had to take a call. My agent, calling from New York with an offer. I was talking to her, walking around the podium for an exit because we could barely hear each other, when—" She drew in a deep breath. This part was well-known. "When we were cut off. I was checking my cell, thinking to call her back and then all the lights went out. It was like someone had waved a magic wand and created darkness."

Her voice had gone up in a tremolo. She clenched her teeth, getting herself back under control. Or at least as much control as she could manage.

"But there were candles on the front tables, an array of them. They were going to dim the lights and they'd threaded the floral arrangements with tea lights. My mom insisted because she loves—" Isabel's eyes widened in horror. Her mom didn't love candles anymore. Her mom was in the cold, cold ground. Together with her father and three brothers. Her throat spasmed and she had to cough to loosen it. "*Loved.* My mom loved candles. There were also big wax bowls with several tea lights inside, surrounded by the floral arrangements. Beautiful. But more than that, they shed light."

An eerie light, she remembered. Like footlights in theaters in the nineteenth century, lighting faces from the bottom, leaving features indistinct. Leaving the eyes in shadow.

And at the same time the world came to an end.

"There were—there were screams from all around the room. And a ripping sound."

"AK-47s," Joe murmured.

"Guns, yes," Isabel said. "Machine guns. Those were in my dreams. There were men everywhere, it seemed. I couldn't count them. Dressed in black, with black ski masks and black goggles. What you said was night vision gear. Outside the front tables which were lit by the candles, it was pitch-black. So they could see in the dark and we couldn't."

Her heart burned. Such a horrible cowardly thing. Shooting innocent people in the dark when they could see! Not even allowing for the possibility of anyone defending themselves, innocent unarmed people in the dark, against armed men who could see. "People were screaming in the dark, scrambling to get out of the way, and then they started falling. One masked terrorist planted himself on the other side of the tables with candles and opened fire on the podium. As if he were shooting ducks in a gallery in the county fair. Left to right." She closed her eyes but the scene she'd repressed for months was painted on the inside of her eyeballs. Her memory had come roaring back to life and it was exactly as if she was living it again. "My mom, my kid brothers. Mowed down." She shook.

Joe put his arm around her and bent low to her ear. "Honey, you don't have to—"

Joe meant well but he was wrong. Isabel pushed away. "Oh, but I do, I do. Teddy—a bullet shattered his head. He dropped to the floor and there was only mist spattering my mom and Rob. Mom had already been shot but she was still on her feet. She was turning to put herself between the shooter and my father and Rob but the shooter got her in the back."

How could the memory have been wiped? How could

she have possibly forgotten it? Dead people on the podium, her wounded mother, blood pouring from a shoulder onto her pretty cream-colored suit, turning with her arms wide, wanting to catch her kid brother except the only thing she caught was a bullet.

"It sometimes took two bullets, but the guns killed everyone. Methodically, coldly. The gunman was making his way across the podium. Dad was struggling with—with Hector. Dad was trying to get to Mom and my brothers but Hector was holding him. Wait."

Isabel held up a finger and stared into the distance. No one in the room moved. No one even breathed.

She ran through the sequence in her head. She almost didn't believe herself, but the events rang true somewhere deep inside her.

"This is what happened. The gunman was picking off the people on the podium, Dad was trying to get to Mom and the boys but Hector was holding him. At that point, another gunman shot the man next to me and he fell on top of me. He was a big man, knocked the breath out of me. The gunman killed the man standing next to Hector. Cyrus Lowry, the former secretary of state. Dad went to school with him. Cyrus fell, the gunman pivoted…" Isabel closed her eyes, saw everything. "Hector was standing next to Cyrus. The gunman all of a sudden pulled his machine gun…*up*."

"Like he didn't want to shoot Blake?" Joe asked.

"Exactly. Exactly as if he had orders not to shoot Hector. And the two exchanged glances. Both nodded. Then the gunman, oh, God!" She reached for Joe's hand, found it. "The gunman brings his gun down, aims and kills Dad. Hector was spared. Deliberately."

Silence.

"So Blake was last man standing on the podium." Joe's voice was harsh. Isabel looked around at her little audience. The women looked shocked, pale. The men looked grim, as if unsurprised at this example of human wickedness.

"Yes. And he turned away, but before he did, he—"

"What, Isabel?" Lauren asked softly. She still held the portrait of an eminently recognizable Hector Blake between two fingers.

"He saw me. I was on the ground, half-crushed by this man, but I was able to lift my head. We were both in the small circle of light thrown by the candles, the rest of the huge hall black and filled with bloody corpses. And…and he *saw* me. Saw me watching him just as he was turning away. There was still a huge amount of noise. The machine guns were still firing and, though the moans and screams had died down a lot, there was still screaming. So Hector gestured to the man who'd killed everyone on the podium to catch his attention and then pointed at me on the floor. I imagine what he wanted wasn't immediately apparent because the gunman's head was swiveling, trying to see what Hector wanted. And Hector's face tightened…and I have never seen that expression on a man's face before. Pure malevolent evil."

Joe nodded. Douglas and Metal and Jacko were listening, looking grim. They were warriors. They'd seen pure malevolent evil before. They knew what she was talking about.

"The gunman is still looking. He doesn't see me, doesn't see that I am alive. So Hector checks his watch and makes this gesture—" She twirled her index finger in the air. "And Hector and the gunman run out the door behind the podium. I was drowning in blood and I was trying to get out from under this dead body and there was an explosion and…everything went black. The next thing I knew it was ten days later and I had a concussion that was twelve on the Glasgow Coma Scale. And I'd lost all memory of that night until—until now."

"What do we do now, Mystery Man?" Felicity asked in a loud voice.

Mystery Man?

"Depends," a metallic voice answered. It was one of those anonymized voices, like kidnappers had in the movies. Had someone been kidnapped? Isabel looked around. Had the voice come from Felicity's computer?

True, Felicity's computer was magical but now it had developed into a person?

"Is someone inside your computer, Felicity?"

"Sort of." Felicity didn't smile. Usually any mention of the magical wizard-like properties of her computer made her smile, but she wasn't smiling. She looked deflated and sad. "An ex-CIA guy who is investigating the Massacre."

"Can he see us?"

Felicity nodded.

Isabel walked over and addressed the monitor directly. Who knew who was on the other end? Former CIA. Then he'd have known Hector. "Are you investigating the Massacre undercover? Not officially?"

"Not officially no."

But unofficially, yes. And presumably Mr. Former CIA knew a lot about what actually happened. So Isabel had to ask the question. And the answer would divide her life into two. She almost wanted to cling to her precarious mental state. Poor Isabel, who was blown up and can hardly stand, what does she know?

Because if she was right…if she was right…

"This is the guy who told me to protect you," Joe said.

Isabel faced the monitor. "Do I know you? What am I to you?"

"You're one of the very few survivors of the Massacre. And the only one close to the podium to survive, except for Hector Blake, who in his official statement during the Senate inquest says that he was knocked out and came to after the explosion. He was found with a few cuts and scrapes."

Isabel hadn't been called to the Senate inquest. She'd barely just woken from her coma and would have been unable to testify to anything. She hadn't even been asked.

So. This guy in Felicity's computer seemed to know a lot. She'd spent so many months in which her memory was a blur. In which putting one foot in front of the other was painful and hard. In which merely surviving seemed to be the most that she could hope for.

These sudden memories were sharp, almost too sharp. She had to ask.

"So tell me. Am I—am I crazy? Or do I remember what really happened? Is my memory reliable?"

"Your memory is reliable, Isabel."

Isabel stepped back a moment, in shock, and Joe was right there. He had her back in every way there was. She leaned back for a moment, leaned into that wall of strength, then straightened. Whatever happened from now on in had to depend on *her* strength, not Joe's.

"Do you have any idea why on earth Uncle Hector—Hector—would be involved in this?"

Everyone exchanged glances. "What?"

"Well, honey," Joe said gently. "We aren't in his head. So we don't know if that was the motive. But the side effect of the Massacre was that three trillion dollars were drained from the United States into holding companies owned by Chinese companies. And that Hector Blake personally gained over a billion dollars. Which is a big motivator."

A hot wind blew through Isabel, scorching and scouring so hard it felt like her skin was removed. It blew away all her insecurities and anxiety. It blew away the past six months and it blew away all her fears.

She hardly recognized her own voice, hoarse and raw. "Do you mean to tell me that Hector Blake killed my family, orchestrated the Massacre…*for money?*"

Joe shifted on his feet, watching her carefully. "It looks like—"

"For money," the mechanical voice said. *"But maybe this is also part of a larger plan to destabilize the US economy. Or even destabilize the country."*

Isabel barely heard the mechanical voice. Her mother, father, three brothers. Aunts, uncles, cousins. Hundreds and hundreds of innocent people. *Murdered. Murdered for money.*

She had no idea she could feel such rage.

Isabel pulled her cell phone out of her purse and started scrolling furiously.

Without looking up she could feel the eyes of everyone on her. "What?" Damn, where was that number? Her fingers were trembling, making the delicate screen jump around.

"Who are you calling, Isabel?" Joe asked. When she didn't answer, he put his hand on her shoulder. She shrugged it off. "Who?"

Aha! There it was! "I'm calling that son of a bitch Hector Blake and I'm going to accuse him of mass murder. And I am going to bring that bastard down!"

"Stop her!" The mechanical voice said, urgency even in the artificial tone, just as Joe snatched her phone from her hands.

Isabel turned to him, fury in her voice. "Give that to me!"

Joe's face was sad but firm. "Sorry, honey. Ask me anything else and I'll give it to you, but not this."

She slapped her hand against his chest, feeling hard muscle. She hadn't hurt him, but she wanted to. She wanted to strike and scream and hurt. "Give me that phone!"

He was holding it away from her and if she knew anything at all, it was that she had no chance of grabbing it, none at all. He was bigger than her, taller than her, stronger than her.

The way of the world. The biggest guys won.

Tears burned in her eyes but she refused to shed them. She would never cry again. She looked at everyone in the room, looked directly in their eyes, stared at the monitor where this ghost man resided, then looked Joe squarely in the face.

"You're not going to let him get away with this!" She looked around. "All of you. Hear me, hear what I'm saying. We have to do something. I'm going to call every single reporter I know, and I know a lot of them, including Summer Redding, who runs the political blog *Area 8*. She's not afraid of anything, and neither am I!"

Joe's face was tight, nostrils wide, white lines around his mouth. He wasn't happy keeping her phone from her. But he was doing it.

"Goddamn it, Joe!"

He just shook his head. *Not giving it to you, sorry.*

Isabel rounded on Metal. "Joe told me your story, Metal. How you lost your whole family on 9/11, father and brothers. And your mother dying of a broken heart a week later. Your entire family, wiped out. What would you do if you could find the men who did it? Actually come face-to-face with them? What would you do?"

"I'd rip their hearts out," Metal answered.

"And I will rip Hector Blake's heart right out of his chest," she replied, meaning every single word.

Metal let out an audible breath. He was with her.

"Honey, listen—" Joe began.

"If you go to the press now, if you confront Hector Blake without a plan, you are letting him win," the metallic voice from the monitor interrupted.

Isabel twirled. "What do you mean?"

"I think that the Massacre was just the opening salvo of a bigger campaign. Hector Blake has enormous resources. If you face him alone, you will lose. And your testimony will be lost, too. And we will lose any advantage we have. Right now Blake has no clue anyone is on to him."

Strong fingers cupped her chin. Joe turned her head toward him. "He's right, honey. We need to go after him carefully. We don't know where he has allies. And if he's got allies in the CIA, we could end up incarcerated, at a black site or dead."

Isabel stared him in the eyes. "He cannot be allowed

to get away with this." She looked around. "He cannot be allowed to get away with this," she repeated.

Her bedrock bottom line.

"No, he cannot be allowed to get away with this," the metallic voice answered. It was really hard to read emotion into the altered voice, created by software, but somehow an underlying determination came through.

"Do you have any hard evidence to bring him to the authorities' attention?" she asked the computer. She gestured with her thumb to Nick. "I think we can count on Nick to push this through the FBI. It's the country's top law enforcement agency. If you've got something, they can run with it."

"Bet your ass," Nick growled. "If the Massacre was planned and carried out by Americans, they are going down. I won't rest, none of us in the Bureau will rest, until justice is done."

"Blake has covered his tracks well."

"If you've found something, others can, as well."

"Mainly what I have is a money trail. Which could disappear not overnight, but in the course of two minutes."

"That's true," Felicity said. "I can almost guarantee that there will be another set of anonymous accounts where Blake can drain his money and pour it into them. And he can do it fast. A hint of the fact that someone is on to him, and he'll be gone and it will take months to find him. As a matter of fact, with the right software and with someone who knows what he's doing, or someone who can hire someone who knows what they're doing, he could create a shell game, keep the money moving from account to account so that you might know where the money has been but you never know where the money is going to be. So you'll never nail him."

Just the thought of Hector moving his blood money around and getting away with mass murder made her sick. Made her shake with rage, as if every cell in her body were alive with fire. And yet if she knew one thing about Hector, she knew he was smart. If Felicity said that it was possible to keep his money moving, then it was on the move.

"He needs to confess," she said.

"Riiight." Jacko's deep voice chimed in full of sarcasm. "All we have to do is ask him. Nicely. And he'll spill the beans on everything."

"*We* won't ask him," Isabel said. As she spoke, certainty settled in her bones. She could do this and she was going to do this. "I will."

"The fuck you will," Joe said immediately. "You're staying a continent away from this guy. He killed hundreds of people. He's not going to stop at killing you. He's already tried anyway."

"Joe is right," Mystery Man said. *"Stay out of this, Isabel."*

Isabel's spine shot up straight as if someone had given her a shot of adrenaline. "Excuse me? Because you all have done such a good job of catching him, exposing him. Look at you, you don't dare use the CIA and you have to call the FBI in surreptitiously. And Nick is here as a simple citizen, not representing the Bureau. You're all scared to death that you are going to stumble on a mole or that he will be warned. Has anyone thought that he was going to run for the presidency as my father's political heir? And he could have won, too. We could have had a mass murderer and traitor as our president! Has anyone thought of that?"

"Every day," the voice said. *"Every fucking day."*

"We have to stop him. Right now. Because if he is part of a conspiracy, they are planning something else. Or else he's going to be happy with his billion dollars and is going to disappear to a Thai island."

"We're going to stop him," Nick said. "Guaranteed."

She whirled on him. "You are one man. You're here alone without the force of the Bureau behind you. I know Joe and his friends called you because that guy—" she pointed a shaking finger at Felicity's laptop, "—wanted someone from the FBI and Joe knows you're one of the good guys, like he is. Like everyone here is. But you are part of a huge security machine that involves congressional oversight. I've been around politicians all my life and they talk. They love to talk. Can you guarantee that a juicy bit of news that the man who was supposed to be the next vice president before the Massacre, a possible presidential contender, was behind the Washington Massacre will stay secret? Can you guarantee that?"

"Yes," Nick said. "Absolutely."

Isabel got right up into his face. Nick didn't flinch or back down. "I don't believe you. People talk and Hector is very plugged into the national security apparatus. How are you going to investigate something this big without tipping him off? He'll be gone at the first whiff of an investigation. I wish I could just take a gun and kill him. He's getting away with mass murder and we can't stop him! What can we do?"

Silence. Utter, complete silence.

"There might be a way," the robot voice said finally.

"I DON'T LIKE IT," Joe said, crossing his arms. He put a lot of emphasis in his voice, making it deep, using his command voice. The one that had young recruits flinching. Because no way was Isabel doing this.

"I like it," Isabel said. "Let's do it."

Joe heart beat painfully in his chest. He wanted to put his foot down, hard. He wanted to stop this craziness. Isabel was straining at the bit and that was dangerous for Navy SEALs who trained day in, day out for years for missions, let alone a beautiful young woman whose most dangerous assignment was wielding sharp knives in the kitchen.

But there was no stopping her.

That was another reason his heart was hammering. This was an Isabel he'd never seen before. Not the gentle, wounded, grieving woman who made him want to wrap himself around her and never let go.

No, this woman was electric, sparks flying off her. Eyes wide, shiny, a flush under that ivory skin. Even her hair crackled. She walked up and down as CIA guy and the ASI team discussed the outrageous plan as if it was in any way feasible.

Which it wasn't.

She would do this over his dead body.

The only thing was—it looked like she was willing to do just that. Step right over his stroked-out body as if he was invisible and carry out the plan to get Hector Blake, because there was no stopping her.

"Let's go through this again," the Senior said. He was good at strategizing, which was fortunate because though Joe was good at strategizing, too, right now his brain was MIA. Whatever electricity had fired Isabel up had been leeched from him because it felt like his very bones were weak. Like someone had zapped him.

It was terror like he'd never felt before. Because they were planning on using Isabel as fucking *bait.* Bait for the man responsible for the Massacre. And she was up for it, oh, yeah. No stopping her, in fact. Joe had tried, he really had, but Isabel wasn't even listening to him.

The plan was fairly simple so Joe absorbed it through his skin because his head wasn't working right. It was filled with images of Isabel shot, Isabel knifed, Isabel dead. Fucking Blake finishing off the job he'd started in Washington.

And then someone said something that was like a cattle prod. "Fuck no," he said. "I'm going to be right beside her."

Because someone had talked about the ASI guys—and that included him—being in the back and hidden behind bushes and there was no way. Just—no way.

Isabel looked at him impatiently, as if he was a few bricks shy of a load. "The only way this is going to work is if he thinks I'm alone. I mean cosmically alone. I know him down to the ground and if there's one thing he is, it's vain. I can get him to talk but he would only talk to me. To Isabel Delvaux, victim. The only survivor of a family he slaughtered. If I play it right—and I will—he's going to want to brag. How clever he was, how he deceived us all. How no one will ever believe me."

"No one will believe you because you'll be dead." Joe looked everyone in the eye, cool and calm, though his back was covered in sweat. "This is not gonna happen."

It was as if he hadn't spoken.

"Okay," Senior said. "Let's go through this again. From the top." He pointed a long finger at Isabel.

She nodded briskly, made an imaginary phone out of her hand. "I call him. I call Uncle Hector. The man my father grew up with, who has been a family friend forever. I've called him Uncle Hector since I learned to speak. All of that will be in my voice and my demeanor. Utter trust and faith in a man I've known all my life. So I call him and I'm puzzled. I'm turning to him because I don't have a father or a mother anymore and my big brother is dead."

Her eyes narrowed and her lips tightened and something fierce passed over her face. She made a hand phone again. "So who else would I turn to but the man who had been like a father to me all my life? My dear Uncle Hector. So, Uncle Hector—you know what? I've been having dreams, terrible dreams. Of that night. Yes, I'd lost my memory, isn't that sad. But what if—what if my memory is coming back, Uncle Hector? Because I see flashes of things and somehow—isn't this crazy?—somehow you are always in my dreams. What do you think that means? What do I do?"

Isabel stopped for a moment, looked around. Everyone but Joe was nodding. Were they all fucking *nuts?*

"He's not going to go for that! He's—"

Isabel's voice overrode him. "So I suggest that maybe we should meet, talk it over. I mean I know you're a busy man, Uncle Hector, but I really need to talk to you. What? Come to Washington? I don't know… I'm not feeling well these days. It's a long trip. Do you think you could…you could? Oh great. Whenever you can make it. Yes—thanks so much, Uncle Hector. You've always been there for me."

"After which—" Senior began.

"After which I call him about an hour before our appointment. There's been a leak in the water mains, the house is a mess. Can we meet downtown in a nice place called Three Windows? And I go in all wired up."

"With me," Joe said. "You go in with me."

She didn't even look at him. "You're going to be with the others, Joe. All of you guys will be within a minute's reach."

Joe's body hairs still hadn't settled. Jacko knew the owner of Three Windows. They belonged to a biker club together. Which was weird because Three Windows was definitely upscale and trendy. Whatever. The owner was a former marine and was going to give them whatever they needed. Jacko was on the phone with him for half an hour, not telling exactly what the op was, but his marine buddy didn't need to know. He'd offered his entire restaurant to them without asking questions.

"And we're gonna be armed."

"Well, of course." Isabel deigned to look at him for a split second. "Because I'm secretly hoping that you'll all shoot him full of holes. But I do understand that might create legal problems for you all, killing a man who could have been president. So we won't kill him, we'll just ruin him."

"That's my job," Nick said grimly. "With any luck, he'll never see the light of day again after tomorrow."

"I would love it if he never saw the light of day again because he was in a box in the ground, but I'll take what I can get." Isabel consulted a notepad. She'd been listening very carefully as the plan took shape. "So, I'm wired up, the flowers on the table will be bugged, my earrings will be bugged, when they bring the Brie hamburger the French fries will be bugged. The entire place will have a billion hidden video cameras. The door will be surreptitiously turned into an invisible metal detector that gives a silent signal to—" The phone became a gun that Isabel pointed at Felicity. "You. You'll be in a back room coordinating all the electronics."

Felicity nodded. "Count on it. Every image will be crisp and all the sound will be crystal clear. Every word the man says will feature large in court. The jurors won't have any trouble understanding every word that is spoken."

"You guys." Isabel looked at them all, then took his hand. "And you, Joe. You'll be absolutely invisible until dear Uncle Hector confesses. That's my job. To goad him until he spills his guts."

Joe felt his own guts roil. "There, you see? That's not a good idea. To goad a guy who's responsible for the deaths of hundreds of people. Can't you all see that?" He turned to people he'd considered his friends, people who had turned insane.

"We can," Metal said gently. "But we can't let this guy get away with murder."

"So let Nick take care of this! That's what he does, goddamn it! Nick—" He rounded on his FBI buddy. "You tell them."

Nick rubbed the back of his neck. "Well, that's the thing. There isn't any hard evidence to prove his guilt. Our friend from the CIA has said as much. Blake has covered his tracks and is still covering his tracks beautifully. The instant evidence forms, the money disappears again. And I tell you, there's no love lost for the CIA in the Bureau but we're part of the game, as well. We can't go tossing around accusations about moles in the CIA and the man who might have been president. If we're wrong we'll lose face, lose power."

Nick held up a big hand as Isabel opened her mouth. "I'm sorry, Isabel, but that's just the way power rolls. The big guys have an almost automatic get-out-of-jail-free card. You have to have some powerful proof to get at them. And though Sanders—" the current head of the FBI, "—hates Blake, he'll stand by him. Because power at the top stays at the top and that's one of the ways it does that. They don't attack each other. And before you say anything, I'm not protecting my career. To put the man responsible for the Washington Massacre behind bars, I'd trash my career in a heartbeat."

"You'd always have a job here," Senior said in his gravelly voice.

"Thanks. Though it would entail working with these bozos here. But they're still better than most of the Bureau pukes I have to deal with." He turned to the computer monitor. "So. Ex-CIA puke, do you have any evidence that would stand up in court? Because Blake would lawyer up fast with the best mouthpiece money can buy. They'd line up to defend him in a high-profile trial. Did you follow the laws of discovery in tracking down Blake?"

"No. I know he's guilty but cannot prove it in a court of law."

"There you have it," Isabel said. "So when do I call? When do we start this?"

"Tomorrow," Joe said.

"Right now," Isabel said and picked up the phone and scrolled through her contacts again.

"It's 8:00 p.m.," Joe protested.

"That makes it only 11:00 p.m. in Washington. Hector is a night owl."

Before Joe could stop her, she'd pressed the number, on speed dial. Everyone could hear the phone ringing, hear when someone picked up.

And Isabel's body language changed instantly.

She'd been standing ramrod straight, eyes flashing, face tight. The instant Blake picked up, she seemed to lose a couple of inches in height. She slumped, her face grew soft and sad. Her hand trembled. Her voice trembled.

"Uncle Hector?" she sounded apprehensive, frightened. "It's Isabel." She sighed. "No, I'm still in Portland. You knew I moved over here, right? Yeah." She listened. "Not too great, Uncle Hector, to tell you the truth. I can't seem to move on. And I'm having…" She made an audible swallow. "I'm having nightmares, Uncle Hector. Terrible nightmares. Sleeping pills don't help, alcohol doesn't help, nothing helps. I keep having this same nightmare over and over and somehow *you're* in them. Always. It's so…so *horrible*."

She started breathing heavily. Tears were in her voice. Joe had to check to make sure she wasn't really crying. Her cheeks were bone-dry, but you'd swear she was crying. "I don't know what to do, who to turn to." A long sigh. Her face radiated sadness. She perked up. "Oh, God *really*? You can? When? Tomorrow? Oh, thank you, Uncle Hector, you have no idea what that means to me. I'll text you my address. Thank you." Her voice throbbed with gratitude. "I'm looking forward to it. Bye."

She pressed End and straightened up, the lost look gone, voice strong, staring into the phone screen as if she was seeing him. "I'm looking forward to tearing your heart out and eating it, you scum-sucking son of a bitch." She looked up. "We're taking that fucker *down.*"

The new Isabel rode back with him in his SUV. It was icy, so Joe had to pay a little attention to the driving, but most of him was focused on her. On the Isabel who wanted to eat Hector Blake's heart

Of course, Joe was down with that. Blake *was* an evil, scum-sucking douche bag, but Joe was used to being the one who planned revenge. It was all he'd done as a soldier. He'd joined as an eighteen-year-old right after 9/11, just like Metal. He hadn't lost his immediate family, like Metal had, but his country had been attacked and his country was his family.

So through all the harsh training that led to his acing BUD/S and surviving Hell Week and all the years of ops, he'd had one thought—revenge. He was going to get back at the fuckers who'd fucked with his country.

This was the very first time that he was contemplating revenge on a man, or men—because Blake couldn't do what he'd done without a team behind him—who were fellow citizens.

And he wasn't even the one who was going to exact revenge. Isabel was. He was merely backup. The muscle. It freaked him out every time he thought about it.

"Stop worrying so hard," Isabel said with a sidelong glance at him. "I can actually hear the worry vibes. It's distracting."

"Sorry. They come naturally."

"You're a navy SEAL. You guys aren't supposed to worry or feel anxious."

True. He'd never felt anxious when going out on an op. He and his team were as well trained and equipped as it was possible to be. They went out, got the job done and came back. Alive.

"I'm just backup this time. You'll be on the front lines. If that isn't crazy making, I don't know what is."

"I'll have you guys with me. All of you are former navy SEALs, even Nick. Felicity on the computer. What can go wrong?"

Joe's sweaty hands tightened on the steering wheel. "God. Don't say that! That's like the pretty young chick who goes down into the cellar alone in her baby doll nightgown when there's a serial killer on the loose. That's just inviting trouble."

"You think too much," she said. "Don't think and drive."

Joe shot her a glance then back to the road. Or rather, took his eyes off her enough to glance at the road. Because Isabel was an eye magnet. So beautiful it hurt and right now she was crackling with energy. What drove her was the thought of whacking a man, or at least putting him behind bars for the rest of her life, but what she made Joe think of was sex. Hot, sweaty sex. She looked almost aroused. High color, eyes gleaming, lips full and pouty with a pillowy look. Thank God she was wearing a down coat and he couldn't see her breasts because he'd take odds that her nipples were hard.

Or maybe that was wishful thinking because under his coat he was hard as a rock.

Can it, he told himself. No sex tonight. He would hold her and comfort her and give her courage. She also needed to sleep. She'd said she hadn't had a good night's sleep since the Massacre. Tomorrow Isabel was going to face a mass murderer. She was going to walk a dangerous tightrope and needed to be firing on all cylinders.

So sex was out tonight.

He clenched the steering wheel harder with wet palms because just thinking sex in the same context as Isabel made his dick kick in his pants. It was going to be hell holding Isabel all night with a massive woodie but he was a SEAL and SEALs were the ones who did the hard things.

His face twitched. Hard was not a word that should be in his head at this moment.

Was Isabel thinking about sex? Who knew what was in *her* head?

Joe swerved and parked his vehicle. Usually Isabel waited until he got out, rounded the vehicle and opened her door. It was still icy slick and she was often unsteady on her feet. Now, though, she was already halfway to her door by the time he got out. She punched in the code, had it read her thumbprint then just as the heavy steel door they'd put in snicked open she looked over her shoulder at him and the hair rose on the back of his neck.

The look she gave him was trouble. Pure sex, pure trouble. He leaped up the three steps in one bound, pushed the door open above her shoulder and ushered her in. He could hear his blood pulsing in his ears.

Isabel shoved him against the door, stepping forward until she was pressed against him. "Now," she said in a low voice that sent shivers up his spine.

Now.

Oh, God, yes.

Joe was holding her tightly, lost in her kiss, aware that his arms were full of…down coat. Her mouth was soft, warm, tongue licking his lips.

He lifted his mouth for a second. "Off."

Smart girl, she understood. Good thing, because he wasn't capable of full sentences. Gloves off, hands undoing the buttons of her coat, then unzipping his. Outer layers off. Now he could feel her shape, the long line of her back, the small waist, the rounded hips. He cupped her ass, lifting her up against his hard-on and she breathed out heavily and bit his lip.

An electric shock ran through him and now it wasn't just his dick that was hard. He was hard all over, as if his skin was too small to contain him. Muscles tense, solid as rock.

"Clothes," Isabel said when he lifted his mouth from her to get a better slant. "Now."

"God, yeah," Joe muttered.

It became a contest to see who could get naked first. He could hardly tell whose hands were doing what because all the blood in his head had gone straight to his dick.

His shirt, her sweater. Pants, jeans.

Something ripped. He didn't give a fuck because suddenly his hands were full of warm soft smooth woman, naked breasts pressed against his chest, soft belly against his. He smoothed his hand over her backside, pressed her against him. The lips of her sex opened over him and he rubbed himself against her, up and down, feeling her warm and wet.

It was insanely pleasurable but it wasn't enough.

Joe picked her up, turned her around and placed her against the closed door, hoping he wasn't slamming her because a drumbeat of urgency was throbbing inside him and he couldn't think much beyond that.

He hitched her up. "Put your legs around my waist,"

he muttered against her mouth and she did, instantly, and there she was, open to him.

Slowly, he told himself and he tried, he really did. He clenched the cheeks of his ass and moved into her as gently as he could and oh, God, she was like wet silk.

"Move," she ordered.

Everything about Isabel was open to him, welcoming him. Her mouth, her arms, her legs, her sex. She was signaling with her entire body that she wanted him. Joe found her mouth with his and pushed forward, as slowly as he could, until he was firmly embedded inside her. He went slowly because he didn't want to hurt her but also because there was red-hot pleasure so intense he wanted to savor every second, every inch. They were holding each other tightly, kissing deeply, there was nothing anywhere but Isabel.

"You're driving me crazy," he said.

"Good." She licked his ear. "Now move."

It was like a storm, hot and wild. Joe slammed into her over and over again, not asking if he was hurting her because she was with him every step of the way. Her arms and legs were tightly wound around him, holding him, meeting him. Her head was thudding against the wall so he cupped her head and her kisses deepened.

She went first, with a wild cry in his mouth, clenching hard around him. She threw her head back, white throat exposed and he kissed her there, his tongue feeling the beating of her heart in her neck. He could feel the beating of her heart in her sex, too, throbbing and clenching.

He was covered in sweat and thrusting into her in hard little stabs because he couldn't bear the thought of pulling back too far because that meant leaving her heat. So he set his legs and pressed into her, circling her, stabbing hard and his heart stopped and the top of his head came off and he spilled into her, hard spurts that made him shake.

When he was finally done, he put his palms against the wall near her head to hold himself upright. Isabel slowly lowered her legs to the ground and he slipped out of her.

They were panting, both of them.

Isabel's legs were shaking and her knees gave. She slid to the floor and he slid with her, rolling until it was his back against the cold floor and Isabel was lying on top of him, eyes closed, mouth upturned in a mysterious smile.

Joe lifted his head to watch her then let it fall back with a thud. He was completely wiped out.

"Forget killing Blake," he said when he got his breathing under control. "You're going to kill *me*."

She laughed.

Washington, DC

SHE KNEW. The bitch knew, somehow. She had to go. It was time.

Blake had thought of this over and over again. Leaving Isabel alive was a security risk. But she'd been so broken he'd let it ride and all things considered, she'd had a good run. He'd let her live six months. Her memory was returning, and he knew exactly what she was remembering. Isabel alive was now an unacceptable risk, but it was good that it had taken time.

No one was going to connect the suicide of a troubled young woman with the events of months ago.

And soon Blake was going to be busy with phase two, and he wouldn't have time to deal with her if she all of a sudden woke up and remembered halfway through a presidential campaign. So, it was time.

He arranged a rock-solid alibi then called his personal pilot. The pilot would fly him under an assumed name, flying a plane that was registered under a company it would take forensic economists months to trace back to Blake.

And why should they?

Hector Blake in Washington would have nothing to do with the suicide of a young woman across the country.

He could actually deal with this himself, with the help of his pilot and Kearns, his man on the ground.

He called Kearns. "Our little dove is going to fly away." Their code for it's time to get rid of the little bitch.

There was just enough of a silence to annoy Blake. Had the moron already forgotten their code?

"Ah. Okay. In Washington?"

Blake closed his eyes. Kearns would be the next to go. He wasn't smart enough to take part in phase two, let alone phases three and four. "No, where her nest is."

Portland.

"*Nest* nest?"

Meaning—in her home?

"Any objections?" Blake asked coldly.

"Well...she, um, seems to have made friends with a—a lot of people on her street. Maybe they'd report right away if something—something happens to her. Or someone might...interfere. I think we should, um, isolate her."

"None of that was in your reports. That she had made friends on her street."

"No, um. I didn't think it was worth mentioning."

A small vein throbbed in Blake's temple. At the first opportunity, Kearns was *gone.* But for the moment, Kearns was on the ground and right now, Blake felt that he should be moving fast. Eliminate this small threat before it grew into a big threat.

"Okay. I'll call her before the meeting and say I have to meet her downtown. Say at the bar of the Hotel Monaco. In the meantime, book a room in her name at the cheapest motel you can find. Here's her credit card information—" Blake read off Isabel's Visa number. He kept close tabs on her. It pleased him that she had very little in her checking and savings accounts. "I'll email you a prescription for twenty capsules of Trevilor. Little Miss Dove is going to have a sad ending. Any questions?"

He'd better not have questions.

"No, sir."

Next Blake spoke to his pilot and arranged a noon departure for Portland, a six-hour flight, arrival 3:00 p.m. local time. Plenty of time to get set up. He'd arrange for a 5:00 p.m. meeting.

Once Isabel was eliminated he'd fly straight back to DC, where at least four people would swear in court that he'd never left.

He paid them more than enough for a little perjury.

ELEVEN

"COMMS CHECK, AGAIN," Joe ordered.

Isabel didn't complain, didn't roll her eyes. As if she'd been an undercover agent for the past ten years, she simply ran through their systems one more time. The tenth time. Eyes focused, no wasted movements, completely serious.

An operator.

"Check," Felicity said.

Okay. It was late afternoon and they were in the back of Three Windows and Jacko's friend had been absolutely ace. They had the placed fully wired. Nothing was going to happen that they didn't know about. Joe had personally tested the metal detector at the front door, going through again and again with a weapon, with a knife, with knuckle-dusters. You couldn't tell it was a metal detector and what he was carrying only showed up on Felicity's screen at the back.

The metal detector worked.

If the fucker showed up with a fucking metal toothpick Joe was going to be all over him, he didn't give a fuck if he blew the op.

The place was positively seeded with mini-mikes, almost invisible, incredibly powerful. Several were going to be piped into Bud Morrison's office, an ASI friend. Former marine, now head of the homicide department and slated to become police commissioner soon.

Bud was chomping at the bit, as was Nick. Neither of them was territorial, either. Both of them just wanted to take that fucker down. They didn't care who got the credit.

This was a team just raring to go. Even ex-CIA guy was communicating with Felicity via computer.

Everything depended on Isabel. He shot her a glance. The hot sexy woman he'd made love to last night was gone. In her place was a serious woman willing to risk her life to bring a criminal down.

They'd gone over the plan again and again and she knew every step, every facet. She'd had Felicity walk her through the eyes and ears they'd have until she understood everything.

Nick had given her an intro into interrogation techniques and she'd absorbed them quietly. They'd gone through a number of scenarios and in each one, she kept her cool.

Jacko and Metal were the designated shooters. If Blake so much as touched Isabel they would shoot to maim and stop, not kill. That was a collective decision and Isabel had been hotly opposed to it. She had a shoot to kill policy and it had taken a lot of talking to bring her down.

She accepted the reasoning—he needed to be alive so he could be interrogated about the conspiracy, so he could name names, so he could point fingers at the moles that had to exist in the US government for something like this to work. She accepted the reasoning but she didn't like it.

Isabel looked calm and ready but Joe knew she was out for blood and that scared him. The only thing he could do was be ready to jump in and protect her. That was his designated role. He'd be in the open, just another guy in the bar situated way across the room, to the left. Drinking a beer, back to the room, seemingly absorbed in his tablet just like any other guy watching a game. What he'd be watching was Isabel. There was a camera trained right on her face. They'd worked it out so he had a clear view of everything, down to her eyelashes. It was the only way he could be persuaded to not be sitting next to her.

"Ten mikes," Nick's calm voice sounded in his earbud. Ten minutes to the arrival of Blake. The earbud was invisible. On Joe's screen, Isabel blinked three times. A prearranged signal for everything's okay. Blink twice and Joe was pulling his Glock from his shoulder holster, turning and shooting the fuck's brains out from across the room. No, he told himself. As satisfactory as it would be to paint the walls with the inside of Blake's head, he wouldn't shoot to kill. Wouldn't. No, sir.

Nick was with Felicity in Jacko's friend's office, monitoring everything. He'd brought along handcuffs, just waiting for Blake to slip up.

Joe watched Isabel's face on his iPad. Before an op he was as focused as a human could get. Focused but with situational awareness. He realized finally that he was completely out of the game because he found it hard to tear his eyes from her face. It was the face of his future.

He was going to grow old with this woman. He was going to have kids with her, a family, and they'd eat really, really well for all the years of their lives. He'd work for ASI because they were great but they wouldn't have every part of him the way the navy had. Because his heart belonged to Isabel.

He shook himself. This op was the most important

one of his life because his life was sitting quietly on a chair near the window waiting to accuse a monster of mass murder and treason. A man like that would have no problem killing Isabel.

So he had to stop thinking of her and go over lines of fire and escape routes in his head.

"Five mikes."

So far everything had gone smooth as shit through a goose. Joe had been by her side when she took Blake's call at ASI. Felicity had routed it so that it looked like her cell was being used in her house.

When Blake had called, Isabel had been brilliant. She sounded flustered, depressed. *Bathroom pipes broken, water everywhere. Let's meet somewhere nice. It's been a long time since I've been anywhere nice. Hotel Monaco? No, it's really busy. Let's meet at this nice restaurant I know, Three Windows. In an hour. I'll finish up here and meet you there.*

"Contact," Nick said quietly in his ear and sure enough, on Joe's monitor the tall, very elegant figure of Hector Blake appeared in the doorway and walked over to Isabel. The metal detector didn't register any weaponry.

He was wearing a full length black overcoat and a black fedora, sunglasses. A thick scarf covered the bottom of his face.

Joe shifted uneasily. If he didn't take that scarf off there would be no facial recognition possible.

He stopped by Isabel's table, sat down, took her hand. They were talking. Isabel looked so sad, so vulnerable.

Joe's skin prickled.

And then the lights went out. His tablet went dark.

"HELLO, ISABEL," Hector Blake said as he stood next to her.

During the planning, Isabel had promised herself she would remain cool, not go for his throat. Not stare at him with hatred. And while promising herself that, she hoped she could do it.

She could. She could stay in character.

She gave a small smile, dipping her head. Sad Isabel, seeing an old family friend. "Hello, Uncle Hector. Nice to see you."

He sat across from her, without taking off his hat or unwinding his scarf. A prickle of alarm ran through her. If he was planning on staying only a few minutes she wouldn't have time to get him to incriminate himself.

"You're not staying?" she asked, indicating hat and scarf.

He didn't answer. He simply reached across for her hand. Oh. So this was how they were going to play it? Dear Uncle Hector, holding her hand while saying all over again how sorry he was she'd lost her family?

He held her hand in his gloved one, palm up, thumb over her inner wrist.

"Your heart is racing," he said, with a cold smile. "You know, don't you?"

Oh. So *that* was how it was going to be.

"Yes." She gave him the cool smile right back. "I know everything. And you're not getting away with it." Her smile broadened. "Guaranteed."

The lights went out.

Isabel looked around briefly and felt something cold against her wrist. She looked down and saw a white ceramic knife with a very sharp blade pressed against the inside of her wrist. Held by Hector in such a way that with one swipe he could slice right through the artery. She'd bleed out in seconds.

She looked back up into that face, not bothering to hide her hatred anymore. She could barely see him. It was dark in the restaurant, people murmuring, stirring. She blinked twice.

"I am getting away with it. I'm not here at all. I have all sorts of people back in Washington willing to swear in court that I am there. Not that it will ever come to that, of course."

"People know you are here."

"Yes?" He looked around. "I don't see anyone I know. If you have friends who are watching this over a video feed, too bad. Because I just killed everything with a chip in a hundred-yard radius. Nothing is being recorded, nothing will be recorded and you—" He pressed down hard on the sharp knife and she felt him slice through the skin. Blood welled up at the knife's edge. "You are coming with me."

"No." She looked up steadily at him.

"Developed a backbone, have we?" Hector murmured, words muffled by the scarf. "Be the first one in your family. Just so you know, I have a sniper watching through night vision optics and he can see perfectly clearly. The first person who comes up to you gets one right through the head. Maybe a waiter, maybe someone you've recruited, maybe even a friend, but someone gets killed. So move."

Joe was seconds from running over to her.

Heart thudding, Isabel stood.

Hector was good. He managed to keep the knife at her wrist without it looking awkward. They walked to the door and Isabel kept her gaze down, at the floor.

A sign she desperately hoped Joe would interpret as *stay away!*

Hector had already cost her everyone she loved. Mother, father, brothers. Aunts, uncles, cousins. She wasn't going to give him Joe, too. Not sweet, brave Joe. She'd rather die herself.

It was dark inside the restaurant and outside, too. No lights at all. If Joe was coming out, he was coming out blind. He'd shown her night vision and she knew that whoever was out there with a sniper rifle could see just fine, and they were blind.

Whatever Hector's plan was, though, Joe and his guys were smarter.

They were crossing the threshold of the restaurant, Hector pushing open the door into the cold night. Behind her, restaurant patrons were murmuring. She knew her team would be scrambling to deal with the situation.

"Forget about anyone coming after you," Hector said, bending toward her. An uncle out with his beloved niece. "I just set off a limited EMP. That same EMP that killed video cameras and cell phones and any tracking devices you might have on you? It also killed any vehicles with electric circuitry. But I have acquired a vehicle that doesn't have electronic circuitry. Ah, here we are."

A dilapidated van screeched into the driveway, backed up. The rear doors opened and before Isabel could react, she was shoved inside and Hector climbed up next to her.

The doors were pulled shut and she bounced against the hard steel wall as the van took a corner and sped away.

Hector was wrapping something soft around her

wrists in a figure eight. He knotted the ends and let her go. She tried to free herself but they were like handcuffs, only soft.

The van was moving fast. Every few minutes the driver took a sharp turn. She was lost in minutes.

Hector was looking out the back window with binoculars. "Don't even think of trying to get away, my dear." He put the binoculars down and spoke to the driver. "Nobody following us. We're clear."

She was trapped in a van with a man who wanted to kill her. Who had killed her entire family. Nobody knew where she was and no one could find her.

Hector was going to win this.

"Fuck!" Joe wanted to scream but he knew he couldn't. Silence on an op had been beaten into him. He was blind. And deaf, he discovered as he tapped his earbud and got a whole lot of nothing. Complete silence. He couldn't go running toward Isabel in the restaurant, that would tip Blake off.

What was happening out there?

Joe had to find out the old-fashioned way. By looking. Actual looking with his actual eyes because sure as fuck his electronic eyes were shot to hell.

He peered around a corner, trying to find Isabel and Blake in the sudden gloom in the restaurant. People were standing up, having patiently waited for the lights to come on. Now that they weren't, they were getting agitated.

With the restaurant-goers milling around he couldn't see the table at the front windows where Isabel sat. He moved through the diners as quickly and unobtrusively as he could, head on a swivel and as he moved toward the windows he saw Isabel and Blake outside. Who knew what he'd done to convince her to go with him but the fucker was wrong if he thought he was going to be able to kidnap Isabel.

In a fury, Joe took off, but in the darkness, a couple stumbled in his way and by the time he'd shoved them aside, Isabel was gone. *Gone.* In an old van with mud on the license plate, red brake lights winking as it took a corner. It had come racing to the entrance and in a second, Blake had pushed Isabel in then climbed in after her.

He hadn't had a straight shot otherwise he'd have killed the fucker.

Joe raced to the back where the crew was.

"She's gone!" he shouted.

Felicity slammed her computer shut. "Damn thing is fried. All comms are down. Must have been some kind of limited EMP. If he killed my computer, he's going to be sorry."

Metal and Jacko ran in, grim-faced, carrying their rifles. "Our vehicles won't start," Jacko growled.

Joe punched a wall. "Contact Bud Morrison! Get a description of that van out in a BOLO!"

Jacko's friend Chuck, the owner of the restaurant, held up his hands. "Guys, sorry. The cells are fried and I don't have a landline. The nearest public pay phone is a mile away. East to Stone Avenue. We're completely cut off here. And I gotta get out there and deal with the customers."

Joe was clenching his jaws so hard it hurt. Even running, it would take them minutes—minutes they didn't have—to get to the public pay phones. By then Blake would be long gone. Joe had no doubt that they'd be finding Isabel's dead body somewhere far away, on some roadside, tumbled down a remote hillside or fished out of the river.

He'd never felt so fucking frustrated. On any op there was always something you could do. But now? Any step could be wrong, waste precious time. It scared the hell out of him.

For the very first time since he signed up to be a warrior, he didn't know what to do.

Metal and Jacko and Nick were looking at him, all three of them with their useless cells in hand. Felicity was looking at him, too, fingers touching the closed cover of her useless laptop.

Time was rushing by like a flood, Isabel was getting farther and farther from him with every passing second and he didn't know what the fuck *to do!*

A vehicle slewed to a stop outside the back room, in the loading area, spewing gravel. It was ancient—with more primer than paint, two dented fenders. A jalopy.

A man got out, tall, with dirty blond dreadlocks. He was moving fast and Joe drew his weapon. The man had an athlete's body but he looked like a homeless person, clothes rags, boots ancient. Hands and face grimy with dirt. And with a lump on his hip under the filthy long overcoat.

Was he sent by Blake?

"Hold it right there! Hands up!" Joe held his Glock two-handed at chest level. If this guy was sent by Blake he was going to kill him where he stood, homeless or not. The guy wasn't raising his hands. "There are two snipers behind me. You reach for your weapon you're a dead man."

The man was frowning. "Goddamn it, we don't have

time for this shit! You let them take Isabel! She's getting farther from us every damned second."

Joe lowered his weapon.

The bum glared at Joe. "Name's Jack Delvaux. I'm Isabel's brother and you've been talking to me on the computer. Blake must have used a miniature, controlled-pulse EMP so whatever tags you put on Isabel are useless. But I've got a hardened tag on that fucker Blake, so you and your friends hop in, we're going after the son of a bitch."

"YOU'RE NEVER GOING to get away with this." Isabel kept her voice steady as she rode in the back of the van on a bench set along the side. Hector had been leaning forward conferring with the driver. She couldn't hear what they were saying over the loud engine noise of the ancient vehicle.

Hector's eyebrows rose as he looked back at her. "Oh, but I am going to get away with it. As I told you, I'm in Washington, DC, right now." He sat back down next to her. "You've been rich all your life so you should know this. Money can buy a lot of things, a lot of people."

"And you've made plenty of money," she spat.

"Plenty, yes. With more to come. But that won't concern you, my dear, because you'll have taken your own life. Poor, broken Isabel checked into a cheap motel and took enough pills to kill a horse."

She tried to still her hammering heart. He sounded so certain, so matter of fact. But he couldn't fake her suicide, could he? "People know I'm with you."

Blake shook his head. "People know you're with *someone*. Maybe an old lover, maybe the guy who filled your prescriptions for you. All anyone knows—if they even saw it in the dark—is that you willingly went with someone and drove away. No one could possibly know it's me. And I put out a small electromagnetic pulse and anything with a chip is fried. My hat—" he tipped the brim of the fedora, dark eyes sardonic, "—has infrared lights in the brim. In case the cameras caught my face for one second before everything was switched off, all they'd get was a glow. I wore gloves. Even if someone saw me all they could say was that they saw a man in a black coat, hat, dark glasses and a scarf over the bottom half of his face. No one could possibly recognize me."

"My friends will know I didn't kill myself! You're crazy! They won't rest until they get the truth."

"Your friends can make all the noise they want. You checked into the motel under your own name with your own credit card, records showing you bought a huge stash of pills back in Washington, DC, will be uncovered. You tried to build a new life for yourself in Portland, but sadly that didn't work out. You decided to end it once and for all. The autopsy will show a lethal dosage of a commonly prescribed antidepressant in your system. No signs of violence. Oh, and there will be some very sad—very, very sad entries in your journal and in your computer. No, my dear. No one will question this and if they do, we can buy the coroner, any PI they hire, any investigative journalist. We have more money than God."

Smug and composed, he leaned forward once again to talk to his thug.

Isabel tried to think against the rising panic. He couldn't possibly get away with this! Could he? But then, he'd gotten away with the Massacre. He'd hidden in plain sight. The worst terrorist attack on US soil since 9/11 and no one had a clue who had orchestrated it.

Three trillion dollars had been drained from the economy, which was enough to buy off every single government bureaucrat in the chain. Of course Joc and his friends couldn't be bought, not for anything. Nick couldn't be bought off. And the way they spoke of him neither would their cop friend, Bud Morrison, be bought. But it wouldn't be the first time someone was murdered and the murderer got away free.

They'd raise a fuss and maybe some journalist or blogger would mention her.

But in the meantime, she'd be dead.

A suicide.

But—for it to be a plausible suicide by ingesting pills, the body had to show no signs of violence. If there were signs of violence on her body, even the most corrupt cop would have to investigate.

Violence like—

She banged her head against the van wall, once, twice. She changed the angle and banged her head hard against a bolt and felt skin tear. It hurt but being dead was worse. She beat her head, her shoulder against the wall, tearing at the soft fabric holding her wrists together, twisting them so that her hands started turning blue from lack of circulation.

She kicked her ankle, hard, against the bench they were sitting on. So hard blood showed through her pant leg. She kicked again.

"Hey!" Hector looked astonished. "What the fuck are you doing?"

Ankles, head, hands. She banged her shoulder against the van wall, over and over again, raking her hands over a nail, writhing, kicking. She was in a frenzy now. If they were going to kill her then *by God* no one was going to think she'd killed herself. No way.

She launched herself at Hector, biting him, scratching his face. There'd be his DNA under her fingernails. *Talk that one away, you son of a bitch!*

He understood, and tried to keep her away with his gloved hands but Isabel was having none of it. The point was not getting away. She knew she'd never escape, she could only foil his plans.

This was the man who had killed her family. The most wonderful people in the world and he'd killed them for *money!* Blood was running over her face from a cut in her forehead. She swiped at it and smeared it on Hector, smeared it on the van's bench.

He was backing away from her but there was no room to avoid her. A low inhuman growl escaped her throat as she beat her bound fists against him, getting in close and unstoppable.

Screams of rage came from her throat now as she kicked, swung her fists, turned her fingers into claws, bit away a chunk of his cheek.

Blood. She tasted his blood and it drove her insane. He should bleed and he should *die*!

They tumbled around the back of the van as it turned corners fast, sometimes sliding on the icy roads. That was fine, that was *great*. The more bruises the better. She lunged forward and her elbow caught the driver on the side of the head.

"Hey!" The driver turned, eyes wide and white in the darkness. Isabel turned on him, too. He was perfectly willing to kill her and she was perfectly willing to hurt him. She shoved one foot in Blake's face and grabbed the driver's arm.

"You crazy, lady?" His voice was high-pitched, scared. She was right behind him, he couldn't see her in the rearview mirror, so he was driving with his head on a swivel, watching the road and trying to see the crazy lady behind him. "The fuck? We're on a fucking bridge, you want us to go over?"

Yes! A voice roared in her head. *Explain that to the police!*

She launched herself so that she was facedown on the passenger seat, Blake pulling at her legs, the driver trying to punch her but she was unpunchable. She was Isabel the unpunchable, the unstoppable, full of rage, out for revenge.

The overhead streetlights of the bridge lit the driver's face then left it in darkness and each time it light up he looked more desperate, more wild. His one-handed punches had no effect. She could feel the van sliding on the street and with one last lunge—*this one's for you, Mom and Dad, Teddy and Rob and Jack*—she pulled the steering wheel as hard as she could to the right and felt something crunch against the fender and then they were sailing, flying out into the night.

Hector and the driver screamed and Isabel savored their fear, but not for long because the van hit the surface of the river and started sinking.

THE OLD JALOPY pulled away before Joe could even get the door closed.

The car was filled with gear. The homeless guy dumped a small monitor and IR binocs in Joe's lap. There were handguns and four Maglites in the footwell.

"Watch the screen," he said.

Joe looked but couldn't figure out what he was seeing. The man—Jack Delvaux—gave a disgusted noise. "I can't believe my sister picked such a moron. Look at it, goddamn you! Blake had access to a small EMP generator, it's the only thing that makes sense. We had intel that the Chinese had come up with something like this only we'd never seen it. But I had a hardened tracker embedded in a plastic that is indistinguishable from human skin and I slapped it onto Blake's neck. It's functional. Check that green dot."

Joe looked down and sure enough, a green dot was running along the river.

"They won't know we can follow them." Jack looked briefly over his shoulder. "You two, you're shooters, right?"

Metal and Jacko nodded. Metal aimed a thumb at Jacko. "He's the best shot we've got. But I'm a medic, too. If anything happens to Isabel, I'm there."

If anything happens to Isabel. Code for Isabel being shot to death, knifed to death, strangled… A pulse of fear so strong it bathed his body in sweat went through Joe's system.

Jack shifted his eyes without moving his head. "You. Joe. Former navy SEAL. Keep your fucking head in the fucking game. That's my sister and we're bringing her back. Alive."

"Yeah." His voice was so hoarse he could hardly talk.

"Believe it. See it, live it."

Jacko punched Joe's shoulder from the backseat. Hard. "Yo. I can't believe you're letting a CIA punk give you a pep talk. 'Smatter with you?"

"Help me on this, Joe," Jack said, watching the road

ahead. "I can't do this without your help and the help of your friends."

And just like that, Joe's head was back in the game. Isabel was in danger and she needed him to be cool-headed. She needed him to be an operator, she didn't need this sweating terrified man. He blew out a breath and checked the monitor.

"Two blocks up, turn right. Then three blocks down turn left. If you go fast we can catch up."

Jack's lips pressed together and he pushed on the accelerator so hard it was like being in a rocket. The car looked like it had been rescued from the junk heap but, man, it was eating up the miles. They were breaking every speed law on the books, but Joe leaned forward, willing it to go faster. To catch up with Isabel, in the hands of a murderer.

"How come this car works when ours don't?" Metal asked.

"I bought it for cash and had it tuned," Jack said. "It's all mechanical. I have been pretending to be homeless and at times I slept in it, but it's a real lucky break because Blake's EMP killed everything that has electronics within a hundred, hundred fifty yards. He's driving a van that doesn't have electronic components either. I parked a block down, anyway. So my car and my gear work."

And his foresight might save Isabel's life.

"So," Joe said, glancing over. Beneath the filthy dreadlocks, stubble and grime, he could see the resemblance. "Isabel's brother."

"Yep."

"Thought you were dead."

"So did Blake. That was the point. And I had to stay

dead. If Isabel knew I was alive, she wouldn't be able to hide it. I've been investigating, but I don't have proof yet. But I will. There are other people involved in this and they are not done yet."

"How'd you hide for six months?"

Jack flashed a grim smile and pointed to himself. "You'd be surprised how invisible the homeless are. That's how I slapped that tracker onto Blake. Pretended to be a homeless vet at a rally, he had to shake my hand. Looked right into my eyes and he didn't recognize me. Didn't even really see me. Where are they?"

"Turn this corner and—" Joe looked up and saw the outline of an ancient van. "There it is!"

Impossibly, Jack stepped on the accelerator harder and they shot forward. "We need to be careful, I don't want Isabel hurt."

Joe lifted the IR binocs to his eyes. "I see them," he reported. "Three outlines. Isabel is sitting on a bench." Shoulders slumped. In the hands of the enemy. She had no idea they were coming after her. She thought she was alone, abandoned. On her way to her death.

Hang on, honey. Just hang on a little while longer, we're coming for you.

"Where's Blake?" Jack asked.

"Sitting next to her," he answered. "And Isabel is—" He stopped. What was he seeing? The red outlines that were heat images were churning.

"Isabel is *what?*" Jack shouted.

"Fighting," Joe replied, surprised the word came out. It felt like there were rocks in his throat. "She's fighting Blake and—oh, God." He watched as she beat at Blake with handcuffs or restraints on her wrists, then started whaling on the driver. He was torn between cheering her on and screaming at her to stop it. They were undoubtedly armed. What the fuck was she thinking?

Though she was magnificent.

The van ahead fishtailed.

"She's fighting the driver." Joe couldn't take his eyes from the binocs. It was like watching a train wreck.

The van swerved onto the other lane, then veered back into the right hand lane. Isabel was a red-gold ninja, limbs moving almost too quickly to follow in the IR lenses, so quickly her movements left a red-gold trail, like manifestations of ghosts.

The van turned onto the Morrison Bridge, wobbling. Thank God there was very little traffic on the roads.

"What?" Jack asked urgently. "What's happening?"

"She's putting up a real fight," Joe said, terrified, trying to keep the pride out of his voice. "She's got her head real close to the driver's face. I think, um..." He held the monitor up to try to decipher what was going on. Isabel's and the driver's heads together formed one big red-yellow blob. Isabel pulled away and the driver took a hand off the wheel to place it against his head. "I think she bit him. Or kissed him."

One or the other.

The van swerved again only instead of righting itself, it curved even farther to the right.

"Hey!" Joe shouted at the driver of the van. "You crazy fuck! You're going to go off the bridge!"

The van speeded up as it rammed the bridge spars, broke through them and plunged straight down into the cold water of the river.

"Stop the car!" Joe screamed.

Jack stood on the brakes and Joe opened the door before it came to a complete halt. He studied the black water as he tore his boots and jacket off, figuring out his moves, figuring out how to get to Isabel because not saving her was not an option. He was either going to come up with Isabel or he wasn't coming up at all.

He'd clocked in four and a half minutes underwater during training but only after super oxygenating and not moving in the water. On a rescue mission he could last two minutes, tops. That wasn't important, though. The only important thing was how long Isabel could last.

He only had time to pull in two deep breaths, filling his lungs up completely with air then exhaling deeply by the time he stood on the edge of the bridge where the van had crashed through the barrier.

Isabel was a civilian and civilians didn't last long underwater. She'd be terrified and panicky and flailing. She'd last thirty-forty seconds before she tried to pull in a terrified breath and breathed water. At least the water was freezing cold which slowed things down a little. Make that fifty seconds, tops.

Joe started the clock in his head as he stood barefoot on the edge of the bridge just long enough to calculate the entry point of the dive.

The van's roof was disappearing underwater. There would be some air trapped inside the cabin and Isabel was smart enough to take advantage of that. He had to dive as close to the vehicle as possible. One second to calibrate and he dove.

The water was freezing cold and black. The van's headlights were on and he used that as guidance as he fought the swirls of water displaced by the sinking van. In a few hard strokes he was there at the front passenger door, barely able to see inside by the glow of the headlights. Isabel was still flailing and for a second he couldn't understand why as he floated just outside the window.

Ten seconds.

Then he saw that the driver was still attacking her.

Goddamn it. He had his Glock in its shoulder holster but he couldn't use it underwater, much as he'd like to just shoot the murderous fuck in the head. On some missions his Glock had been equipped with maritime spring cups that protected the firing pin but this one didn't have it. Beyond that, the shock wave could damage Isabel's internal organs, could even kill her.

He pounded on the window to get her attention and she turned, face lighting up when she saw him.

Goddamn. His heart simply turned over in his chest. She'd just fought off two murderous men, she was in a vehicle that was submerged in water, he had no idea if she could even swim, she was surely terrified and the love in her face when she saw him nearly blew him apart.

No one had ever looked at him like that before. He was not going to lose this woman. He was going to save her and if she'd have him, he was going to marry her. And if she wouldn't have him, he'd just keep asking.

Twenty seconds.

The driver was reaching for her again, movements impeded by the water rushing in.

Joe motioned Isabel away. By some miracle she understood and moved slightly to one side and Joe drove the butt of his Glock with all his strength against the glass pane. It broke, shards of glass floating in the water. Too bad. If they got cut, they'd get stitched up. The important thing was to get to the surface.

He quickly broke away all the pieces of glass clinging to the window frame, reached in past Isabel and with a quick movement of his hands broke the driver's neck, then put his hands under Isabel's arms and pulled her out.

Thirty seconds.

From the backseat, a hand reached out, flailing. Blake. Joe watched coldly as Blake's desperate face appeared, bubbles around his head. He was drowning.

Good. Joe hadn't bought into the whole bringing-Blake-to-justice thing anyway. The fucker deserved to die.

The heavy vehicle was pushed sideways by the swirling water, crashing into his leg, dragging a shard of glass with it. His blood darkened the water. There was no pain—the water was too cold for that. But if his leg wouldn't function, it would take longer to get Isabel to the surface. He pulled her completely out of the window just as the van settled on the bottom, hoping no remaining glass was cutting her open.

His right leg wasn't working right. Fuck. The plan was to hold Isabel and propel them both upward with the strength of his legs. But with only one leg functional, there was only one thing he could do.

Forty seconds.

There wasn't enough light for Isabel to follow gestures so he took her arms and placed them tightly around his neck and hoped to God she understood. She did. She held on tightly as he began to rise in the water using the full power of his arms and his one leg.

Fifty seconds.

It felt like it took forever, hauling both of them up through the dark, freezing, muddy water. Almost immediately he lost the light of the headlights of the van and could see nothing, nothing at all. Not even Isabel's face so close to his.

Damn.

He knew she was alive because she was holding his neck but he thought he felt her grip lessen.

Please God.

Please don't let this brave, beautiful woman die. Take me instead. But if he was too slow, he'd live because he was a navy SEAL and had trained for a year to dive and come up in dark cold water. He'd live but Isabel would die.

Fifty-five seconds.

Isabel's grip was loose. She was dying.

Light! Faint, barely perceptible. He aimed his face up and pulled as hard as he could.

Fifty-eight seconds.

Joe broke the water on a huge gasp, just as Isabel went loose in his arms.

His head swiveled as he looked up at the bridge where the men had angled the headlights to shine over the water. Jack was shining a powerful flashlight into the water.

"Rope!" Joe screamed just as a rope hit the water five feet from him. He was bearing Isabel's full weight now. Her eyes were closed and through chattering teeth he started praying.

Don't die on me, honey. Don't die. Don't die. Please God, don't let her die.

He wrapped the rope three times around his fore-arm, his other arm around Isabel. She needed to get the water out of her lungs but he couldn't do it here. He had to get her onto that bridge where Metal could work his magic. Metal had saved men's lives countless times.

He'd saved lives other medics couldn't save. He knew what Isabel meant to him, he'd save Isabel.

He had to.

The four men pulled them out of the water, Joe hanging from the rope, holding Isabel tightly to him.

Her eyes were closed. She looked like she was sleeping. He couldn't do anything—one hand was holding on to the rope pulling them out of the water and the other was grasping her. All he could do was stare at her face, willing her eyes to open.

His gasps were clouding the frigid air with steam but there was no steam coming out of Isabel's mouth.

Oh, God.

And then they were pulled over the bridge onto concrete and Metal was bending over Isabel and Joe was on his knees, gasping, coughing out water. Blood pooled around his leg. Metal looked over at him, big hands compressing Isabel's chest, but Joe waved him away.

"Take…care…of… Isabel."

Metal was counting under his breath, big hands compressing Isabel's chest hard. Isabel was so cold and still, beautiful face deathly white.

And then—the most glorious sound he ever heard. Isabel, coughing. Metal put her on her side as she weakly coughed out the water she'd swallowed. She looked ice white and battered. The most beautiful sight he'd ever seen.

Joe's leg wouldn't bear him so he crawled over to Isabel, putting his arms around her, holding her tightly, patting her back as she coughed. He pulled back and looked down at her face, wanting his face to be the first thing she saw when she opened her eyes.

Her eyelids fluttered, she coughed again, then opened her eyes.

"Is he dead?" was the first thing that came out of her mouth.

Joe laughed weakly, and it turned into a cough. "Yeah." His voice was gravelly. "He's dead."

"Good." Her eyes closed again.

Joe tapped her cheek. "Honey. Honey, don't go off just yet. There's someone you have to see."

"Don't want to see anyone," she said, her voice drowsy. She was falling into hypothermia. They'd wrap her up in their jackets and get her to a hospital fast but first—first she had to know something. Joe lifted his hand and beckoned to Jack. Jack hunkered down on his haunches next to Isabel.

Joe turned her face toward Jack. She blinked. Blinked again.

"Jack?" she whispered, holding out a hand.

Jack grabbed it, put it against his filthy, stubbled jaw. "Sis."

Tears welled, fell down her face. "You're alive!" Her mouth formed the words, though there was no sound.

She gave a sob, then another, then lifted from Joe's arms to throw herself into her brother's arms, crying and laughing at the same time.

Metal stood. "Gotta get her warm and to a hospital," he said, but he didn't stir. It was an incredibly moving moment. Jack's head was bent over Isabel's and though he wasn't sobbing, tears were falling down his cheeks into his beard.

Jacko and Nick held out their hands and lifted Joe. He couldn't put weight on his right leg, but they were strong men and they were there for him. Everything in Joe's world felt heavy with the sense of rightness.

His woman, in her brother's arms, crying out her happiness. His buds, holding him up.

It was going to be all right.

Isabel turned her face, held out a hand. Jacko and Nick shuffled forward with Joe between them until he could reach her, take her hand.

"You—alive. My brother—alive. Blake—dead," she whispered. "Happiest day of my life."

EPILOGUE

The Grange, Mount Hood
Two weeks later

IT WAS A GREAT PARTY. The place was fantastic. It was a sunny day and the place was filled with light. Built of wood and glass the reception hall was huge, airy, magnificent. A cathedral to the art of living well.

And eating well.

There were whole stretches of time when the entire ASI crew—a rowdy bunch normally—fell completely silent as a new dish appeared on the fifty-foot-long table. Isabel had designed the menu and had done some of the cooking and it was spectacular. She'd absolutely refused to rest after near drowning and had been working round the clock on the menu.

Joe glanced over at her for the billionth time. So far there'd been ten toasts to her and she was rosy and smiling and so goddamned beautiful it nearly blinded him. She'd begun her blog again—just a few posts so far but the reaction was overwhelming. Each post now clocked up a hundred thousand hits and the numbers were climbing fast. She'd dusted off the file of the book on food she'd been writing. Joe let her be, didn't push her in one direction or another, because she was finding her own way back just fine. But he was incredibly proud of her.

Her brother Jack was sitting on her other side. He'd cleaned up for the occasion after his months of staying under the radar, pretending to be a mentally disturbed homeless person. He and Nick had been huddled together for the past two days, planning the next steps.

The FBI had handled the removal of Hector Blake's body back to Washington, DC, where soon the former senator would drown for the second time in a tragic accident in the Potomac. The Portland driver had been ID'd as a former member of the Clandestine Service who had quit after a fuckup in Pakistan.

Nick and Jack were patiently combing the records of former Clandestine Service members and they were being investigated for possible involvement in the Washington Massacre. They were both going back to DC tomorrow to ramp up the investigation, but they had given themselves today off. Amidst all the death, it was time to celebrate life.

There was a kids' table and Isabel had prepared a perfect kid menu and they were gobbling food down like the apocalypse had come. Lily, Suzanne and Midnight's amazingly gorgeous little girl, sat at the head of the kids' table, completely in charge. At four, she was a little princess.

The servers wheeled out a huge cake that was an exact replica of the ASI compound, down to the chocolate trees with mint leaves, the walls made of something Isabel called ganache. It looked amazing and doubtless tasted amazing, too. The servers were pouring champagne.

Pretty soon Midnight would stand up and make a speech and then the Senior would, too. His bosses. For real, this time. Though Joe's leg was going to take another month to heal, he had absolutely insisted on coming in to work and he was starting to get a handle on their workload, on their clientele and had made a couple of suggestions that had been gratefully received. And as soon as he got the doctor's okay, he was going operational.

So everything was going just dandy, except for one thing.

He and Isabel were together. She made that clear. But she never, ever spoke about a future together, which was what Joe wanted more than his next breath.

So he was approaching it as an op. Carefully calibrated, step-by-step. He had his strategy all planned out.

First step—unite the houses. Then their lives.

Joe leaned into Isabel and refrained from taking a big sniff, like a dog. God, she always smelled so damned good.

Be calm, he told himself. *Relax.*

This was worse than going on a mission downrange, because then it had been only his life in the balance. Here it was his heart.

"Hey, honey," he said casually. "Look what Suzanne designed." *For us.* He swallowed the words because, well, for Suzanne to design something for them, there first had to be a *them.*

He had his tablet with him and scrolled through the images. Suzanne was as magical with design as Isabel was with food.

She'd taken their two houses, united the gardens and built a glass walkway between the two. In the images the walkway was transparent but in actuality it would be made of one-way glass so that the long corridor got all the sunshine but nothing would be visible from the outside.

And it united their two houses into one, making for one big house with a huge garden that would be a great family home.

Isabel watched the carousel of images silently and Joe quietly began sweating. The corridor Suzanne had planned was full of hothouse plants and benches, with a living-room-like arrangement at one end, so light-filled it would be like taking coffee in a garden, even in winter.

Suzanne had called it an orangery, only he didn't see any orange trees.

It was gorgeous, guaranteed to delight a chick. No? Isabel didn't look delighted, she didn't look anything.

Fuck.

Had Joe miscalculated? Presumed way too much? Was this a bad move? Shit, he thought he was being really clever, presenting united houses before proposing to unite their lives.

Maybe she didn't want to unite their houses *or* their lives. Maybe she was just fine with the way things were. Maybe...maybe she was planning on moving on. Moving away from Portland.

God.

He watched her face carefully for some sign of what she was feeling, but couldn't discern anything.

Finally the carousel of beautiful images stopped and Isabel looked up at him.

"Joe Harris!" Her voice rang out loud and clear. Everyone stopped talking and looked at them. Even the servers stopped and looked at them.

Oh, fuck.

"Yes, honey?" He tried to smile.

Isabel tapped the glassy surface of the tablet. "Is this by any chance a proposal of marriage?"

Yes it was, but it was a subtle one. It was supposed to *lead* to a marriage proposal. Eventually. She'd seen right through it and he had no way to back down now. If she was going to refuse him it was going to be in front of everyone.

"Uh, yeah," he croaked.

She looked severe. Disapproving. The ASI crew and Suzanne's people watched, fascinated. Metal and Jacko were smiling sardonically.

Joe had made the mistake of putting on a dress shirt and a tie. He hated dress shirts and ties. Especially ties. They made him feel like a noose was around his neck. He loved it that ASI didn't have a dress code. He ran a finger around his shirt collar to loosen it up a little so he could pull in some air.

Isabel frowned. "This is the most half-assed marriage proposal I have ever heard of. Do it right."

Joe's eyes widened. *Do it right.*

Okay.

Joe stood, using the table for balance. But there was no frigging way he could get down on his knee, not with that injured leg. He threw desperate glances at Jacko and Metal and they manned up. Both came around and each took an arm. They were holding almost his entire weight. That was okay. He wasn't up to his full weight yet and even when he was, Jacko could bench-press him.

They lowered him to the floor so he could kneel on his good leg.

Ring. Jesus fucking Christ. Ring. Not in his wildest imagination had he thought he'd need a ring so soon.

The table had been set with pretty crystal napkin rings. He snatched his up and held it out to her on his sweaty palm. She picked it up, looked at it carefully, then put it on her left-hand ring finger. It was so large she couldn't close her hand but she still held her hand out as if admiring an ordinary ring.

Isabel looked down at him and finally, finally smiled. "It'll do. For now. Then you get me a proper one."

Joe was breathing hard. "Is that a yes?"

She signaled Metal and Jacko and they hauled him back up.

"That is a definite yes," she said and kissed him.

The whoops shook the rafters.

* * * * *

To purchase and read more books by Lisa Marie Rice, please visit Lisa's website at www.LisaMarieRice.com/books.

Keep reading for a sneak preview of MIDNIGHT FIRE by Lisa Marie Rice, coming in print in June 2016 and available now in digital.

ONE

Washington DC
National Cathedral
Memorial Service for Hector Blake

FUNERALS BROUGHT OUT the worst in everyone, Summer Redding thought. Particularly when the man being buried was universally hated.

Well, maybe not everyone hated him, but certainly no one loved Hector Blake, former US Senator, survivor of the Washington Massacre, the man who would have become the Vice President of the United States if Alex Delvaux had lived.

But Alex Delvaux hadn't lived. The entire Delvaux family—a huge clan—had died except for Isabel Delvaux. Even Jack Delvaux had died—and he'd been so beautiful, so full of life, so amazingly charming you'd think he could outcharm death itself.

But no.

Hector Blake, however, had survived. Like one of those proverbial cockroaches that would survive a nuclear apocalypse.

Summer had never figured out how Hector had survived when so many others had died in the Massacre the evening Alex Delvaux was supposed to announce that he was running for the office of President. By all accounts Hector should have been in the stone-cold ground six months ago instead of mysteriously drowning in the Potomac two days ago.

His funeral service was amazingly long and tedious. Just about everyone who was anyone had climbed up on that podium on the mosaic hardwood dais and droned on and on about how wonderful Hector Blake had been. Not one person who spoke believed a word they were saying.

Hector had been a mean, nasty piece of work with no redeeming virtues beyond being a childhood friend of Alex Delvaux, who'd been a good guy. Hector had also been a relative by marriage of Summer's, for about fifteen minutes a million years ago.

The National Cathedral Chorus started up "I know that my Redeemer Liveth." Beautiful piece of music for such a miserable asshole.

Summer was there professionally because there was a lot about the Massacre that made no sense to her and she'd always felt that Hector was the key to unlocking the mysteries. For just a moment, though, she allowed herself to get caught up in the gorgeous music. She let it run through her, the harmonies reverberating in her, the genius of the music lifting her soul.

She found herself doing that more and more often lately. Switching off for a moment to listen to music, to read a poem, to take a walk in the park. Because more and more it felt like mud was seeping into the world from some secret putrid underground source, making everything filthy, tarnishing everything that was fresh and clean.

Her political blog/webzine, *Area 8*, was highly successful. It was incredibly successful because political wrongdoing—her specialty—was so popular lately.

These past years it seemed you couldn't turn around without a congressman or senator or cabinet secretary taking money from the wrong people, diddling a teenager or crashing cars while drunk or high. Sometimes all three.

It was like some kind of epidemic of crazy.

Area 8 covered these in loving detail. When you took the long view, and squinted and put a little Vaseline on the lens of life, it was funny-grotesque. But Summer took a closer view and was often heartsick at the blatant wrongdoing, the betrayal of the public's trust.

She found herself seeking out concerts of all types, whether in small churches or large concert halls, and she'd sit at the back, close her eyes and let the music wash over her, through her, like she was doing right now. More and more, she would take time out from her busy schedule to drive to Rock Creek Park and walk for an hour, two. Breathe in the fresh air, watch the squirrels, bask in living things that weren't cheating each other and cheating on each other.

She'd reread all of Jane Austen four times last year.

Even she recognized she was on the verge of burnout.

But she had to keep going because there was something even nastier than usual swelling underground and the Washington Massacre was part of it and Hector Blake had been in the middle of the Massacre.

Summer didn't have any hard data, nothing she could take to the authorities, or at least to authorities she trusted. No documents, no files, no videotape, no recordings. Just gut instinct and a few signs of blood in the water.

The last lingering notes of the choral music shimmered in the air, rising to the immense coffered ceiling, then dissipated. The music was over, alas. Now for some more fragrant bullshit.

Marcus Springer, the CIA's Deputy Director of Central Intelligence, took the podium. Fussy and prissy, he shot his cuffs, carefully placed a sheet of paper on the podium and slowly withdrew his reading glasses from a fancy steel tube in his front jacket pocket, movements slow and deliberate. Expression serene, the very opposite of grief-stricken.

"We're here to celebrate the life of a great American, Hector Blake," Springer intoned and Summer tuned out. Another fluff piece.

Blake's life was of little interest to her. She knew the highlights. But there was something really wrong with Blake's death. The coroner's office had been extremely terse in its findings after the autopsy.

Basically, Hector Blake had drowned. Somewhere.

Maybe the Potomac, maybe not. Maybe in his car, maybe not. That was the sum total of the info given in the coroner's report. The full report was unavailable for reasons of national security. Summer had a really good informant in the coroner's office—coroners saw a lot of mischief and her informant could be bribed by tickets to concerts—but this time her informant, James Hadson, who had a secret crush on her, was completely mute. He gave her zip. Nada. He could not put his hands on the report, which was in a separate file that required a password James didn't have. And James hadn't assisted in the autopsy. Strangely enough, for the autopsy of such an important man, it had been carried out solo by the coroner of Washington DC herself, who had since taken unpaid leave and was nowhere to be found.

It all stank to high heaven.

Summer had no problems imagining someone whacking Blake—but who?

In her head a very long imaginary line formed of people who'd like to off him.

Her Aunt Vanessa, for one. Aunt Vanessa had been briefly married to Blake, so there was a connection to Summer, though not a blood one. Sharing DNA with Hector Blake…eww.

When her parents had died she'd landed on Aunt Vanessa's doorstep for two months, waiting to go to boarding school. Aunt Vanessa and Hector had been going through a vicious separation that would lead to a hotly contested divorce.

Those two months would have been unbearable if it hadn't been for the Delvauxes who stopped by often and invited her over often. She ate a lot of meals at their house and would probably have gone hungry otherwise. No one at the Glades ate in the house and they didn't care whether she was eating or not.

Isabel Delvaux had been two years older than her and had been kind and fun. And Jack—when Summer first saw him, her jaw had dropped, the first time that had happened to her in all her twelve years. She was sure he jump-started her puberty.

He'd been fifteen and drop-dead gorgeous. From his sun-bleached tousled blond head down to his perfect feet which she spaced out on when they spent the afternoons at the backyard pool, he was beautiful boyhood incarnate.

She'd lost sight of Isabel but had met Jack again her first week at Harvard.

He'd done a double take when she'd shyly said hello to the dazzling senior, even more gorgeous than before.

A handsome man instead of a beautiful boy and oh, just looking at him was such a pleasure. He'd been really nice to her and then he'd bedded her and it had been as if her life were finally coming together. But Jack was like a sun god, too magnificent to stay with a lonely freshman. He'd seduced Summer, her dorm roommate and two other girls on the floor in one month and then he'd disappeared.

He'd been her first and her last for a long, long time.

He'd given her blinding pleasure, she'd so foolishly thought it was true love, and he shattered her heart. All in a few days.

And then he vanished into smoke. She never saw him again. And now he was dead, too, in the Massacre.

He'd broken her heart but he'd also been brimming with life and joy—the golden boy who should have had a long and happy life, now dead in the cold, cold ground.

Summer shivered and shook herself.

Hector's funeral was affecting her too much. She was here as a reporter, an observer, searching for clues to the Washington Massacre, she wasn't here to reminisce. Springer's droning voice came to an end and the entire audience seemed to wake up.

Summer looked around at all the well-coiffed heads atop elegantly clothed bodies. More or less anyone who was anyone in Washington was here. They had even set up a Jumbotron outside for those who wanted to follow the memorial service but hadn't been invited. Summer hadn't been invited either, but there was a section set off for journalists and she'd found a place to sit by coming an hour early.

The funeral was over and a hidden organ began playing leave-the-church music. A huge perfumed rustle of expensive clothes and everybody rose, chatter buzzing immediately.

"One more wanker gone," a sour British voice said next to her. "Good riddance." She glanced to her side, recognizing the man. Billy Atkins, formerly of the *London Times* until he was fired for uncovering one too many royal scandals. Now he freelanced in Washington and drank. She could smell the beer coming off him.

"So what do you think of that coroner's report?" Summer asked, curious. Billy was a cynical drunk, but he had a first-rate journalistic nose.

"Cover up, lass," he replied and moved away before she could question him any further. Maybe sometime this week she could invite him to a beer or two or seven, loosen up his tongue.

Someone somewhere had to know something.

People were shuffling out of the pews, spilling into the huge aisles, heading for the big open doors at the back. Sunlight streamed in through the blue-and-pink stained glass windows but all of a sudden, like everyone else, Summer craved the real thing. Craved sunlight and open air.

She made a beeline for the big open doors, uncaring that there were a thousand contacts for hundreds of possible stories all around her. She didn't care, the air in the cathedral was stifling and she couldn't breathe.

Everyone wanted out. The line moved swiftly to the exit, propelling her out onto the large cement porch. It was chilly but sunny, the cold sun turning the hilltop lawn a bright green, the buildings down below as white as snow.

For some reason it made her think of the Delvaux

compound in Virginia. Bright green grass, white buildings…

Unsettled, Summer turned to snake her way through the throngs pouring out the doors and down the stairs. Hector Blake's funeral was stirring up things she had put in a box long ago. The bewilderment after her parents' deaths, her heartbreak at Harvard when Jack had dumped her like an ice cream cone he'd licked and found decent but not special. At Harvard there had been so many tastes for him to savor.

It had taken her *so long* to get over him. An embarrassingly long time. Good thing he had essentially disappeared and she didn't have to see him on campus with a different girl every week on his arm. She'd been so shaky at the time, it would have broken her heart even more.

Good thing she was strong now. No man would ever—*could* ever—break her heart again. Certainly not Jack or anyone like him. Too handsome for words, utterly charming, a lightweight.

Around her, several people pulled back quickly, almost violently, one woman stepping on Summer's toes. The woman didn't even turn around to excuse herself. She was being crowded by the person in front of her.

Summer wasn't tall, so she had to go on tiptoe to see what was going on.

Oh. A homeless guy. A tall vet, dressed in filthy, tattered BDUs, smelling of urine and body odor, long lank greasy dirty blond hair hanging in dreadlocks over his face, down his back, an unkempt beard covering half his face.

Well. Though her own heart swelled with pity—with the economic downturn there were a lot of homeless vets on the streets—she understood the people in front of her jerking away from him. Homeless vets didn't fit into the elite's mind-set. They shouldn't exist and when the elite came across them, they shied away.

The vet turned his face toward her for a second and that's when their eyes met. Sharp, bright blue eyes. Eyes she'd seen in her dreams a thousand times. Eyes that had stared into hers when they'd made love.

He turned immediately and ran. Though Summer pushed through the crowd brutally, stepping on toes and elbowing people aside, she lost him.

The vet was nowhere to be found.

Summer stood, frozen, unable to believe her eyes, yet knowing exactly what she'd seen.

Jack Delvaux, dead these past six months.

FUCK! SHE MADE HIM!

Jack Delvaux vaulted down the great stone steps of the National Cathedral, pushing people out of his way. But they parted for him anyway. He looked bad, he smelled bad and Washington's elite simply broke ranks to let him through because the alternative was him touching them and their skin crawled at the idea.

Good.

Pretending to be homeless had kept him alive these past six months since the Washington Massacre. Everyone thought he was dead, which was just fine by Jack.

Because the Washington Massacre hadn't been carried out by jihadi terrorists. No, the Massacre had been carried out by homegrown monsters, masquerading as terrorists. The Massacre hadn't been about terror, it had been all about money, and dear departed Hector Blake had been right in the middle of it.

Jack had been present when Hector had really died. Had been part of it, actually. Hector had drowned in the Willamette River in Portland, Oregon, four days ago while trying to abduct Jack's sister, Isabel. Like him, she was one of the few survivors of the Massacre that had taken the lives of their parents, their younger twin brothers, their aunts, uncles, cousins and about seven hundred other people in the Burrard Hotel.

Jack's heart still burned when he thought of it.

He wished Hector were still alive so he could kill him all over again.

But Hector had left a lot of secrets behind. A deep conspiracy that reached into the upper levels of the American intelligence community, including Jack's former employer, the CIA, and Jack wasn't going to rest until he unveiled it all and saw the conspirators in jail or in the ground. Preferably the latter.

Everyone thought Jack had been killed in the Massacre. Jack had stayed off the grid by pretending to be homeless, while living in a hidden safe house no one else knew about, set up by his former boss, who was now dead.

Pretending to be a homeless vet made him invisible. People didn't want the homeless around at all. And homeless *vets*? No way.

Jack had bought old BDUs from the Salvation Army, pissed on them a couple of times a week and kept them out on the safe house's little balcony where they got rained on and snowed on and grew more and more filthy.

He showered but took care to never wash his face. He shaved his head regularly and wore a filthy dreadlocks wig and pasted a scraggly beard on his face every time he went out, to confound the facial recognition bots. It worked. He didn't even recognize himself.

For the entire funeral, Jack had watched from the edges of the crowd outside, keeping an eye on the Jumbotron, looking for clues, looking for *something* and wasn't once recognized in the city he'd grown up in.

Except for Summer.

Damn.

She'd always been too smart for her own good.

He vaguely remembered the summer she'd been around at Hector's place—she was some kind of relative of one of Hector's wives—after she'd lost her folks. She'd been a funny looking little thing, eyes and mouth too big, a messy mass of reddish-brown hair sitting on her head like a bird's nest. Stick-thin and quiet as a mouse. It was the summer he'd had the crazy idea of training for the Olympics as an archer but it had turned out to be too much work and interfered with his social life. Life had been really good back then. He'd been pretty busy all that summer training and competing and partying and hadn't really paid her much attention.

Then she disappeared. People were appearing and disappearing from his life constantly in those years because he was too clueless and self-involved to pay attention.

And then in his senior year at Harvard he'd run across her and—whoa. Her face had grown so the eyes and mouth were sexily big without looking weird. She didn't have a rat's nest at all, but a smooth auburn bob and had filled out nicely. Very nicely.

He'd barely recognized her and had been able to place her thanks to her voice. She'd grown up abroad, dragged to a thousand places by her hippie parents. She spoke beautifully but with a tinge of an exotic accent that had made him smile when she'd been twelve and made him sweat when she was eighteen.

And then he'd fucked her and left her. Which was what he did on a massive scale in those years, thinking with his little head and not his big head.

It felt like ancient history, something you'd study in a textbook. The Years of Fucking Around: 1997-2001.

He had to get out of here, fast, because Summer would follow her instincts and try to catch him.

His years in the CIA's National Clandestine Service had taught him to walk really fast without appearing to hurry. He just lengthened his stride and made sure he wasn't pumping his arms.

He didn't really have to worry about anyone other than Summer, because no one noticed him, except to draw back or even cross the street to avoid him. Down the hill from the Cathedral and four blocks away was a black SUV with mud on the license plates and smoked windows. It looked exactly like every other official vehicle in the city.

Jack jerked the passenger door open and sat down.

"Well, that was fun," Nick Mancino said as he started the engine. Nick wrinkled his nose. "Man, you smell."

"That's the point," Jack said. "Now drive."

The SUV pulled out and headed for Jack's safe house. "So?"

"I think I was made," Jack said sullenly. Six fucking months without being made in a city full of intelligence operatives and government agents and one girl—woman—made him in an instant.

"Well...fuck," Nick said, driving fast. Nick, a member of the FBI's elite Hostage Rescue Team, was under unofficial cover. Only one person knew he was here investigating the Massacre, the Director of the FBI. With possible CIA involvement, it was the hottest of hot potatoes and so far, the investigation was off the grid.

Officially, Nick was on leave from the FBI and would stay on leave until they unmasked the conspiracy. He was almost as driven as Jack to find the fuckers responsible. Almost.

Jack had lost his entire family except for his sister, Isabel. He was going to find out who was responsible or die.

"Who made you?" Nick's eyes swept the side-view mirrors and the rearview mirror in a constant rotation. Jack was a good driver but Nick had taken combat driving training at Quantico.

Jack clenched his teeth. "Summer Redding."

Nick's eyes widened and he flicked a glance over to Jack. "Summer Redding? The blogger? *Area 8?*"

Jack nodded.

"Well, hell." Nick shook his head. "That is very bad news. Redding is one sharp lady. Are we going to read about you being alive after all in today's blog? If so, we're fucked."

They *were* fucked. If Summer posted that he'd been seen today—alive—the entire mission was endangered. It wasn't just a question of himself. Jack knew that forces inside the CIA were working against the country. The Massacre was just the first of what he felt might be more attacks coming soon.

A drumbeat of dread thrummed through him.

Just before the Massacre, Jack had stepped on some kind of trip wire. He'd first come across whispers in Singapore, where he'd been posted for the past four years. An informant had contacted him about a secret plan at the highest levels of the Chinese government to destabilize the United States with the help of a few very highly placed American citizens, including a few in the CIA. When Jack heard that, every hair on his body had stood up.

The plan had several steps and the first one had been the Massacre and the second one was going to be an attack on US soil. He had nothing more than that. No timetable, no indication of where.

And then the informant had disappeared and reappeared as a floater in the Singapore city morgue. The corpse had been so bloated it had taken the coroner an hour to discover the slit across the informant's throat.

But it had been serious enough for Jack to fly home to talk to his boss, the head of the National Clandestine Service, Hugh Lownie. He'd been meaning to fly home anyway because his dad, against the entire family's advice, had announced his intention to declare his candidacy for the presidency. His mom had gone into panic mode, frightened to death that someone would assassinate him. Rumor had it that they were fighting, close to a divorce, but that was bullshit. His parents loved each other deeply.

His dad was an idealist, wanted to run, and Jack had come home.

He'd met with Hugh in a park with no microphones anywhere because he didn't trust anyone or anything at Langley. Hugh had promised to start an in-house investigation.

That night, the night his father was slated to declare his candidacy at the Burrard Hotel, Hugh had called him. Jack had been on the podium because whether or not he agreed with his dad about running for President, he loved the guy and would swing his support behind him.

Everyone he loved had died that night with the exception of his sister, Isabel.

Nick wrinkled his nose. "Dude, do something. You fucking reek."

Jack unfastened the seat belt, took off the stinking jacket and slid out of the uniform pants. He also snatched the smelly wig off his head. He hated it almost more than the sweat and piss-soaked BDU. The wig itched and was heavy as fuck. Underneath, Jack kept his hair shorn and did it himself. Looking at himself without the wig, he looked like a prisoner of war. He pulled the beard off, too. The beard was stuck on by a miracle glue like that on Post-its that he could apply and tear off without pain.

Nick kept his eyes firmly on the road. Jack reached behind him for a hoodie and sweat pants, put the stinking homeless uniform in a plastic bag, tied the handles together, and put the bag in a gym bag. The funk factor in the vehicle dropped by about a thousand.

"Thanks," Nick said, sighing with relief. "So, what are we going to do about Redding? She made you, she's going to put it in her blog. We have to stop that, stop her. It would be a disaster. She can't write about it. Not now, it would put the entire mission in jeopardy."

"Whoa," Jack shot up in the seat. "We're not touching her. The hell you talking about?"

"Calm down, bro." Nick clutched the steering wheel harder. "I don't mean hurt her, Christ, what do you think I am, CIA?"

Jack let that slide. A couple of years ago he wouldn't

have taken any abuse from an FBI puke, no, sir. The CIA wasn't perfect but he'd been proud to serve. At least in the beginning. Then later…

And now? Now someone in the CIA had killed an informant, carried out the Massacre and moles—he had no idea how many—were plotting to bring his country down. So he kept his mouth shut. Slumped back into the seat. "We're not touching Summer," he repeated. "She won't post anything, she never posts anything without some kind of proof. So we're okay."

He hoped.

Nick narrowed his eyes at the road and slapped his hand against the wheel. "You fucked her. That's what this is about."

Jack sighed. "Yeah. About a million years ago. I fucked a lot of the women who were at the funeral. I was a man slut. So what?"

"So you were imprinted on her, that must be it. Because no one else noticed you. And if that's the case, she'll be like a dog with a bone. Must have been some fuck."

Jack stiffened. Nick was a good guy but no one could talk like that about Summer. Jack swiveled his head and glared. "Say anything like that again and I'll rip you a new one," he growled, meaning every word.

Nick's eyes widened. "Dude. Sorry. Whoa, didn't mean it that way. Hell, she's an incredible woman. She followed the trail of Senator Rowland's abuse of the family au pair like a terrier with a bone. If we have one less shit in the Senate, it's thanks to her. I read *Area 8* regularly, love it." He blew out a breath. "So—now that we've got that out of the way—we still got a problem. A big one."

Jack clenched his jaw.

"Problem. We've got a problem. You see that, don't you? Talk to me, Jack." They were at the safe house and Nick pulled into the covered alleyway in the back. "What are you going to do about it? One of the most well-known bloggers in America knows you are not dead. How do we remedy that?"

Silence.

"Jack?"

"I'm going to go talk to her," Jack said finally.

* * * * *

ABOUT THE AUTHOR

Lisa Marie Rice is eternally thirty years old and will never age. She is tall and willowy and beautiful. Men stop at her feet like ripe pears. She has won every major book prize in the world. She is a black belt with advanced degrees in archeology, nuclear physics and Tibetan literature. She is a concert pianist. Did I mention her Nobel Prize? Of course Lisa Marie Rice is a virtual woman and exists only at the keyboard. She disappears when the monitor winks off.

Check out her website at lisamariericebooks.com and sign up for her newsletter.